HE WA

"No one defies me or intentionally provokes me here, and certainly not a—"

"A woman? Is that what you were going to say?"

He grabbed her so quickly she didn't have time to react. He pulled her out of her saddle, halfway across his lap. His hard chest crushed her as his mouth found hers in a burning, searing kiss that sent currents of heat down her torso.

He had expected her to fight him. He had not expected to become caught up in this irresistible spiral of desire that threatened to devour him.

Books by Deborah Cox

Desert Dreams
From This Day Forward

Available from HarperPaperbacks

From This Day Forward

 DEBORAH COX

HarperPaperbacks
A Division of HarperCollins*Publishers*

HarperPaperbacks   *A Division of* HarperCollins*Publishers*
                   10 East 53rd Street, New York, N.Y. 10022

Cover illustration by Jim Griffin

First printing: August 1995

Printed in the United States of America

HarperPaperbacks, HarperMonogram, and colophon are
trademarks of HarperCollins*Publishers*

❖ 10 9 8 7 6 5 4 3 2 1

For my critique partners—
Lorraine Carroll,
Sherrilyn Kenyon and Rickey Mallory.
Thanks for putting up with me!

And the measure of our torment is the measure of our youth.
God help us, for we knew the worst too young!

—Rudyard Kipling
"Gentlemen Rankers"

Prologue

New Orleans, Louisiana, March 1885

Dear Jason,

I am pleased to inform you I have located a suitable candidate to fulfill the position of wife and companion. Her name is Caroline Marshall. I am well acquainted with the lady and can say without hesitation that she meets the requirements you set forth in your letter. I am confident you will find her pleasing to the eye and an intelligent companion.

I am most gratified with your decision to marry. I have sensed a growing loneliness in your recent letters. Melanie and I believe that you have made a splendid decision.

Therefore, the marriage by proxy has been performed and preparations are underway for

*your bride's departure for Brazil. I will write
again when passage has been arranged.*

I wish you both happiness and good fortune.
                                    Your cousin,
                                    Derek

"It's done." Caroline Marshall Sinclair placed the
quill in the inkstand and stared at the letter on the
desk before her. Quelling the doubt that rose in her
breast, she reread the missive. "Tell me I've done the
right thing."

Melanie Sinclair lifted the letter carefully, studying it for several seconds before replying. "It's amazing. I've seen Derek's handwriting hundreds of
times, but I could never have duplicated it so
closely."

"Well, I suppose if this doesn't work out I could
make my way as a forger."

Melanie laughed and returned the letter to the
desk. "I've never known you to be fainthearted,
Caroline. You were so sure this morning."

Sunlight from the open window glinted off the
ring on the third finger of Caroline's left hand,
reminding her of the vows she'd taken today, vows
that tied her forever to a stranger.

"Have you ever met Jason?" she asked, though
she knew the answer. She'd asked the question more
than once and had received a different reaction each
time. The words were always the same—*"No, but
Derek has told me so much about him, I feel as if I
know him."* The difference lay in the expressions,
the physical reaction which ranged from dreamy
contemplation to cautious optimism.

"No," Melanie replied, her mood reflective this

time. "All I know of him is what Derek has said over the years and what I've gleaned from—"

Surprised by the variation in Melanie's response, Caroline stopped studying her wedding band and glanced up at the other woman who stood gazing pensively out the window at the traffic on Tchoupitoulas Street. "What? Gleaned from what?"

"Oh," Melanie murmured as if she'd been called back from some faraway place. "Oh, the requests he's made over the years. Jason has very definite ideas about what he wants—the exact kind of books, the exact kind of furnishings, the exact kind of fixtures and glass and door facings for what must be a giant of a house."

A tremor of fear rippled through Caroline's body. Yes, Jason Sinclair had been very specific about what he wanted in a wife. But she knew that what he thought he wanted and what he needed were not the same thing at all. He needed a strong, independent, intelligent woman who wouldn't mind the isolation of the jungle or the hardships of such a life. He needed a woman who understood him, who could offer him the loving kindness he had never known as a child.

"Derek says Jason was scarred by life," Melanie said, as if she'd read Caroline's thoughts. "That's why he's hidden himself away in the wilds of Brazil for all these years. They were never close, not really. Jason grew up in a different world, a world of poverty. They lived on opposite sides of town. When his father died, Jason came to work for the company. He was only seventeen when his mother died and he left for Brazil. Fifteen years in the jungle."

Fifteen years, Caroline thought with a shudder, trying to imagine it. What would a man be like after fifteen years in the wild? She remembered reading accounts of men who had lived among the Indians of the American West twenty or thirty years ago and had become savages themselves. It seemed as if there was something primitive inside men, and whenever they were separated from civilization for too long, they reverted to a baser nature.

She was generalizing; she knew it. She could almost hear her father scolding her even from the grave. There were plenty of other accounts of men who had gone into the wilderness and tamed it, and that was obviously what Jason Sinclair had done. He had built a house, ordered books and other comforts from home, and now he wanted a wife. He hadn't lost the capacity to read and write. His letters had revealed a fiercely independent spirit, a dependable, hardworking man with the soul of a poet.

In short, Jason Sinclair was the absolute opposite of Wade Marshall, her first husband. He'd allowed life to rule his world, whereas Jason Sinclair obviously ruled life. Jason had decided on a course, set a goal and accomplished it. The obstacles he must have overcome would have crushed Wade.

All Jason needed was the right woman to bring him out of his shell of loneliness and self-imposed isolation. And Caroline knew that she was that woman.

Guilt squeezed her chest. The candid descriptions in Jason's letters of his childhood had been intended for Derek. But until she'd begun writing Derek's responses, Jason's letters had been dry and businesslike, without a hint of intimacy. It was as if something in her words had prompted him to confide in her—in Derek.

"Please don't let me upset you with my rambling," Melanie said, trying to sound lighthearted. "I suppose now is not the time to be telling you these things. I'm sure it's nothing to be alarmed about. I think it's terribly romantic. Falling in love through letters. . . ."

Unsure which of them Melanie was trying to convince, Caroline tried to focus on other things. Thinking back over the past year, she couldn't say exactly when she'd fallen in love with Jason Sinclair. His letters had spoken to her heart from the first one her employer, Derek Sinclair, had given her to read and answer.

At first, Derek had approved each response before she'd posted it, but as time passed and her skills in copying his handwriting increased, Derek's scrutiny had become less and less thorough. Eventually, Caroline became Derek's voice with his cousin. When the letter came from Jason requesting a wife, Derek was out of the country. Acting on Derek's behalf, and without his knowledge, she'd chosen the one woman who understood Jason better than anyone else—herself.

How well she understood the desire to shed the past and start over in a new place. Because she refused to live by the standards imposed upon women by New Orleans society, she'd been ostracized. She chose not to hide the fact that she was capable of using her mind for something other than picking the right color draperies for the sitting room. As a result, men looked at her with suspicion, as if she were a freak of nature.

Women distrusted her because she enjoyed the world of business, a world she shared with their husbands, a world entirely closed to them. Both men and women disliked her because she threatened the status quo. She'd been unwilling to compromise, to lower her standards in order to fit their mold, and so she'd been treated like a pariah.

Only Melanie had befriended her, and she'd repaid her kindness by entangling her in this desperate plot.

"I just wish I could have left you out of this," Caroline said sincerely. She picked up the envelope containing the other letter, the one to Derek, and gave it to Melanie. Her hand trembled slightly as she thought of what she was doing, what she had done. "Answering Jason Sinclair's request for a wife without so much as showing Derek the letter was shocking enough, but involving you. . . . He'll be furious."

"He'll get over it," Melanie assured her, her brown eyes dancing with mischief. "I'm glad to have helped. It was actually very exciting. How many women get the chance to be a groom in a wedding?"

Caroline laughed in spite of her doubts. "That was a stroke of genius."

Melanie shrugged dramatically. "Whoever said the proxy groom had to be a male?"

Caroline touched a finger to the writing on the letter she'd just finished. Satisfied that the ink was dry, she folded the paper quickly and slipped it inside an envelope before she lost her nerve.

Sealing the envelope, she stood and gathered her things, gazing one last time at the small wooden desk and chair that had been hers for the past year.

"You know, I think I'll actually miss this place," she said sincerely.

It was a shame most women were never allowed a glimpse into the exciting, dynamic world of business.

Here at the Sinclair Coffee Company, she'd felt needed, competent. And there was a certain satisfaction that came from earning one's own way.

"And I shall miss you." Melanie smiled a sweet, melancholy smile.

The two women embraced, and when they drew apart, Caroline's eyes brimmed with tears. "And I you. I—I've never had a friend like you before." Caroline laughed. "I've never had a friend at all, not really."

"I am your friend always," Melanie assured her, her tone solemn, her expression serious. "Remember that."

Caroline nodded, unable to speak past the emotion that clogged her throat, trembling as a shiver of apprehension crawled up her back. Was she doing the right thing? She prayed God she wouldn't regret this decision a few months from now.

Straightening her shirtwaist, she followed Melanie to the door, where she stopped, glancing around the familiar dark lobby.

She might miss the vigorous world of the Sinclair Coffee Company, but she would be glad to leave New Orleans behind, glad to escape the strictures of a society into which she had never fit, a society that had always tried to crush her independence.

Bolstering her courage, Caroline walked through the front door and into the noisy bustle of Tchoupitoulas Street for the last time.

1

Caroline stood on the pier, watching uneasily as the mail boat rounded a bend in the river and disappeared from view. She dabbed her face with a damp handkerchief and gazed around, unease threatening to become genuine fear at the vast wildness of the jungle. A screech she now recognized as a macaw pierced the other sounds, sending an army of goose flesh up her arm.

At least he could have sent someone to meet me.

The jungle sweltered with tropical heat, even though the sun had begun to set in the western sky. A fragile breeze set the foliage at the tops of the tall trees in motion. She longed for its soothing touch to chase away the heat and the incessant gnats that hovered around her unprotected face. But the air at her level remained unaffected.

Unbuttoning the top few buttons of her bodice, Caroline dabbed at her moist throat, glancing at the dirty white sack the boat's pilot had dropped on the dock. Logically, she knew that if the inhabitants of this isolated, remote wilderness didn't know when to expect the mail boat, they certainly couldn't know when she would arrive. Still, the boat's captain had blown the whistle several times as they'd approached the pier. Surely someone must have heard. How long would she have to wait before someone realized she was here?

A feeling of unreality gripped her. During all the preparations, Brazil had seemed a world away, a vague dream. All she'd been able to think of was escaping the dull emptiness of her life in New Orleans and grasping at what might be her last chance at happiness. Now, as she stood on the very threshold of a new life in a savage wilderness awaiting a man she'd never laid eyes on, her heart grew faint.

A loud splash at the edge of the river startled her, and she gazed up to see a *cayman* slither slowly into the water, disappearing beneath a mantle of red and gold water lilies. They were smaller than the alligators in Louisiana, but here in the Amazon there were no cities bustling with people where the creatures wouldn't dare venture. This was their domain, and she was the intruder.

Fifteen years in the wild.

What would he be like after being cut off from civilization for so long? As she'd read his letters, she'd formed a mental image of Jason Sinclair as a polished, refined gentleman planter. But her long journey west from the mouth of the Amazon had opened her eyes to the primitive conditions he'd lived under. The towns where they'd stopped along the way could hardly be called towns at all, with the exception of Manaus, which had stood out in this boundless wilderness like a ruby in a pig's ear.

The few homes she'd seen along the way had been raised Indian huts. Most of them barely passed as dwellings. Some didn't even have walls but were just wooden frames with thatched roofs.

And the heat and the insects! She'd thought they were bad in New Orleans, but they were nothing compared to what she'd experienced here. Somewhere between the Amazon and the Rio Branco, she'd stopped wearing a corset—until today. Today she wanted to look her best, but the torturous garment had quickly become soaked with perspiration. The cloying fabric caused her skin to itch miserably.

Movement at the edge of the jungle caught her attention. A figure emerged from the rich verdure, moving toward her with the casual grace and strength of a jaguar. Her mouth went dry and she began to tremble with anticipation. Was this man walking toward her with long, sure strides her husband?

The closer he came, the larger and more commanding he appeared and the smaller and more vulnerable she felt. Tan breeches hugged muscled thighs, disappearing into black knee-high boots. She caught a glimpse of broad, muscled chest as he shrugged into a white shirt and worked at fastening the buttons.

The sultry air vibrated with male power as he drew near. He brought to mind the animals she'd seen at the circus—restrained for the moment, but always there was the sense of wildness just below the surface.

A lump formed in Caroline's throat. What had she done? This wasn't the Jason Sinclair of her fantasies. In fact, the reality was so at odds with the picture she'd formed in her mind that she almost convinced herself that this man couldn't be Jason Sinclair. But as he stopped before her, she saw the resemblance between Jason and his cousin in the curve of his mouth and the shape of his stubborn chin.

That was the source of her disillusionment. She'd expected him to look like Derek Sinclair. Derek was a tall, handsome man, and Jason Sinclair was certainly that. While Derek possessed a certain refinement and elegance, those traits seemed completely lacking in this man. Where Derek was polished and sophisticated, the man before her was rugged and earthy, not at all the genteel plantation owner she'd hoped for. His clothes were dirty from working in the orchards no doubt. His dark blond hair looked as if it had never known a comb, and his large hands resembled a sharecropper's instead of a gentleman planter's with their calloused skin and dirty fingernails.

His gaze met hers briefly, and she caught a glimpse of arresting blue eyes, eyes the color of periwinkle. They captivated her for an instant before he looked past her over her head, searching the dock for something or someone. When he realized the dock was empty, he glared down at her as if she'd suddenly sprouted horns, taking her measure in a restrained, yet angry manner.

"Are you Jason Sinclair?" she asked tautly. He was head and shoulders taller than she, and he stood so close she had to tilt her head back severely to look into his eyes. Did he do so intentionally, she couldn't help wondering, and if so, why?

"I am." Suspicion showed plainly on his expressive features as he waited patiently for her to speak again.

His gaze dipped to her unbuttoned bodice. Her heart pounded as hot color flooded her throat and face. She'd been ogled by men before, but his gaze turned her bones to liquid, and a quiver of something like fear radiated through her.

She fought the urge to close the gaping neckline, knowing that to do so would only draw more attention.

"I am Caroline Marshall Sinclair," she said, trying to sound casual. Never before had she been so aware of a man. It was as if she'd stumbled across man in his natural state in the wild. Jason Sinclair exuded a raw maleness that took her breath away.

Taking a step back, she extended her hand, trying with all her will to extinguish the tiny spark of fear that threatened to devour her. She tried desperately to remember why she'd come here, but she could think of nothing beyond the stranger standing before her.

"That's impossible," he said, moving closer, his tall, powerful body dwarfing her.

She withdrew her hand, wiping it on her skirt in a nervous gesture as she fought the urge to back away from the displeasure in his eyes. He acted as if she'd arrived on his doorstep uninvited when *he* was the one who had requested a wife.

Anger hardened her resolve, and she glared contemptuously at him. "I'm afraid it's not only possible, it's true. I am Caroline Sinclair."

For a long moment, he said nothing, just stood there studying her so intently she could almost see his mind working furiously behind his eyes, before he spun on his heels and moved away from her, assuming she would follow.

"Come along, Mrs. Sinclair," he said over his shoulder, "I'll show you to the house." He stopped and turned back to her with a smirk. "Unless you'd rather stay here and wait for the next mail boat."

"How long would I have to wait?" she asked under her breath, not entirely in jest. A lump of apprehension clogged her throat, but she managed to swallow it. "Are you always so charming, Mr. Sinclair?"

Jason Sinclair smiled without humor. "If you wanted charm, you should have stayed in New Orleans."

Turning, he started walking away from her once more, but her words halted him. "Wait! What about my bags?"

Jason gazed past her at the pile of trunks and satchels on the wooden dock. "I hope you have something in those trunks more suitable for the jungle than what you have on."

Caroline glanced down at the pale green muslin dress she'd chosen so carefully that morning. It brought out the color of her hazel-green eyes and contrasted perfectly with her dark hair. Besides, it was light and cool and the nicest thing she owned.

"Leave them," he growled. "I'll have a couple of servants bring them up."

Speechless for the first time in her life, Caroline could only stare at his departing back in shock. He was the rudest, most infuriating man she'd ever met. How could she have been fooled so completely? A poetic soul? Hah!

Grasping the handle of her father's black medical bag, Caroline lifted her skirts and hurried after him, afraid he would leave her behind.

The narrow, sharply inclined path wound its way through the jungle. At every step, she forced lizards and beetles from their resting places. Long, green branches reached out from both sides, their prickly green fronds scratching her hands. She brushed them aside, ignoring the slight pain. Gathering up her long skirt, she tried to step around the mud holes, but that soon proved to be impossible. Instead, she held her skirt as far out of the muck as possible, but the hem quickly became soaked, the weight draining her strength.

As the house appeared before her, she tilted her head back, running her gaze up the white-washed stone wall that rose toward the heavens. Melanie had been right when she'd guessed at its size. It reminded her of a Moorish castle with its pointed arches and interlocking circular plaster work. Colorful flowering vines hugged the walls, as if to remind the owner that the jungle only tolerated its presence here—for now.

Captivated by the huge, sprawling structure, she missed her footing and fell to the ground, catching herself with her hands. Up ahead, Jason Sinclair kept walking, oblivious to her predicament.

"Stop!" she cried. "Wait!"

He turned impatiently, shaking his head in utter exasperation. He started toward her, but Caroline pushed herself up before he could reach her. She'd humiliated herself enough by falling. She wasn't about to give him the satisfaction of pulling her to her feet as if she were a helpless child. Angrily, she brushed her muddy hands on the front of her ruined skirt.

She gazed up to see Jason Sinclair bearing down on her, a long, lethal-looking knife in his hand. A cry of terror rose in her throat as she backed away from the fury in his eyes. Grabbing her skirt, he sliced the bottom ruffle off with two quick swipes of the knife, then sheathed the weapon in his boot before turning and walking away again.

"Fashionable frocks have no place in the jungle." He bit out the words, turning a few feet ahead and waiting impatiently.

It was a moment before Caroline could gather her shattered wits. Her heart finally calmed to a degree, and she looked down at the damage done to what had once been her best dress. He'd ruined it, and in the process, he'd left her ankles and booted feet exposed.

Embarrassment and fury seethed inside her. Lifting her chin defiantly, she retrieved her father's medical bag and trudged through the mud toward him. Admittedly, the shorter skirt increased her ease of movement tenfold. Still, he had no right to attack her so unexpectedly. The least he could have done was explain his actions. He'd frightened the daylights out of her.

"Why are you in such a hurry?" Her lip quivered with anger and injured pride as she glared up at him.

"This is a coffee plantation, madam," he said impatiently. "I have work to do."

Caroline bristled at his harsh words. He thought of her as a bother, a nuisance that was keeping him from his work.

He waited for her to catch up to him, and when she stood before him, she said, her voice trembling slightly, "I'll try not to detain you longer than necessary. How stupid of me not to know how to get to a house I've never seen before."

"I don't like sarcasm in a woman," he informed her before walking away toward the house.

"And I don't like rudeness in a man!" she cried after him, but if he heard her, he didn't respond.

Caroline followed her new husband through an arched entranceway. Ahead was a wide, square courtyard around which the house was built. In the center, a large fountain gurgled, and in each corner, a wrought-iron spiral staircase led up to the vine-draped balcony that completely encircled the courtyard. Jason led her up the left staircase.

Stopping before the first door at the top of the stairs, he pushed it open and stepped across the threshold onto a pale rose-colored stone floor scattered with small rugs of muted pastels. The white-walled room contained a variety of small, inlaid tables, two divans of white silk, and a richly carved brass-bound chest. On one of the tables stood a vase of fresh orchids. Their scent filled the small parlor, and Caroline breathed deeply of the sweet aroma, heartened at the care and attention to detail apparent in every feature of the room.

Jason crossed to the wide, arch-encased windows on the opposite wall and opened the shutters. Brilliant sunlight flooded the room. The interior was as bright as the outdoors, thanks to a gilt-framed mirror that almost completely covered the wall to her right and reflected the light, despite the damage wrought on it by the harsh elements.

Placing the medical bag on the table that held the orchids, Caroline lifted a bloom to her nose, closing her eyes as she savored the aroma. When she looked again, her new husband's impatience showed plainly in his blue eyes. He gazed at the medical bag as if seeing it for the first time.

"It belonged to my father," she said defensively.

He made no reply, just nodded toward a door to her left. "Your bedroom is through that door."

Caroline glanced away quickly, feeling the heat of embarrassment suffuse her face, trying not to think of the intimate nature of their relationship.

"Thank you," she murmured. She was virtually alone here with him. Of course, there was nothing improper about that; he was her husband, after all. But propriety had nothing to do with the elemental fear in her heart.

Glancing at her new husband surreptitiously, she found him studying her with a frown creasing his brow, whether from impatience or concentration, she couldn't say.

"I trust you will be comfortable here," he said indifferently.

"It's lovely," Caroline managed to reply.

With a nod, Jason Sinclair turned and was gone, leaving a puzzled Caroline to stand in the middle of the room and stare in mute astonishment at the doorway through which he'd disappeared.

She released her breath, unaware until then that she'd been holding it. Closing her eyes, she tried to remember the words of the letters that had prompted her to make this journey. At the moment, nothing came to mind, but as soon as the servants brought her baggage, she would dig them out and read them again for reassurance. Could she really have been so wrong about him? Had she read things into his letters that hadn't been there? Was she so desperate for marriage that she'd given Jason Sinclair attributes he didn't possess?

Where was the gentle dreamer she'd glimpsed in his words? Where was the scholar who ordered crate after crate of hand-picked books?

A light smattering of huge rain drops began to fall

quietly beyond the open window. The scent of damp earth and leaves filled the room and stirred her senses. Her house in New Orleans had always made her feel a bit claustrophobic. Cramped and cluttered with her possessions, the small structure, though meticulously clean, had possessed little charm. It had been too close to the fish market to open the windows throughout most of the year because of the stench and the insects. But here above the trees, not even the gnats would bother her.

At least Brazil had lived up to Jason's description in every way—beautiful, wild, savage. She would never feel cramped or claustrophobic here.

She moved to the windows that lined the far wall of the small salon. Would she be able to see the coffee orchards Jason had described so poetically in his letters from here? The house was built on a hill, so she was able to see over the tops of the giant trees that had spread their canopy of leaves so far overhead on her long journey through the jungle. Between them, the Rio Branco snaked its way through the valley toward the setting sun. She could even see the dock on which she'd met her new husband, but no orchards.

No mail boat either, she thought, realizing that she had half expected to see it in the distance, hoping against hope that it would turn around and come back. She was stranded here, alone with the man of her dreams, dreams that were fast turning into nightmares.

She'd have to make the best of it and try to find in this dark, brooding ogre something of the sensitive, vulnerable man she'd fallen in love with. First impressions could be misleading.

She would rest for a few minutes until the men brought her baggage up, and later she would go down and have a civilized meal with her husband. He would learn soon enough that he couldn't treat her so offhandedly.

Caroline sat at the huge oak dining room table, the only sound in the room the tapping of her fork against her water glass. She glanced at the empty chair across from her with an angry scowl. Today marked the third morning she had awakened in her new home and the third morning she had eaten breakfast alone. This morning she'd risen early in order to catch her elusive husband, but even that had failed. What time must he get up?

She was beginning to wonder why he'd wanted a wife in the first place. It certainly wasn't for companionship, and if he truly wanted an heir as he'd indicated in his letter, he was going to have to get a lot closer to her than he had so far! Just how long did he plan to ignore her?

Heat rushed to Caroline's face at her own thoughts. Naturally, she was relieved that he'd given her time before claiming his marital rights, but she'd hoped to use the time to get to know him, to dig until she found the man who had written those lovely letters.

Oh, the letters, those damned letters! If not for those letters, she wouldn't be here at all. She'd reread them all, every one of them, and their impact was no less powerful now than it had been the first time she read them. It just didn't make sense.

The natural rhythm of life here comforts and invigorates me, he'd written. *I look out over the*

*orchards full of trees my men and I planted as
saplings only a few years ago. Now those same trees
are heavy with coffee berries. Watching them grow
to maturity and yield fruit year after year gives me a
feeling of connectedness with the earth, something I
never would have experienced had I not left the city.*

"You are not eating, *senhora*."

Caroline glanced up to see the cook, Ines, standing
over her, her hands on her hips, her expression
reproving.

"I'm not hungry." Caroline pushed her plate away
for emphasis.

"It is not good. You must eat to be strong."

Smiling ironically, Caroline studied the small
woman who spoke to her like a mother would a
child, despite the fact that she was two years
Caroline's junior. Ines had provided Caroline's only
human contact since that first day. Their growing
friendship had kept her from losing her sanity.

"When did my husband leave the house this
morning?" she asked.

"Oh." Ines stopped in the motion of clearing the
table to give the matter her undivided attention.
"Oh, before daylight."

"Do you know where he might be?"

"*Sim, senhora*. He will be at the *benefício*."

"What is that?"

"Coffee house, where the beans are dried and
processed."

Caroline rose. "And how would I get there?"

"Oh, *senhora*, you cannot go there alone," Ines
cried. "The *patrão*—"

"Then one of the servants will have to escort me."
Caroline's unwavering gaze locked with Ines's. She

was struck anew by the woman's eyes. They were old eyes, old and hard.

"But the *patrão*, he will be unpleased for you—"

"I am going, Ines," Caroline said emphatically, coming to her feet.

"*Sim, senhora*," Ines acquiesced. Her expression clearly conveyed her displeasure and her belief that Jason would be equally unhappy with her actions. "Vincente will take you where you want to go. He will meet you in the courtyard."

"Thank you." Caroline sighed with relief that Ines had given in so easily. She didn't care if Ines disapproved. She didn't care if Jason would be "unpleased." At least displeasure was an emotion. It would be the first she'd seen him express since the surprise he'd evinced on the dock that first day. "I'll be ready in fifteen minutes."

Ten minutes later, Caroline stood on the patio in her brown riding habit, waiting for Vincente. She didn't have to wait long before she was joined by a tall, wiry Portuguese youth who, to her chagrin, spoke very little English.

At least he seemed to know where she wanted to go. They rode slowly along the narrow path that led into the heart of the jungle. Caroline swatted at swarming insects as her horse followed the path with no prodding from her. It had obviously traveled this way frequently.

The sound of voices and rushing water reached her as the *benefício*, a low, wide stone building covered by a flat, red-tiled roof, came into view. All around the central structure, workers in straw hats used hoes to spread the golden coffee beans over broad patios that extended in every direction.

The aroma of coffee permeated the thick, sultry air as they approached. Caroline studied the orchards that surrounded the building. Other workers wound their way between the rows of trees, picking the ripe coffee berries and filling baskets slung over their shoulders.

She watched the narrow trail ahead as they turned a corner, and she pulled her mount to an abrupt stop. Her eyes fastened on the man who stood on one of the unused patios.

Jason Sinclair. He was completely naked.

2

She couldn't move, couldn't tear her eyes away from his powerful, superb body. Her heart lurched, pounding forcefully against the wall of her chest as her mouth went dry and her face grew hot.

Water gushed from an overhead spigot in a steady stream that pummeled his body with bruising force. His every movement spoke of symmetry and strength. How could she have imagined he was less elegant than his cousin? Despite his larger frame and dwarfing height, he possessed all the predatory grace of a jaguar. His shoulders and arms were powerful enough to challenge an ox, and his broad, muscled back, made darker than his legs by constant exposure to the tropical sun, tapered into a narrow waist and sleek, narrower hips and buttocks.

She made no sound, but he seemed to sense her presence and turned to face her. A light feathering of golden hair covered his chest, growing darker and thicker as it plunged down his flat belly to cradle his sex.

Even after two years of marriage she had never seen a man naked, not completely naked, not like this, never like this. As a medical student, she'd learned the rudiments of the male anatomy; it had always seemed a shameful, embarrassing thing. But here was masculinity in its purest form, stripped of the restraints of civilization.

Her gaze returned to his face and locked with his rigid, unreadable expression before he cursed under his breath and reached for a towel. His movement broke the spell that had possessed her, leaving her dazed and mortified. With a violent jerk on the reins, she turned and plunged into the jungle, not knowing where she was going but trusting the horse to find its way back to the stable.

The horse had barely come to a stop when she leaped from the saddle and ran through the archway onto the patio. There she stopped, gazing around at the deserted courtyard, wondering where to go, what to do, to erase the images from her mind.

Her heart pounded erratically in her breast, not from running, but from some unnamable sensation. Leaning against the stone table before her, she took several deep, calming breaths.

She wouldn't think of it, she would not!

It took her all morning to regain some measure of composure. As long as she stayed busy, she could keep her thoughts from wandering back to the *beneficio* and Jason Sinclair's nakedness.

She occupied herself by playing the piano until her fingers ached, and even then she played on, pouring into it all the emotions she couldn't express or even identify. The music consumed her, coiling itself around her, inside her, until she and the music became one. By the time Ines came to announce luncheon, she felt almost completely serene once again.

But her fragile composure evaporated when she entered the dining room to find that Jason Sinclair had chosen today to grace her with his presence for the afternoon meal.

Her face flushed with the memory of what had taken place that morning, Caroline made her way to her customary seat at the long table on legs that had turned to rubber. He stood as she hesitated beside her chair until one of the servants pulled it out for her and they sat simultaneously.

A taut silence stretched between them as the meal was served. Caroline couldn't resist studying him. He seemed to concentrate all his energy and attention on his food, while she was forced to concentrate all of hers on merely breathing in his presence.

Had she really been disappointed when she'd first met him on the pier? She must have been exhausted and nearly blind from her arduous trip up the Amazon.

He was the most beautiful man she had ever seen, in a rugged, utterly masculine way. His features were pleasing to look at, despite the fact that his brows seemed to knit together in a permanent frown and his nose was slightly crooked, as if it had been broken. His was a strong face, a face etched by time and, she suspected, experience. Pain and pride and hatred had moved across that face and left their indelible mark on it.

Without warning, he glanced up and caught her

studying him. She looked down quickly, concentrating on her food to keep from staring at him.

To her shame, she realized that she wanted to see him again like that, to run her hands over the hard ridges of muscle that had played upon his back and chest.

"I'm afraid I'm not accustomed to having a woman around," he told her. His voice held a rich, deep texture, like a soft breeze over dry sand, that shivered down her spine.

Caroline glanced up and met the full force of his ice-blue gaze. A tremor pulsed through her body but she refused to look away.

"Especially such a curious one," he added sardonically. "We were clearing some land this morning and I stepped into a sinkhole. It was more convenient to bathe and—"

"You needn't explain," she told him a bit breathlessly, not at all anxious to discuss the circumstances that had led to her happening upon him that morning.

Just the mere mention of it brought the images vividly to her mind, not that they had been far from it all morning.

"You're right, of course, I don't have to explain," he agreed in a tone that conveyed the message, *I am king here and you'd best remember it.* "I was only trying to—If you want to see the *fazenda*—"

"*Fazenda*?"

As if drawn by a magnet, his gaze flickered downward over her body for the briefest instant. When his eyes returned to hers, a dark fire shone in their pale depths.

"Plantation," he explained, his voice deep and coarse. "If you want to see the plantation, you need only ask and I'll take you on a tour, but I must insist that you not venture forth on your own. My men are no more accustomed to having a woman around than I am."

For a moment, Caroline was unable to speak. She'd been so intent on watching his facial expressions, that she forgot to reply, though she knew that a response was required.

Clearing her throat nervously, she picked up her fork and began pushing her food around on her plate. It gave her something else to concentrate on while she spoke. "But I wasn't alone, and besides—" It was on the tip of her tongue to mention that Ines had evidently been on the *fazenda* for some time. Instead, she mustered as much enthusiasm as she could and said, "I would like that."

He stopped eating and gazed at her, his face a mask of confusion. "Pardon me?"

"The tour," she reminded him. "I would like to see the *fazenda*, if you really meant what you said."

He looked at her as if seeing her for the first time, staring at her as intently as a scientist would study a specimen under a microscope. His gaze left her face and slid down her throat to her bosom once again.

It took a force of will on her part, but she managed not to squirm as his glance touched her like a caress.

"If you'd like," he said, slowly lifting his gaze back to hers, as if reluctant to do so.

"Shall we go now?" she asked, wondering if he were aware of his effect on her, if he guessed at the tumult he caused inside her.

He laughed, a short sound that was more a snort. "Not now. It's too late in the day. I'll show you the premises first thing in the morning before the sun gets too hot."

She started to protest that she had been active at high noon every day of the journey up the Amazon and the Rio Branco, but something stopped her. She hadn't been able to dispute his authority that first day, and she couldn't now.

It annoyed her that she could not seem to argue with him, but when he turned that proprietary glare on her, that look that brooked no disagreement, her throat tightened and she fell silent against her will. He was obviously a man accustomed to having his own way.

"Tomorrow morning, then," she agreed with a tremulous smile.

"And now, if you will excuse me, madam—"

"Caroline," she interrupted, halting him in the motion of pushing his chair back from the table. "My name is Caroline."

Smiling crookedly at her, he settled in his chair again. It was the first time she'd seen him smile, and the way the gesture transformed his face amazed her. How could he appear so stern and formidable one moment, and the next smile in a way that made him look like a little boy? Perhaps there was a gentle soul beneath that gruff exterior after all.

"I know your name," he assured her, his brow furrowing in concentration. He was studying her again, appraising her.

"You know precious little more about me than a name," Caroline said, emboldened by the undercurrent of humor she noted in his voice. "Aren't you even a little curious about me? I mean, after all, I am your—"

"My wife. Yes, I know. And perhaps I am a bit curious," he admitted.

"Then why have you been avoiding me?"

His hand clenched into a fist, the only sign of emotion in his otherwise serene manner. "What makes you think I've been avoiding you?"

"Haven't you?" she asked, and she witnessed the most profound emotional withdrawal she had ever observed. It was as if he had recoiled into a hard shell. The barrier between them seemed almost physical.

"I didn't mean to offend you," she muttered.

Jason stood quickly and strode toward the French doors that led to the patio. With one hand braced high against the doorframe, he placed his hat on his head and turned to face her as if he would say something.

Caroline waited expectantly, but he only stared at her with features obscured by the shadow of his hat brim before stepping through the door into the hot Brazilian sunlight.

The profound darkness of the jungle embraced the white-walled fortress that had been stolen from the wilderness. Nightjars trilled close by, their song loud and repetitious. In the distance, a tree rat called, while millions of insects chirped high in the trees. The rush of water from the nearby river pulsed through the quiet like a heartbeat. Not a sliver of a moon nor a single star marred the empty black sky; not a whisper of a breeze stirred the thick, moist air.

Jason Sinclair paced back and forth across the courtyard around which the house was built, finally coming to rest on a heavy stone bench. He reached across the table of the same material and wrapped his hand around a tall bottle.

Out of raw wilderness, he thought. When he arrived here, there had been nothing but jungle. He'd built an empire. He'd chosen a plot of land and had subdued it. He'd broken ground and built a mansion, a fortress. He'd gone as far into the jungle as he dared, farther than anyone had ever gone and tried to make a successful coffee *fazenda*. But he'd done it.

Lifting the bottle to his lips, he turned it up. Whiskey burned a path down his throat in a steady stream, and he gasped with satisfaction at the searing. He lowered the bottle and wiped the back of his hand across the prickly stubble of a day's growth of beard. It wasn't the taste he enjoyed so much as the fiery burning in his gut—and the forgetfulness.

He'd put enough distance between himself and his demons to ensure his peace. He'd surrounded himself with enough jungle so that nothing could topple this little kingdom. And yet, he still didn't feel secure enough. What would it take to make him whole?

A child? Would having his own child and doing everything *right* blot out the past and allow him to live like a normal man?

You'll never amount to anything, you good-for-nothing lout! His father had told him over and over again.

He'd proven himself, by damn. He'd proven that he could make something of himself. He'd proven his father wrong, but the son of a bitch had gone and died before he saw his worthless son build his empire.

"To hell with him," Jason murmured. "Filthy bastard."

He looked at the half-empty bottle in his hand and snorted.

His father had been a violent, hard-drinking man, who had abused his wife and children until the day he'd died. While his brother, William, had overcome his humble beginnings and made something of himself, all Cullen Sinclair had managed to make of himself was a drunkard. His sudden disappearance twenty years ago had caused much speculation. Some said he'd run off to escape the law or the thugs who had lent him money he couldn't repay. Others said he'd gotten drunk and fallen into the river and drowned. And though he knew none of the stories were true, Jason rather liked the latter. There was a certain poetic justice to it.

"Like father, like son," he laughed, then sobered suddenly. That was the greatest fear of his life, that he would turn out like his father.

He was taking a terrible chance marrying. He might never know what he was capable of if he never had a family.

Would he find out that he was a man capable of the kind of violence his father had exercised, violence against those who were weaker than he? Against the very people who should be able to turn to him for protection?

Why risk it? Was it the loneliness? Was it the idea of having one human being in the world who would love him unconditionally and look at him with something other than contempt or pity or fear?

He turned and glanced up at the closed door on the second floor. She hadn't looked at him with pity or contempt. But then, she didn't know him yet. Give her time. Judging by the intense curiosity and razor-sharp perception he'd seen in those hazel eyes, she'd ferret out every secret in his black heart if he wasn't careful.

Perhaps it had been a mistake to bring her here. He'd come here to escape the world, to a place where no one knew or cared that he was Cullen Sinclair's son. The last thing he needed was a curious, inquisitive wife to start rattling the skeletons in his carefully sealed closet.

"Caroline Sinclair," he said aloud, rolling the name around on his tongue.

She wasn't what he'd expected at all. She was so damned strong, so self-reliant. He'd expected a much younger woman, a woman he could control and mold into what he wanted her to be, a woman who would stay out of his way for the most part so that he wouldn't ever have to face the demon that dwelled inside him.

Why have you been avoiding me? she'd had the temerity to ask.

Damned if she wasn't the most direct female he'd ever met. Granted, his experience with women was limited. Contact with the fairer sex in the Amazon jungle was practically nonexistent.

And just why the hell had she accepted this insane proposition and come to Brazil, unless she too was running away from something?

That thought stilled him, and he squinted his eyes toward that silent door, as if he could see through it all the way into her soul by dint of will.

He'd surrounded himself with fresh, new things. He didn't like antiques and the secrets they brought with them. He didn't like secrets at all, even his own. He gave a snort and decided that thought deserved another drink.

Still, he had to admit she was a beautiful woman, a woman who exuded an aura of sensuality that kept his blood in a constant uproar. His hands ached to feel the texture of her pure, ivory skin, to caress that glorious rich brown hair. He yearned to taste the sweetness of her mouth, hold her body against his, bury himself deep inside her and make her his own.

His hand trembled as he brought the bottle to his lips once again and drank deeply, wincing at the burning sensation that spread throughout his body. Returning the bottle to the table, he held his hand before his eyes and studied it critically—the rough skin, the calluses, the dirty, broken fingernails. He didn't know if he could bear to touch her. There was something fine about her, something elegant and pure. Just looking at her made him feel dirty and unworthy.

She'd been right, of course. He had been avoiding her and avoiding the inevitable consummation of their marriage, the very inevitability of which was a sweet torture, one that he savored even as it tormented him. It gave a special edge to every moment, making him feel more vitally alive than he had in a very long time.

Sweet agony, it was. Sweet agony.

Perhaps she welcomed the respite. He had believed she would, being a woman and naturally timid. At least he'd thought so until she'd come in search of him that morning. Goddamn her timing!

He'd been so stunned by her sudden appearance that he hadn't even had the presence of mind to cover himself. She should have been mortified at the sight of a naked man, but she had absolutely ogled him.

He came to his feet with a brutal curse, flinging the whiskey bottle down onto the patio to splinter into a thousand shards of glass.

The breath tore through his chest with such force that he couldn't move for several moments, and then he began to pace, back and forth across the patio like some caged beast in a carnival.

Out of the corner of his eye, he caught the movement of shutters at the window on the second floor. She had obviously heard the crashing of the bottle against the brick patio, and now she stood at the window, her body only the whisper of a shadow through the glass. But it was enough to set his blood afire.

She stood there watching him. He knew it, though he couldn't see her eyes. Damn her boldness! Why didn't she turn away and go back to bed and leave him in peace? Why did she stand there like a statue, looking at him, examining him, trying to break through his defenses?

Cursing savagely, he turned away, furious that she had forced him to be the one to break the tableau. A blinding rage shuddered through him as he stalked toward the stairs and bounded up them. When he emerged onto the balcony, Caroline no longer stood at the window. Allowing himself a triumphant smile, he grasped the doorknob and rattled it viciously, more to frighten her than to break into her rooms.

Not so bold after all, he mused, only slightly ashamed of his victory. What did she think? That he'd flown up the stairs to throttle her or ravish her?

Did she think a door would keep him out should he choose to do so?

After a while, the terrible noise abated and Caroline released the sigh that had been wedged in her throat. She waited, listening, her back against the closed bedroom door. Though her eyes remained dry, sob after wretched sob racked her body. She trembled so violently she feared she might be ill.

Soon she heard his booted footfalls retreat from the outer door, and her body sagged with relief.

What had she done? She'd married a madman! And now she was trapped here in the remotest Amazon.

Trapped. Defenseless.

The jungle may seem cruel, he'd written, *but there is no senseless violence in the jungle, except that wrought by man. Man is truly a beast to be feared above all others.*

Shivering, she went to stand at the open bedroom window, gazing down at the night-shrouded jungle, wondering if Jason himself were a beast to be feared above all others.

Caroline paced back and forth just inside the stable, waiting impatiently for Jason to arrive. After awakening to the crashing sound on the patio below her window and taking part in a silent battle of wills with Jason—a battle she had lost miserably—she hadn't been able to get back to sleep.

That moment of fear had kept her awake all night. He'd wanted her to fear him, she realized in the early hours of the morning as she tried to sort out all that had happened since she arrived.

Was he displeased with her, or would he have treated any woman with the same contempt and anger? She didn't know how to approach him, how to reach the man inside, but in those dawning hours, she'd decided he was worth the effort, even if he did sometimes frighten her with his rages.

So she had dressed just before dawn and come to the stable, determined that he wouldn't slip out without her today. Whatever it was that made him so angry, that made him lash out at her, she would make him face it. There was only one way to do that, and that was to confront him and not let him intimidate her. As appealing as the idea of remaining safely locked away in her room might be, she had to face him and carve out a place in his life or she might as well pack her bags and leave now.

She didn't have long to wait. Jason strode into the stable dressed much as he had been that first day—tan breeches tucked inside knee-high boots, ivory shirt stretched across the broad muscles of his shoulders.

At sight of his master, the large bay stallion that had been standing sedately while the young groom, Julio, saddled it, began to whinny and toss its head in recognition.

Jason regarded Caroline casually, then walked past her without a word and began murmuring softly to the horse, petting the animal with surprising tenderness. How could he be so gentle with an animal and so harsh with his own wife?

"He's ready to go this morning, *patrão*," the groom said with a smile, and the talk between the two men quickly turned to coffee cultivation.

Caroline had learned quite a lot about the other side of the coffee business while working for the

Sinclair Coffee Company—receiving cargoes, packing for resale. If she could somehow learn about coffee planting and harvesting, she would be able to converse knowledgeably with her husband about the one subject that seemed to consume him.

Caroline made a mental note to ask her husband if there were books on the subject in the library. Or maybe she could find someone on the *fazenda* willing to teach her.

Jason approached, interrupting her thoughts, and Caroline smiled sweetly at him, hoping to disconcert him and succeeding. His bemused frown turned quickly into a scowl, but that instant of dismay satisfied her—for the moment. If he thought he could intimidate her by prowling around beneath her window all night and lunging at her like a wild beast, he would soon learn otherwise. He'd taken her by surprise last night. It wouldn't happen again.

Jason walked past her into the yard. The groom followed, leading the horses, and Caroline trailed behind. Jason took the reins of the bay stallion and swung effortlessly into the saddle.

The groom helped Caroline mount and she hurried to catch up with her husband, drawing alongside him as they started down the path she had taken yesterday to the *benefício*. Her whole being quickened at that memory, and she forced her mind away, concentrating instead on her surroundings.

Lovely banana and palm trees grew along the path, but the absolute cleanness of the jungle floor still amazed her, as it had on her journey up the Amazon. Unlike the forests around the Mississippi River, undergrowth was virtually nonexistent here in the Amazon Valley.

"It's so isolated here, so primitive," she said, a bit in awe. "You could almost forget the rest of the world exists."

"Almost," he replied, and Caroline couldn't help wondering at the bitter smile that curved his lips.

As they rode slowly, the complete isolation of the jungle closed in around her and she wondered how he endured it. Did he even feel the loneliness?

I am so far removed from civilization here, he'd written, *that sometimes I forget what it was like to have a casual conversation or to walk down a busy street and hear the sound of carriages passing by.*

Yes, he felt it. But she wanted to hear him say it. She wanted him to talk about himself, to share something of his thoughts and feelings so she could reconcile this reality with those lovely, often poignant letters.

"You've been here so long. Don't you ever get lonely?" she asked.

He gazed sidelong at her, as he gave his horse's neck an affectionate pat. A corner of his mouth turned upward in a half smile as his turquoise gaze traveled the length of her body in a slow, calculated perusal that brought hot color to her face.

"Well, I suppose that's why you're here," he said, wheeling his horse around and plunging down the narrow path.

Speechless for the second time in her life, Caroline watched her husband ride away until he disappeared around a bend in the path. A slow smile curved her lips.

"Maybe the man's not made of stone after all," she said aloud. This could prove to be a very interesting morning.

3

Caroline caught up with Jason at the edge of the orchards. A sea of coffee trees stretched before her in neat, straight rows. Their white blooms reminded her of the snow she'd seen as a girl while accompanying her father on a business trip to Nashville.

Jason sat forward in the saddle, his posture straight and majestic as he surveyed his domain. His spirited stallion tossed its head and snorted as if eager to be moving again. Jason patted it on the neck and murmured softly to soothe the animal.

When he finally spoke to Caroline, his voice resounded with pride. "Everyone laughed when they learned that I planned to grow coffee so deep in the jungle."

"Why?" she asked with genuine curiosity. Everything about this enigmatic, passionate man intrigued her. *Why did you try to frighten me last night?* she wanted to ask.

Jason shrugged. "The difficulty of getting it to market. They thought I'd be spending all my profits on transportation, if I had any profits."

"No, I mean why grow coffee so deep in the jungle?"

"Because no one had done it before," he replied without hesitation.

"But no one has leaped off a cliff and survived either."

It seemed a perfectly logical observation to Caroline, but Jason studied her as if she were some strange animal that had crawled out of the jungle and had the nerve to challenge him. Irritation showed plainly on his handsome features.

"Haven't you ever wanted to do something just to prove you could do it?" he asked, gazing across his domain once again. "I subdued the jungle and planted seeds that took root and became coffee trees. I built a home—"

"It seems more like a fortress to me," Caroline couldn't help interjecting.

Jason straightened in his saddle as if preparing to defend his position. "I suppose it is a fortress of sorts. It keeps the jungle out."

She withdrew a handkerchief from her sleeve and dabbed at the perspiration on her face and throat, determined to remain calm despite the growing ire she sensed in her companion. "Are you sure that's all you want to keep out?"

She studied the kaleidoscope of emotions that moved across his expressive face. Anger showed clearly in the set of his jaw and the fire in those pale slate-blue eyes.

"You ask too damned many questions." He pointed toward a grove dotted with white blooms, diverting her from the subject at hand. "I grow trees that are a combination of Arabica and Robusta. They bloom like Arabica which grows best in the mountains, but they're stronger like Robusta which can grow anywhere. That's why I decided to develop my own strain. The coffee is uniquely mine in flavor, aroma, and smoothness."

"I know. Your coffee always demands the highest price on the market," Caroline said admiringly. Not only was Jason's coffee of the finest quality, his consistently high yields had made the Sinclair Coffee Company one of the most successful companies in New Orleans. "This part of the plantation is as flat as Louisiana bottomland."

Jason studied her, suspicion showing plainly on his handsome face. "It's very similar in composition, too. It's strong but fragile. It's hard to explain. You can't treat it harshly. But if you're kind to the land, it'll be kind to you. It's a simple rule more planters would do well to learn."

"You couldn't possibly grow pure Arabica here," Caroline said, thinking aloud. "Fungus would take it over. But by combining it with Robusta. . . . How very interesting."

"You needn't patronize me, woman," he said sharply, an angry glint in his eyes.

"My name is Caroline," she told him patiently, as if she were speaking to a child, "and why would you think I'm patronizing you?"

"Aren't you?"

"Why, no. I was completely sincere. I've seen what happens to the coffee when it reaches the market in New Orleans. Is it so hard to believe that I might be interested in how it's grown?"

"There's no need," he assured her, his manner, his expression, cold and remote. "I don't expect it."

Caroline watched in mute amazement as he spurred his horse into a canter. She considered his words. What had they meant? That she was not allowed a thought or opinion or interest except those approved by him?

What an extraordinary man! He obviously had little experience with women—educated, outspoken ones at least—if he believed he could dictate her very thoughts.

Caroline caught up to her husband. He saw her and pulled back on the reins, slowing his horse to a brisk walk. They moved down a narrow path that cut through one of the orchards. The scent of coffee and sweet blossoms enveloped them.

Caroline closed her eyes and breathed deeply. She loved the aroma of coffee beans. In New Orleans, she'd always volunteered whenever Derek needed someone to run a message or voucher to the warehouse, just so she could experience the sweet, tantalizing smell. Besides, it made her feel more a part of the company to actually see and smell the product that kept them solvent.

"The trees bloom year round in this climate," he explained, "so there are trees with berries ready to be picked and trees with young blooms in the same grove."

"How much does each tree yield?" she asked.

Jason eyed her curiously. Though apparently doubtful of her sincerity, he couldn't seem to stop himself from talking about a subject that had dominated his life for the last fifteen years. "A pound of coffee per year per plant is a good yield."

"That doesn't sound like much," she said with a frown. Even with coffee prices high, as they had been when she left New Orleans, she couldn't see how he could make enough money to live. "How many trees do you have?"

"Why do you ask so many questions?" he asked impatiently.

"Why do you hate answering them so much?" she challenged, tilting her chin stubbornly.

"I'm not used to—" He didn't have to explain himself to anyone, least of all her. He'd almost admitted a weakness, that he didn't have a lot of experience with inquisitive females. In fact, his experience with women rarely involved conversation. And he wasn't interested in conversation now, just in getting this damned tour over with. "I've got a thousand acres of land under cultivation right now and probably four hundred trees per acre that are mature enough to yield coffee this year."

"Why that's four thousand trees or four hundred thousand pounds of coffee per year. With coffee at twenty-one cents a pound, that means this year's harvest should be worth eighty-four thousand dollars on the American market. That's a fortune!"

Jason's eyes narrowed. Her quick calculations displayed an intelligence beyond anything he'd expected or wanted in a wife.

"It would be if it were all profit," he told her, wondering why he bothered when the last thing he wanted to do was discuss business with his wife. "It takes a lot of money to run a plantation of this size."

"Especially one so isolated."

Jason stiffened, taken aback yet again. Damn her. She had an uncanny ability to put him at ease and make him say more than he intended. Somehow, she'd managed to turn the tables again.

The orchards gave way to jungle. As they emerged into a clearing, the *benefício* came into view.

"You are familiar with the *benefício*," he commented dryly to cover his embarrassment at the memory of yesterday's encounter.

Caroline's insides churned as she looked at the familiar building and remembered the last time she'd seen it.

"Yes," she said, her gaze fixed on the white building, "and a very fine *benefício* it is, so straight and tall and firm. I would have to say that it is one of the finest *benefícios* I have ever seen." She didn't know why she'd said that. It was as if someone else had taken control of her speech as well as her emotions.

"So, you have a wide range of experience with *benefícios*?" he retorted.

Caroline smiled, enjoying the game more than she should. "Not really. But I am sure beyond a doubt that, as *benefícios* go, this is a most splendid one. But, then, I've only seen the outside. I have no idea what goes on inside. Those hard, thick walls must hide some interesting secrets."

Jason pulled his horse to a halt. At the same time, he reached over and jerked the reins from Caroline's hands, forcing her mount to a stop beside his and moving so that their legs were sandwiched between the bodies of the horses. They were so close she could feel the heat and unrelenting power of his body.

"You are a very daring woman!" he said, a hint of disbelief in his voice. His hard, unyielding eyes pierced her self-control, and she glanced away uncomfortably, irrationally afraid that he would see through to her very soul if she didn't break the gaze.

"I—I'm sure I don't know what you . . ." she stammered, hating herself for allowing him to bully her.

"Don't play games with me." The menacing tone in his voice sent a shiver up her spine. "I won't be toyed with. You would do well not to challenge me."

"Know my place, is that what you're saying?" Perhaps he wasn't so different from the men she'd come into contact with in New Orleans and at medical school. All her life she'd been confronted by ignorance and narrow-mindedness. Why had she thought Jason Sinclair would be different?

He drew himself up to his full height and gazed down at her with eyes that glared a warning. "That's exactly what I'm saying."

"And what if I refuse?" she asked, quelling the fear that threatened her composure.

"It would not be wise. No one defies me or intentionally provokes me here, and certainly not a—"

"A woman? Is that what you were going to say? A woman?"

He grabbed her so quickly she didn't have time to react. He pulled her out of her saddle, halfway across his lap. His hard chest crushed her breasts as his mouth found hers in a kiss that sent currents of heat down her torso, scorching a path to her belly.

He had expected her to fight him, and that he could have dealt with, but not this surrender that strangely made her the victor. He had meant to punish her, not to gratify her, not to become caught up in this irresistible spiral of desire.

He had to stop, even though her mouth tasted as sweet as nectar and her body incited him to satisfy the building torment within him. She'd bewitched him, robbed him of his will. By her very submission, she had become the aggressor, and he sensed that he would lose much more than he would gain if he didn't stop this now.

He set her back in her saddle ungently and disentangled himself from her arms that had been locked around him. His chest still burned from the feel of the pinpoints of her nipples, and his breath rasped painfully in his lungs.

He wanted her with a fierceness that nearly consumed him. He wanted to make love to her right here and right now. She'd returned his kisses with a fervor of her own that told him she would not deny him should he pull her from her horse and carry her to the *beneficio*.

It was still early enough that his men would be in the orchards for at least another hour. No one would disturb them should he lay her gently on the empty patio and make love to her.

They were married. By the laws of God and man, he had every right to take her, but he could not, not now. Yes, they were bound by law, but he wasn't ready to make that final commitment, not yet. There were too many things unsettled between them.

When he did take her, it would not be because she'd seduced him or goaded him. It would be on *his* terms—when and where *he* chose.

She lifted a hand to smooth a lock of hair that had come loose from her chignon, and he noticed with some satisfaction that her fingers trembled slightly. Her gaze dropped away from his as if she couldn't bear to look at him.

"I think I've seen enough," she whispered in a

voice that trembled ever so slightly. "Please, take me back to the house."

As he watched her move slowly up the path toward the house, he experienced none of the gratification he'd expected over his victory. Was this what he had wanted? To make her loathe him? To kill the glimmer of admiration he saw in her eyes whenever she looked at him?

The taste of regret bitter in his mouth, he turned his own horse and followed her back the way they'd come.

Propelled by anger and humiliation, Caroline ran up the stairs and into her room, slamming the door behind her. She stopped just inside, her chest heaving with frustration and her hands curled into fists.

Someone, probably Ines, had opened the windows on both sides of her bedroom and a soft, sweet breeze wafted through, dispelling some of the tropical heat. Stripping down to her chemise and pantalets, she fell on her back on the bed, gazing up at the mosquito netting that fluttered slightly in the breeze.

She hadn't come here to be treated like a leper, like something loathsome and not quite human! Her husband had behaved in the most reprehensible manner. He treated her as if she were the enemy instead of someone who had given up everything to be his wife.

"Dear God, did I make the wrong choice?" she asked aloud.

She'd never been a quitter, but in the three years since her first husband had been killed, she'd never been so close to defeat. She was not the same frightened, destitute girl she had been when she'd first found herself a widow. She'd learned much about survival, and she'd learned to depend upon her own wits and skills to make a respectable, comfortable life for herself in New Orleans.

But nothing she had learned in all that time seemed to matter when it came to dealing with Jason Sinclair.

Rising from the bed, she walked to her trunk where it stood in a corner of the room, rummaging inside until she found the bundle of letters. Just touching them reminded her why she'd come here.

She untied the red silk ribbon that held them together and chose one at random, opening it with a loving, tender touch.

> *My closest neighbor visited yesterday for the first time in four months. He had a bride with him, a sallow-faced, terrified girl who nearly burst into tears when I asked her how she liked her new home. I believe he mistreats her, though I have no proof. I could see it in her eyes, the disillusionment and pain. Like Peggy's eyes. Why would a man bring a wife to the Amazon Valley only to mistreat her? I wanted to break him in half, but of course I said nothing and damned myself for the rest of the day.*

"You're a fool," Caroline told herself aloud as she felt her heart soften toward him again. Her mind was already formulating excuses for his behavior.

To be honest, she had provoked him, albeit unintentionally. She had meant to flirt with him but had only succeeded in angering him, and even when she'd realized how angry he had become, she hadn't been able to stop. Her innuendo and double-edged questions had pushed him beyond endurance. What had she expected? She'd cornered him and she had suffered the consequences. It was a mistake she would be careful not to make in the future. She wasn't about to give up, not just yet.

"*Patrão* is not hungry?" Ines asked reproachfully.

Jason glanced up from his plate to see Ines standing at the end of the dining room table, frowning at him. He realized that he had hardly eaten a bite but had been rolling his food around on the plate instead. Dropping his fork, he pushed the plate away as if it were something odious.

"No, I'm not hungry," he growled. The clock on the wall struck the noon hour. "Where is Mrs. Sinclair?"

"She say she eats in her room." Ines cleared his plate away. "I am thinking you are not nice to her."

"Mind your own business, Ines," Jason growled, pushing his chair back from the table.

Ines snorted. "Man don't know what's good for him."

Jason stalked through the open dining room door, trying not to let Ines's words needle him. He'd always treated her more like a friend or family member than a servant, and now he was suffering the consequences. Now she thought she knew him better than he knew himself.

He just wanted to be left alone. That was why he'd come to the jungle in the first place.

There would be no activity on the *fazenda* for the next three hours as the natives observed the customary siesta. When he'd first arrived in the Amazon Valley, Jason had tried to defy the midday heat. He'd soon learned the error of his ways from the exhaustion his labors produced.

Normally, Jason passed the time relaxing on one of the unused patios of the *benefício*, napping beneath one of the several palm trees planted there if he'd had a particularly restless night. And even though last night certainly qualified, he knew he wouldn't sleep today. He strode out onto the patio, willing himself not to glance up at the door on the second floor. At the fountain, he splashed water over his face to clear his head, then ran his hands through his hair, slicking it back off his face.

Damn her. She'd turned the tables on him again. He'd meant to show her what he was, what he was capable of so that she would stay out of his way. He'd meant to frighten her, but when he succeeded, the self-loathing in the pit of his stomach had nearly devoured him. Maybe he didn't have a taste for violence any more.

You'll end up just like your good-for-nothing father, his uncle William Sinclair's voice taunted him from the past. *Just like your father.*

Could a man change his destiny? Could he escape his birthright?

A shiver trembled up his spine and set his neck to tingling. Someone was watching him. He jerked around to find Caroline sitting on a bench behind him. He released a sigh of relief mixed with displeasure. He'd been disappointed and even a little angry when she hadn't appeared for luncheon, but now he found he didn't want to face her again so soon. What could he say to her; how should he approach her? He'd be damned if he'd apologize.

"I don't mean to intrude," she said in a voice that dripped honey. "I usually spend the afternoons here reading."

She had donned a light cotton dress and come to the patio to pass the afternoon. It had not been her intention to force her presence upon her husband again. She didn't relish the thought of facing him so soon after her humiliation. But she'd spent far too much time fleeing to her room, and she wasn't about to do so now.

Jason ran a hand through his damp hair. He stared at her silently, and Caroline watched the changing expressions that always shifted across his face. At first, he seemed surprised to see her, surprise giving way to something she might have interpreted as gladness, if she didn't know how unlikely he was to be glad to see her. Whatever that emotion might have been, it quickly gave way to curiosity.

"I had no idea," he said. "I mean, that you spent the afternoons here."

"How could you?" Caroline asked. "There are many things you don't know about me."

Anger was getting the better of her, and she struggled for control. If she didn't tread lightly, she'd find herself baiting him again. She didn't want to drive him away, so she'd have to use another approach.

She turned the leather-bound book in her hand so that Jason could see the title on the spine. It was *Bleak House* by Dickens. "Your taste in books seems quite eclectic. Your library is extensive."

"I'm glad you approve. Please feel free to avail yourself of anything that interests you."

"I wondered if you had anything on coffee cultivation." Her eyes remained on the book in her hand, but she could feel the heat of his gaze on her. "I can't imagine that you would not. You've got everything from Russian history to Goethe to Jane Austen. . . . If I didn't know better, I'd think that every book in your library was a new edition."

"They are. It's my only requirement. Derek and his wife bought them on my behalf," he told her. "One hundred and twenty yards of books, enough to fill all the shelves in the room."

"You don't . . . ?"

"I don't have time to read," he said.

The skill with which he told the lie chilled Caroline to the marrow. He was very good at it—at lying. How would she ever be able to know when he was telling the truth?

I used to sneak and keep some of the money I made working at the sugar mill to buy books, he wrote Derek. *I'd hide them under my bed and read them late at night after my father passed out.*

The words of the letter leaped unbidden into her mind, jolting her with their significance. Compassion gripped her heart at the thought of that small boy hoarding the money he'd worked so hard for and using it to purchase books, books his father had burned more than once.

Jason was still hiding his books. He guarded his secrets carefully. How would he react if he ever learned that for the past year she and not Derek had taken his detailed lists and purchased the books he'd requested?

"The most I can manage is the month's worth of newspapers we get when the mail steamer comes up from Manaus," he was saying. "And why would you want a book on coffee cultivation?"

Caroline shrugged, trying to appear casual while her mind churned with unspoken questions. "I told you, I'm curious." She held his gaze for as long as she could, but something in those iridescent blue depths forced her to look away before he penetrated her very soul. It was the second time she'd experienced the sensation of being scrutinized, physically and emotionally, by those sharp, inquisitive eyes.

Opening her book to the place where she'd left off yesterday, she tried to dismiss him, but Jason would not be dismissed so easily. He stood still, studying her intently. She read the same paragraph three times without comprehension before finally lowering the book and gazing back at him.

"There are no seasons here," he told her, "not like you're accustomed to at any rate. There's the rainy season when it rains every day, and there's the dry season when it rains every other day."

She smiled up at him serenely, and he frowned and looked away. "I'm not at all what you expected, am I?" she asked.

Jason returned his gaze to her with a shrug. "I don't even remember what I'd expected any more. What about you? Am I what you'd expected? I mean, you must have had some kind of expectations or you wouldn't have come here."

Caroline felt her face burn as she remembered the fantasies she'd nurtured in New Orleans. She was twelve years old when her mother had died, so she remembered what it was like to have a complete family. And she remembered how it had been between her parents—the love, the laughter, the secret glances they shared that she didn't understand at the time. That was what she wanted, what she'd dreamed of. She wanted the kind of marriage her parents had enjoyed, a partnership.

Those dreams seemed quite ridiculous now. She sat in a tropical garden in the heart of the Amazon Valley surrounded by the pervasive jungle with her irascible, unrefined husband, a man who had been cut off from civilization for so long he'd reverted to behaving like a savage.

"I still can't understand why a young, attractive woman like yourself would want to live in such an isolated place," he said. "Or why you would marry a man you'd never laid eyes on. You're obviously not desperate."

"No," she agreed, "only lonely."

She'd been lonely since her father's death. Losing the love and camaraderie they'd shared had left her hungry for that kind of spiritual belonging. Foolishly, she'd turned to Wade Marshall to fill the void.

Her first husband had exuded taste and impeccable breeding, but his dissolute living had nearly destroyed them.

Studying her tall, ruggedly handsome husband, she had the inexplicable feeling that she could be happy with him, in spite of his lack of polish, social grace, sophistication. Somehow those things seemed unimportant, meaningless, even ridiculous.

"May I ask how old you are?" he asked, bringing her back from her reverie.

"Twenty-five."

Jason quirked a shocked eyebrow at her answer.

"You needn't look so shocked. Twenty-five is hardly ancient."

"That's true, but you. . . . I mean, you're so lovely, so . . ." His incendiary gaze seared her flesh and melted her composure. "Why didn't you marry before now?"

Caroline swallowed her fear. Finally, the moment had come, the moment she had been dreading since she answered Jason's request for a wife. The words in Jason's letter rose in her mind—"chaste, tractable, and of child-bearing age"—and her heart settled to her stomach.

"I didn't mean to pry," Jason said a bit defensively. "You yourself said that I know nothing about you."

"I . . . I was married before," she confessed quickly before she lost her nerve, feeling as if she'd just admitted to murder or some other heinous crime.

His face hardened and he stood straight up, dropping his foot from the bench. "Derek failed to mention that detail," he said through clenched teeth. "Didn't he tell you what my requirements were?"

Fear began to coalesce into anger. Caroline clenched her fists to control her rising ire. "I suppose he thought we were suitable . . ." she lied. She knew she'd live to regret it, but she couldn't tell him the whole truth, not when he stood glowering down at her as if he'd like very much to throttle her.

"I'm sorry." She studied him, mesmerized by the bitterness etched across his taut mouth. A cold dread shivered through her body. "I'm a widow. That is . . . I'm not sorry I'm a widow, I'm sorry . . ."

Jason laughed without humor. "This must be Derek's idea of a joke."

"A joke? I hardly think so. I mean, if he knew how you would react, it would have been very cruel to send me all this way for nothing." *Tell him*, her conscience urged, but when she gazed into those fury-bright eyes, her throat closed.

"Well, that's exactly what he's done," Jason assured her, turning away as if to leave.

"Wait!" Caroline came to her feet, and Jason turned to face her expectantly. "You can't just walk away like that. Surely you didn't expect one of the fine families of New Orleans to send a young, innocent daughter to the wilds of Brazil."

"I have quite a lot to offer a wife," he assured her. "Or didn't my cousin tell you that? I think he did. I think that's exactly why you're here. You seemed overly interested in my financial status earlier."

Caroline bristled. She threw the book onto the stone table with all her strength, then stood glaring at him, hands clenched into fists at her sides.

"I never asked you about your financial status." She bit the words out. "If you'll remember, you volunteered that information."

"You did the calculations, Mrs. Sinclair."

"If I were only interested in financial security, I could have found that without traveling hundreds of miles!"

"It would have been better for both of us if you had."

"What are you saying?" she asked apprehensively. "Are you saying that because I'm not a—a—because I've been married, that you intend to. . . ."

"The mail steamer will return in a month. What I

am saying is that you will be aboard that boat when it returns to Manaus."

"But—but we're married!" Caroline sputtered.

"A condition easily remedied," he said, his manner indifferent. "An unconsummated marriage is easily dissolved. You can take care of it when you reach New Orleans."

"Annulment? What if I refuse?" She trembled with outrage and frustration. He was so cold, so unbending.

Jason shrugged. "Then I'll take care of it myself. You misrepresented yourself to me."

Caroline sucked in her breath as if she'd been hit in the stomach. "Don't you think your views are a little outdated? It is nearly the twentieth century, and we're a long way from Victorian England!"

"That is irrelevant."

He turned to leave again, and his apathy fueled her anger. Determined to elicit some kind of emotion from him, she shouted at his retreating back. "It was very wise of you not to consummate the marriage until you decided whether or not to keep me. It avoids the necessity for a nasty divorce. But if I should decide to oppose your suit, how would you prove your claims? A medical examination? I can't possibly profess to be untouched since I was married before, and for the same reason, you can't possibly hope to prove the marriage was not consummated!"

He turned to look at her, his face a pale shade of red that gave Caroline a small measure of gratification. "You are a very blunt woman!"

"Yes, I am," she admitted, tilting her chin proudly. "I am blunt and bold and daring and intelligent, all the qualities you must abhor in a mate!"

He impaled her with his gaze. "How could you possibly know what I abhor or desire?"

"You wanted a girl and you got a woman! You wanted someone you could bully and frighten with your blustering and your—your . . ."

Her words trailed off, and she backed away as he moved slowly toward her until her back was against the stone table. Standing close to her, their bodies nearly touching, he leaned over her menacingly, forcing her to bend backward to avoid contact with him.

"And I don't frighten you?"

"No." She averted her gaze from the violence in his blue eyes, gasping for breath as the very air turned thick with tension like the stillness before a violent thunderstorm.

"Not in the least?" Heat radiated from his body; his warm breath stirred the wayward tendrils of hair at her temple.

"No." Her trembling voice belied the word.

"Then perhaps you aren't as intelligent as I'd thought. You see, I know a great deal about inflicting pain." He touched a callused finger to her chin and she recoiled as if she'd been burned, her heart pounding ferociously.

He wouldn't really hurt her, she tried to assure herself, but the very threat was enough to fill her soul with fear.

"I learned from a master," he went on, his voice soft, mesmerizing. "I know your every vulnerability. I know how to make you beg for mercy. You have no idea—"

"Stop it." Her throat constricted around the words as a genuine fear shivered down her spine. He could easily hurt her. His size alone was daunting, even if she hadn't seen the corded muscles that rippled beneath his skin. He could crush the life from her with his bare hands.

"Pain is a different sensation for women than for men. Certain parts of the body and mind are more susceptible."

"Stop. Please." Tears threatened her control. A part of her, the small part not immersed in fear, almost pitied him. Had he survived the pain of his youth by hardening himself to suffering and learning to inflict pain himself? The thought terrified her. She was very much alone, very much at his mercy, cut off from civilization by a thousand miles of river.

"Have I managed to frighten you now?" he asked tautly.

"Yes. Are you happy? Does it make you feel more like a man?"

Panting with anger and excitement, he moved closer to her, barely brushing her body with his. She placed a hand behind her to brace herself against the table. The other hand she pressed against his chest, pushing against him with all her strength, but he refused to yield. Instead, he twined a hand in her upswept hair and wrapped his other arm around her narrow waist, crushing her roughly against him as his mouth possessed hers in a bruising kiss.

This time she did fight him. She wedged both arms between their bodies and pushed desperately against his hard, implacable chest. He deepened the kiss, forcing her lips apart and assaulting the inner softness of her mouth with the lash of his tongue. Desire began to creep insidiously into her flesh and she stopped struggling and let her body fall against his as his hands moved to her buttocks and he pressed her soft loins against his hardness.

"Are you always so easily aroused?" he asked, releasing her abruptly so that she settled ungently onto her feet.

Caroline tensed at the harsh cruelty in his tone. Anger drove her to recklessness. She reached up, swinging out wildly, feeling the satisfying sting of her hand against his cheek.

Jason chuckled. "Leave it to my cousin to send me a whore for a wife."

"How dare you!" She swung out again, but this time he caught her wrist and held it fast. She tried to pull free of his grip, but he refused to release her.

"Whore or not, you are my wife," he reminded her. "And like everything else in this house, you belong to me. And my word is final here. You will be on that steamer when it leaves for Manaus."

4

Jason stalked from the house to the stable where he mounted his prized bay stallion and sent it flying over the twisting paths to the *benefício*. The building and surrounding patios were silent and deserted, as he'd known they would be.

He unsaddled his horse and let it loose to graze and find shade from the blistering sun, then went to stand on the only empty patio, gazing out across the dark water to the jungle on the opposite side.

A widow.

Hadn't Derek even read his letter? Of all the people in the world, he would have expected Derek to understand his need to surround himself with purity.

He'd never been close to anyone, not really, but he and Derek had been friends during the three years he'd spent working at the Sinclair Coffee Company. And over the past year, Jason had revealed more about his past to Derek than he ever had to any other living soul. Betrayal by the one person he'd thought he could trust cut deeply. He'd poured his guts out to Derek in his letters. Derek should have understood.

He'd wanted a woman without expectations, a woman without knowledge of the world, a woman who would fit easily into the place he'd created for her and not complicate his life with a lot of questions and demands.

All he required was a woman to give him an heir, to give him tenderness when he wanted it, on his terms and without asking for anything from him in return. But tenderness had never been a part of his life, at least not after Peggy. If not for his older sister, his life would have been a wasteland. He'd believed her to be the most beautiful, most loving creature in the world. Peggy had tried to make their pitiful shack habitable. She was always picking wildflowers from the field behind their house and bringing them home or making paper lanterns that their father would destroy in one of his drunken fits of violence. It had been a useless exercise, but Peggy had never given up—not until the end when life and reality had finally extinguished the tiny flame that had been her spirit.

He hadn't thought of Peggy in a long time. It was Caroline's fault. She and his sister weren't at all alike, except that they were both beautiful and they were both dreamers. Peggy might have done something as impetuous as hopping on a boat and traveling to an unknown fate in a savage country, but Peggy would have been doing so to escape. Was that what Caroline had done?

Damn her! He didn't need complications. And why did it matter? He'd already decided she had to go when the mail steamer returned. There was no other way.

He closed his eyes, allowing the pain in his soul to wash over him. To be honest, he'd been looking for something, some flaw in her apparent perfection, something he could use to justify rejecting her. He couldn't bear it, being near her, always wondering when the demon inside him would strike out. She'd pushed him to the very brink of his restraint twice already, and she hadn't been in his house a week. So far he'd channeled his frustration into the escalating desire within him.

She would be better off without him. She could go back to New Orleans and resume her life, forget about him.

He wasn't proud of his behavior, but it had been necessary. He'd succeeded. For the remainder of her stay, she would go out of her way to avoid him. It was a good thing. He didn't know how much longer he could resist her. After all, he wasn't made of stone. Just thinking about her set his blood on fire. The feel of her lips against his, the softness of her skin still lingered vividly in his mind.

He opened his eyes when, without warning, the heavens parted and a drenching rain beat down on the already sodden earth. A wall of water surrounded the *beneficio*, cutting him off from the rest of the world. He breathed deeply of the exhilarating, familiar scent of wet jungle and sultry heat, listening to the sound of the rain battering the red tiled roof.

Work, that was what he needed. The men would be waking from their siesta soon. He'd work himself to the point of exhaustion, leaving no energy for reflection or conjecture.

*   *   *

Caroline looked up from the book that lay open on her lap. Her spirit slumped in disappointment as the sound of rain filled the library. She'd mistaken the noise for approaching hoofbeats that would have heralded Jason's return.

It was no use trying to concentrate on anything. Her mind kept returning to the afternoon's battle. Like generals in a war, they seemed to gather their forces for each skirmish, inflict as much damage as possible on the other side, then retreat to count their losses and tend their wounds in order to regroup for the next battle. The problem was that he played the game much better than she did. His blows struck much deeper than hers.

"Damn him!" she said aloud to the empty room.

Coming to her feet, she began to pace the length of the room as a growing anger roiled in her breast. When she looked back on the history of their little war, she had to admit that she'd lost almost every battle, and it infuriated her. She'd never lost at anything, and the bitter taste of defeat nearly choked her.

Where was he weakest, most vulnerable? If she could analyze his defenses and exploit his Achilles' heel, she could. . . .

What? She could win? At what cost? If she declared all-out war, would either of them be left standing when it was over?

Until now, he'd set the rules and he'd maintained the element of surprise. She'd never known when something she said would set him off. That still might be true, but the next time she would be prepared.

And there would be a next time. He'd said the mail boat wouldn't return for another month. That meant they'd be forced to share this house for a while longer. And then. . . .

Caroline's heart constricted as she considered her options. She couldn't go back to New Orleans. She'd sold everything she owned, including her house, and Derek Sinclair would never rehire her after what she'd done.

Moving in with Aunt Sarah in Memphis was her only option, and the thought made her stomach knot and her heart sink.

Aunt Sarah wasn't unkind, just unbending. Pious to the point of absurdity, Sarah Powers, her mother's matronly sister, detested anything she considered worldly—newspapers, plays, music, paintings, anything more than somber, utilitarian dress. . . . It was a list without end. Once under Aunt Sarah's roof, all of Caroline's hard won independence would be stripped from her, along with her very spirit.

"And I wanted adventure," she said aloud with a snort.

"What is a'venture?"

Caroline jerked guiltily at the sound of the voice behind her, whirling around to watch Ines enter the room with a feather duster in her hand. She turned away with a sigh, running her fingers along the uneven row of book spines that lined the shelf before her.

"Excitement," she explained. "Experience. Maybe danger."

"You have a'venture where you come from?" Ines asked as she began dusting the furniture.

Caroline laughed without humor. "Where I come

from, the only adventure I ever experienced was trying to get to work on the trolley car."

Ines stopped dusting, her brow knitting in curiosity. "This is dangerous?"

"No." Caroline smiled. "No, it's not dangerous. It's not very exciting either, but it is an experience."

"Here it is excitement all the time," Ines assured her, resuming her task.

"Oh, I can imagine."

Excitement was one thing she would never lack in the Amazon Valley. The jungle pulsed with a never-ending struggle for survival. But the one thing she would lack was the one thing she didn't want to live without, the one thing she had come here hoping to find—a sense of belonging, of being needed and cherished.

Her father had cherished her, in his own way, but that wasn't the kind of love she wanted now.

She'd hoped to find that kind of love and mutual need with Wade, but he had been incapable of the depth of emotion she craved.

"So, here you have adventure, yes?" Ines's words drew her out of her reverie.

"No," Caroline replied quickly. "Well, yes, but I can't stay here."

Ines turned to face Caroline with shock and disappointment in her eyes. "But you marry Master Jason and travel across the ocean Atlantic."

"Not exactly, but I did travel a very long way. It—it was very foolish of me. I thought—" Caroline broke off, her eyes filling with tears she refused to shed.

"You don't like it here?"

Gaining control again, Caroline took a deep breath before answering, "I haven't been here long enough to tell. It doesn't matter. Master Jason says I must go and I'm not even sure I want to stay. I don't know what I want."

"Master Jason means what he doesn't say sometimes."

Caroline laughed. "I wonder."

"Master Jason is a good man. I know. Master Jason is not affection, not soft. You know?"

"Believe it or not, I do."

"But in here—" Ines held her fist to her chest. "In here he is soft."

Caroline turned to gaze out the window once again, her mind in turmoil. She'd believed Jason to be soft on the inside. Otherwise she never would have come here at all. But what she hadn't expected was the hardness of the shell he'd crawled into. If he possessed any softness, she wasn't sure any more that she could get through to it, to the man inside.

The rain subsided as quickly as it had begun. The jungle grew quiet and still for an instant before bursting with the noise of trilling birds and chattering monkeys once again. "Ines, he doesn't want me here. He's told me so."

"Man like Master Jason, he not always knows what he want. Sometime he find out what he want when it's gone."

"He has been nothing but rude and outright cruel to me since I've been here. He avoids me or insults me . . ."

"He is afraid."

Surprise forced Caroline to turn and face the other woman. "Afraid? Of what?"

"Of course, of you."

Caroline laughed without humor. "Me? That's

ridiculous. I can't imagine that Jason Sinclair has ever been afraid of anything. Why would you think he's afraid of me?"

Ines stared at her for a moment, and Caroline waited for her to speak. Instead, she turned away and went back to dusting. "I say too much. Master Jason, he is much mixed up inside. He isn't liking it here alone, and he is afraid. . . . He is afraid you will get too close to him and you will not like what is there."

The less you let anyone else know how you feel about anything, the better. It's good business sense.

Jason's words leaped into her mind. At the time, she'd taken them at face value, but maybe there was more to it than that. Business sense or philosophy of life? Could Ines be right? Her heart twisted at the thought that the frightened, injured little boy she'd glimpsed in Jason's letters might still be trapped inside that grown up body.

"You stay, *senhora.*" Ines nodded emphatically and went back to her dusting, as if everything was settled.

"I can't. Don't you understand? He said I have to go back on the mail boat when it returns." Caroline looked out the window again. "I'm not sure I want to stay anyway. I'm not what he wanted, and I don't know if he's what I want either."

"*Sim, senhora.* You want a strong man, not like Master Jason, a handsome man, no? *Varonil?* Yes, I see why you do not want Master Jason for a husband."

Caroline laughed. "Well, I don't know what *varonil* means exactly, but I can guess, and yes, he is all those things, but what difference does it make whether or not I want him if he doesn't want me?"

Ines smiled slyly. "Master Jason is not knowing his own mind, I know. But a beautiful woman can sometimes show a man what he does not want to see, it is not true?"

Jason stood just outside the stable beneath a waning sun, his eyes closed as the hauntingly sweet music surrounded him and penetrated his soul. A deluge of memories rushed at him so quickly he didn't have time to staunch them. The half-forgotten scent of roses filled his nostrils, and an oppressive heat nearly suffocated him, not the heat of the jungle. He'd been transported to Mrs. Longford's parlor in the Garden District of New Orleans. He was a child again, sitting on the bench beside his mother while she played.

A piano had been far out of reach of the Sinclairs' meager income, but Mrs. Longford, one of the fine ladies his mother had done laundry for, had allowed her to play from time to time. Listening to his mother play was one of the few pleasant memories from his childhood.

He blinked against the blinding emotion in his breast. The soft, seductive melody settled like a stone on his heart.

No one in the house knew how to play the piano, no one except perhaps Caroline. Evidently that was one requirement Derek had heeded.

She played well, better than his mother, but then Caroline had probably had more opportunity to practice.

My grandmother had a grand piano in her house in Dublin. His mother's clear, dulcet voice reached out to him from the past. *I used to play all the time when I was a girl, but then the bad times came and we had to leave.*

He didn't want to go inside. He wanted to stay where he was and listen to the haunting music and forget that she would be gone in a month, this woman who made him feel things he'd never felt before.

What was it about her that made him feel that anything was possible? She made him hope, made him almost eager for tomorrow instead of fearing it as something unknown and therefore threatening.

Shaking himself mentally, he gathered his resolve before stalking purposefully toward the open door to the downstairs parlor where the grand piano had stood silently for five years. He stopped just inside the door, captivated by the sight of her sitting on the bench, her hands moving magically over the white and black keys as she elicited sounds from the instrument, the sweetest sounds he'd ever heard.

His breath caught in his throat as his eyes glided over her body, drinking in her beauty. She wore a white gown, the sleeves of which were little more than strips of material worn low on her smooth, white shoulders. A deep V plunged down her back, revealing delicate shoulder blades and soft, ivory flesh. Her brown hair, as lustrous as the mahogany instrument she stroked, was swept up in a chignon and gilded with one of the orchids he had placed in her room every day.

Caroline reached the end of the piece, her fingers lingering over the last chords. As the melody died away, it was replaced by the sound of clapping. She turned slowly to see Jason standing in the doorway, his body haloed by the red light of the setting sun.

Still angry after their earlier confrontation, Caroline turned away, glancing back at the keys. "I couldn't resist. I suppose I shouldn't have played without asking permission," she said caustically. "I know I had no right—"

"Don't," he said sharply. "You're welcome to play as long as you're here. I didn't know its sound would be so true after all these years in the jungle humidity."

"Why do you own a piano you don't play? Is it just another possession to add to your collection, something else to *own* just for the sake of owning it?" *Calm, calm*, she told herself. She was spoiling for a fight, and if she didn't watch her sharp tongue, she'd end up prodding him into another argument.

"What difference could it possibly make to you?"

"You own books you don't read and a piano you don't play," she said thoughtfully. "What a pity."

"What do you mean?"

She shrugged, trying to appear nonchalant, acutely aware that he had come to stand close behind her. "Anyone who knows anything at all about the piano will tell you that the sweetness and tone only improve with the playing."

"Is that so?"

"Why yes," she replied as demurely as she could. She ran her hand across the keys from low to high. "Of course, it takes a true master to bring her to complete fulfillment."

He moved so swiftly she had no time to react before he slammed the lid on the piano keys, and Caroline withdrew her fingers just in time.

His hand still on the piano, he stood over her, his gaze traveling down the low décolletage of her gown. Her face and throat flushed with hot color as she struggled to control the wild pounding of her heart and her rapid breathing. From his vantage point, he would be able to see deep inside the daringly cut gown.

"And was your first husband such a master?" he asked, his voice thick with desire.

Caroline fought the urge to cover herself against the warmth of his gaze on her exposed flesh. Perhaps she had been too bold this time, but she had to do something if she wanted to stay here. No one was going to convince Jason Sinclair that he didn't know his own mind, but perhaps she could sway his senses by showing him what he would miss when she was gone. And perhaps if she could make him desire her, she could make him love her.

You have almost every young man you meet wrapped around your little finger, but you always want the one who can resist your charms, her father had told her more than once. And whether that was true or not didn't matter in the least. All she knew was that she wanted this man, God help her, despite his gruff, irascible manner. And she *would not* get on that mail boat and return to New Orleans in defeat, not without a fight.

Tension crackled in the scant space between them. Caroline's breath became shallow and her nipples grew taut in anticipation of his touch. She wanted him to touch her gently, to kiss her again.

He had asked her a question, a bitter question, but she couldn't answer. Her throat had tightened and her mind had stopped functioning altogether.

"Run out of clever retorts?" he whispered.

"I . . ."

Her words drifted away unsaid as he ran a finger

along the line of her collar bone, the gentle fire in his fingertips melting what was left of her composure. A dizzying desire possessed her body as he lowered his head, the soft warmth of his breath touching her parted lips. Gasping for air, Caroline felt her body melting into a pool of mindless longing. It didn't matter that he'd been cruel to her earlier. Nothing mattered but Jason and the terrifying demands of her own body.

"Dinner."

Caroline nearly jumped out of her skin at the sound of Ines's voice from the doorway. Jason jerked away quickly, and it took them both a few moments to compose themselves.

Jason smiled sardonically, as if he had been unaffected, as if she had been the only one close to surrender, and she hated him for that smile. Grudgingly, she placed her hand on his proffered arm, her body still resounding with a bittersweet yearning as they walked into the dining room. He held her chair out for her, then took his own place across from her.

Caroline noticed that Ines served the food quickly and made her exit as soon as possible, the traitor, leaving her alone with this man who defied understanding.

Silence stretched between them as they both concentrated on their food. Jason lifted his water goblet and took a long drink. As he returned the glass to the table, Caroline felt the heat of his measuring gaze.

"So," he said, "tell me about this husband of yours."

Caroline stiffened. "Why? I thought you didn't want to know anything about me."

Jason shrugged. "Just trying to make conversation. But if it's a sore subject. . . ."

"He died in a river boat accident three years ago. We were married less than two years. Afterward, I supported myself by teaching piano and—"

"But you haven't told me anything about the man," he interrupted, "what he was like."

She shot him a murderous scowl. "There's not much to tell."

"You mean he wasn't much of a man?" he asked, wiping his mouth with a white linen napkin and placing it on the table beside his plate.

"I didn't say that." He was leading up to something, and she wasn't sure she wanted to follow.

"I'm sure there are plenty of interesting things about your former husband." He sat back in his chair, studying the wine in his glass as he swirled it around.

"What would you like to know?" she asked, knowing full well that he didn't want to know about Wade at all. He wanted her to say something he could attack.

"Oh, his name, what he looked like, how old he was. . . ."

"His name was Wade. Wade Marshall. He stood just under six feet tall, rather slim. His hair and eyes were brown. He was a year older than me and had all his permanent teeth, as far as I knew."

"How did you meet?"

Caroline released a tired sigh. He wouldn't be happy until she answered all his questions, when he had been so reticent about answering hers. "He was one of my father's apprentices."

"Ah, so he was a doctor like your father," Jason said, pretending to give the matter careful consideration. "You must have had quite a lot to talk about."

"He was not a doctor. My father left him enough money to finish medical school but—" She hesitated, the pain in her heart as acute as it had been three years ago. "Well, he lost it and he was never the same after that. It broke his spirit."

Jason was quiet for so long that Caroline grew uncomfortable. Unable to meet his gaze, she rearranged the food on her plate with her fork. She'd told him what he wanted to know. Why didn't he say something? Why did he sit there as if he were analyzing her testimony for flaws, for hidden meanings?

Finally he spoke, his voice soft and low. "If he had no more spirit than that. . . ."

Caroline faced him squarely, outraged at his unwarranted attack. Maybe Wade had been weak, but it was utterly unfair and petty of Jason to slander a dead man. "Not everyone has your strength. Not everyone can survive what you have—"

As soon as the words were out of her mouth, she wanted to retrieve them. How could she have been so careless? She knew him so well it was hard to pretend they were complete strangers. She knew that his parents had been Irish, that his father's name was Cullen, that his sister had killed herself. And she knew that he'd overcome more in his lifetime than most men could have endured. Naturally he would disdain those weaker than he.

But she wasn't supposed to know any of those things. He must never learn that she'd pretended to be Derek and answered his letters, read letters intended for his cousin. Deep in the pit of her stomach, she feared that he would never forgive her should he find out.

She sat as still as a statue, watching him, gauging

his reaction. He leaned forward, his eyes narrowed, his face as hard and cold as granite. "How could you possibly know what I've survived?"

Swallowing hard against the fear lodged in her throat, Caroline measured her words with care. Still she stammered guiltily when she finally spoke. "I . . . It's written on your face, in—in your eyes."

"What did Derek tell you about me?" he asked, doubt and suspicion etched on his face.

Caroline glanced away nervously. "Nothing, nothing really. He said you grew up in New Orleans and you came to Brazil when your parents died. That's all."

"He must have told you something else, otherwise you'd still be in New Orleans."

Oh, dear, how could she explain? To him, they were total strangers. To her, they were longtime friends. He sat staring at her, waiting for her to explain. She had to say something, but she couldn't think clearly. Her mind was still reeling from the fact that she'd almost told him too much already.

"He told me you loved music," she lied with a tremulous smile. "He said that you weren't satisfied in the city where a man's potential is limited by his family connections and his wealth. He said you wanted to make something of yourself and build something with your own hands."

The tension in Jason's face eased to a degree, and she could tell by his expression that he believed her, albeit grudgingly.

"Then you know volumes more about me than I know about you," he said harshly. "I only found out today that you'd been married before. Did you love him? Your husband?"

Caroline bristled, but tried to remain calm. "I don't see how that could possibly matter—"

"It matters to me."

She relaxed back in her chair, unaware until then that she had been coiled as tightly as a spring. She knew what he wanted to hear, and she wasn't about to lie to satisfy his vanity. "Why does it suddenly matter so much? As you said, I'll be gone from here in a month. You've ignored me up until now. Why the sudden change?"

"Like I said, I'm just trying to make conversation."

"That's not conversation. You're interrogating me. Why don't you stop playing this game and just come to the point? There is a point, isn't there?"

Jason studied her for a moment, the stubborn set of her delicate chin, the challenge in her light eyes. Yes, there was a point. He wanted her to admit something, to say something that would make him feel justified in turning her away. He had tried to convince himself her lack of purity was enough, but now he wasn't so sure.

"No," he lied. "There was no point."

Movement on the patio beyond the open French doors caught Caroline's attention a second before one of Jason's workers burst into the dining room, his eyes wide in alarm and his chest heaving from exertion.

Jason was on his feet before the man came to a stop at the far end of the table. "What's happened?"

"*Patrão*, the river!" he gasped. "At the dam—mud slide."

"Dear God!" Jason's chair scraped against the floor as he shoved it back and moved toward the open door. "Injuries?"

"Ernesto and Vincente are trapped."

"Go tell Ines!" Jason ordered.

"I'm coming, too." Caroline said, coming to her feet, amazed at the swiftness of Jason's reaction. Concern showed plainly on his face as he turned to face her, halting her with a look.

"No. You stay here. I have enough to worry about without some blasted female who thinks—"

"I can help!" she cried furiously. "You are the most arrogant—"

"I don't have time to argue with you, Caroline!" He turned and walked away once again, dismissing her. "You'll get hurt. It's dirty and dangerous. Just because your father was a doctor and you carry that damned medical bag around everywhere you go. . . ."

"I went to medical school for two years!"

He turned to face her once more and his gaze swept over her in a cold, almost disgusted manner. "My, but you're full of surprises, aren't you?"

She rushed past him and out the door. "I'll get my bag!"

"Two minutes!!" Jason called after her. "I'll wait two minutes and then I'm leaving!"

5

A cacophony of voices reached out of the darkness as soon as the wagon rolled to a stop. Lanterns swayed crazily as men ran to and fro in a frenzy of activity. Caroline stood in the wagon, straining to see, trying to decide where the greatest need was.

Leaping from the vehicle, Jason rushed toward a group of a dozen or so men, leaving Caroline to climb down on her own. He disappeared into the darkness, swallowed by the night and the confusion.

"Help! Quickly!" someone shouted. "I have found Vincente!"

In the midst of the melee, Jason's rich baritone voice rang out. "Ines! Where are you?"

Caroline couldn't see two feet in front of her, but she followed the direction of Jason's voice, Ines tagging along in her wake as she shouldered her way through the crowd until she stood in the middle of the circle. Jason knelt on the ground beside Vincente, whose pallid face appeared ghostly in the darkness. The boy was in shock, that was the first thing she noticed. Her gaze went to his left arm where a tight tourniquet had been tied. Blood and mud covered the bandage and his arm.

"Have you been loosening the tourniquet?" Caroline asked the crowd at large. She fell to her knees beside the prone body, unmindful of the soft mud that soaked immediately through the thin material of her gown. "How long has it been on there?"

Jason looked up at her in annoyance. "Ines has been tending my workers for years, madam, and she can—"

"Ines is near to fainting, in case you hadn't noticed." She took hold of the boy's arm. His skin was clammy and cold beneath the mud. The circulation to his lower arm had been shut off too long.

"You can't just cut off the blood flow!" she shouted at the men who stood around her in dumbfounded silence. "He'll lose his arm."

"Julio!" Caroline called to the young groom. All her energies were concentrated on the patient, but she couldn't help sensing the incredulity in Jason's silent gaze. "Julio!"

"*Sim, senhora!*" The young man stepped forward. Ines peered around him, her dark face sallow with shock.

"Julio, go to the river and draw me a bucket of water. A full bucket," Caroline ordered.

"*Sim, senhora!*" he cried, rushing off to do as she bid.

Caroline began unfurling the tourniquet. The release of pressure would cause the wound to bleed

again, but she had to get that thing off and do it
right. She glanced impatiently at Jason, who
watched her in rapt silence.

"Jason, I think they need you down by the river!"
she pointed out, then searched the crowd for Ines.
"Ines, come here! I need your help."

"*Sim, senhora!*" Ines replied, standing over
Caroline, gazing down at the bloody mess with
round, horrified eyes.

"Are you sure you know what you're doing?"
Jason asked harshly.

"Go, Jason. I've done this sort of thing before!"
Without thinking, Caroline pulled up her skirt and
tore off a length of petticoat. She shoved it toward
Ines, who didn't respond.

Jason stood and rushed off in the direction of the
river, and Caroline breathed a sigh of relief. This
was going to be difficult enough without Jason questioning her every move.

"Ines, take this fabric," Caroline ordered. When
the other woman didn't comply, she called more
sharply, "Ines!"

"*Sim, senhora,*" came the reply.

"Ines, I need your help. Can you do as I say without fainting?"

Swallowing hard, Ines nodded her head. "I will
try, *senhora.*"

"Good," Caroline said more gently, compassion
for Ines momentarily outweighing the gravity of the
situation. Then she gazed down at the pale young
man and the urgency returned. "When I release the
tourniquet, the wound is going to start bleeding
again. When I tell you, press the fabric to the
wound. Can you do that?"

"*Sim, senhora,*" Ines replied, her voice quivering slightly.

Julio returned with the water Caroline had requested, and she used it to wash away the mud from around the wound.

"Are you ready Ines?"

"*Sim, senhora.*"

"Now." Caroline removed the tourniquet, and Ines replaced it with the wad of fabric as Caroline had instructed, pressing with all her strength to staunch the alarming flow of blood.

Satisfied that Ines wouldn't faint or become ill, Caroline opened her father's medical bag, digging inside until she found a large bottle of alcohol. "When I say now, move your hand and the bandage away from the wound. Julio, be ready. As soon as Ines lets go of the wound, grab him by the shoulders. If he's not too far out of it, he may try to fight against the burning."

"*Sim, senhora.*"

"Now!"

Ines released the wound and blood flowed freely, mixing with the mud and grime that covered Caroline and the boy. Revulsion and compassion rose inside her in equal parts. He was just a boy— hurt, frightened. She spoke to him soothingly, not knowing if he could understand her words but hoping that her tone might comfort him.

"Press the bandage to the cut again," Caroline said as soon as the boy relaxed. So much blood, blood everywhere. She struggled to ignore it, to retain her professional poise, but the bile rose in her throat.

She doused the laceration with alcohol and

Vincente screamed, tried to rise, but Julio pinned him to the ground.

"I've got to close the wound. A bandage won't do it. It's too deep." She reached for the black bag and dragged it to her, rummaging around inside until she found a bottle of ether. She held the ether and another strip of petticoat toward Ines.

"I'm going to take some stitches, and when I start, I want you to pour this into the material and hold it over his nose and mouth. Be careful not to inhale it yourself."

The sound of high-pitched wailing followed Jason as he stumbled away from the river. He tried to close his mind against the pain, but all he could see was the face of Rosita, Ernesto's mother, as she'd thrown herself over her son's body. Damn, he should have been able to prevent this! If only he'd gotten here sooner. He'd known how precarious the earth around the dam was after heavy rains. He should have forbidden them to fish here until the reinforcements could be finished. He should have. . . .

As he approached the place where he'd left Caroline earlier, Ignacio, his foreman, helped a weak Vincente to his feet. The boy leaned heavily against his father, obviously still dizzy from the loss of blood. But at least he was alive.

"*Obrigado, senhora, obrigado!*" Ignacio said, his voice raw with emotion. "Thank you for my son's life."

Ignacio's gaze met Jason's as he turned away, and Jason's throat constricted at the tears in his old friend's eyes. "*Obrigado,*" he murmured.

Affection between a father and son was something Jason could hardly imagine, yet here it was before him. It touched a deep yearning inside him, a hunger he tried with all his will to deny. His own father had hated him. His own father wouldn't have cared if he'd drowned in the river or been eaten by alligators, except that he wouldn't have had the money Jason had earned sweating all day in a sugar factory.

Jason watched until Ignacio and Vincente disappeared into the darkness. On the ground at his feet, Caroline gathered medical instruments, cleaning them as best she could on the soiled material of her ruined gown before returning them to the black medical bag. Wiping her brow with her forearm, she released a great sigh.

How Caroline could be so vulnerable and so strong at the same time was the essence of her mystery. It confounded him, threatened his reality. Women were weak and demanding, but the only thing Caroline had ever demanded was his attention, his company. She'd wanted them to be friends before they became lovers. Was that what courting was about?

Nearly laughing aloud at the absurdity of his thoughts in light of the fact that his wife was up to her neck in mud, Jason asked, "Can I help?"

She gazed up at him, her hazel-green eyes heavy with pain and fatigue. His heart skipped a beat and he wondered for a moment if she'd injured herself in all the confusion. But the pain came from deep inside her, he realized. It was as if she'd taken Vincente's suffering into herself. That depth of compassion couldn't be good for her. If she carried the wounds of all her patients inside her heart, soon she would have nothing left for herself. Was that why she hadn't finished medical school?

Mud and blood covered her white gown, but she didn't seem to notice as she struggled to stand. Jason took her by the arm and helped her to her feet.

"I've never seen anything like that before," he told her sincerely. He'd never seen anyone work so tirelessly, so selflessly for a stranger. "I mean, I've seen doctors work to save lives before, but never—"

"Never a woman?"

Too tired and confused to argue, Jason ignored the question, taking the medical bag from her hand and supporting her as they walked toward the wagon. "You must be tired. Let's go back to the house. There's nothing else we can do here."

Caroline stopped, her gaze searching his blue eyes in the darkness. "The other one—Ernesto. . . ."

Jason shook his head, the guilt and impotent anger rising in his chest. "I was too late."

Caroline jerked her arm from his hold. "I suppose you'll blame me for that."

"Dear God, no!" His heart twisted at her words. Was he such a brute? "How could you think I'd blame you when it was all my fault?"

"If you hadn't waited for me. . . ."

He took her by the arm again, forcing her to look at him, determined to make her understand. "If I hadn't waited for you, Vincente would be dead now, too."

"Maybe," she conceded, pulling away again, her face a mask of bitter hurt that he couldn't for the life of him comprehend. "Maybe Ines could have saved him."

What had he done? What had he said to anger her when he was trying to tell her how much he admired her?

As they reached the wagon, Jason grabbed her by the arm again. Intent on making her understand, he turned her so that he could look into her eyes. "Why can't you just accept my thanks?"

Caroline slumped wearily. "What do you want from me, Jason?"

He released her and backed away to find her weary gaze still fixed on his face. What he wanted was to hold her, to find solace and forgiveness in her arms, to ease her weariness and tell her he admired her courage and her strength. He wanted to comfort her, wanted her to comfort him. But if she knew how he felt, she would use it against him.

He couldn't risk it. She couldn't stay here, so near, so accessible. He could never live close to her day after day and not reveal his heart. And as soon as he showed the slightest weakness, she would destroy him.

"Nothing," he murmured, and whether or not she was satisfied with his answer, she turned toward the wagon and waited for him to help her up. The distance that widened between them saddened him. He climbed in beside her, shook out the reins, and the horses bounded forward.

"What about Ernesto? Will there be a funeral?" Caroline asked tiredly.

Jason's body went rigid as her words plummeted him back in time. He fought to keep the memories at bay.

Shaking his head to clear it, Jason replied, "His family will take care of it. They'll bury him in the cemetery and when the priest comes next month, he'll conduct a ceremony."

"Shouldn't someone say something—a eulogy."

"They'll take care of it, Caroline." He knew what she expected. It was only natural. He was the *patrão*. Ernesto and his father had both been his employees. It was only right that he should be present at the funeral.

They didn't speak again as they rode toward the house, a silence that stretched so long that Jason thought Caroline might have fallen asleep until she spoke, her voice a mere whisper in the night.

"Shouldn't you be there?"

"What?" he asked, pretending he didn't know what she meant. How could he explain without revealing things he'd rather leave unexplored?

"The funeral for Ernesto." He could hear the impatience in her voice, the accusation. "They look up to you."

Jason felt his heart tighten. How could he explain? He must appear heartless and unfeeling to her, and even while he told himself he didn't care what she thought of him, he knew with a sickening certainty that he did care. No matter how much he tried to distance himself, he couldn't help caring about Caroline, any more than he could stop himself from taking on responsibility for the well-being of his people. Their loss was his loss.

God knew he didn't want to care. He didn't want to care about anyone or anything. Caring left you open to hurt. He'd cared about his mother, and look what that had gotten him. He'd cared about Peggy, and he still carried the pain of her death inside his heart.

"Caroline, I'm not good at funerals." He waited for a response, but none came. Either she was asleep or she couldn't think of a reply to such a selfish statement. Either way, he was glad for the silence.

They arrived at the house as the sky began to brighten with the sunrise. Caroline climbed down from the wagon almost before it stopped, dashing his hope that she had fallen asleep.

"Ines!" she called. "Have a hot bath brought to my room please, and then get some rest yourself."

"*Sim, senhora,*" Ines replied, moving past Jason with a disapproving glare. He didn't know if she meant to speak, but he quelled her with a scowl. The last thing he needed was to be scolded by Ines.

Jason fetched the medical bag from the wagon and hurried to Caroline's side. Taking her arm, he walked with her toward the courtyard. "Your gown is ruined," he said inanely, kicking himself mentally because he could think of nothing else to say.

"Good night, Jason," she said as they reached the arched entranceway. "I'm very tired."

Caroline pulled her arm from his grip. Taking her father's medical bag from him, she walked toward the spiral staircase that would take her upstairs to her room.

"Caroline!" He called after her, unwilling to let her go, yet not knowing what to say. She turned to gaze at him, her face drawn and smeared with mud. "Why didn't you finish your schooling?" he asked.

"My father became ill. It took all his savings and mine just to eat and keep a roof over our heads. Then he died and . . . well, that was the end of that."

"He left money for your husband's education. He should have left it for yours."

"He did," she murmured, turning away from him and slowly mounting the stairs.

Two more workers died of the fever yesterday. I suppose they buried them today. Ignacio went for me, to give my condolences. You know I cannot abide a funeral, not after Peggy's, not after I had to lie so they'd bury her in consecrated ground and so the priest would speak over her. I knew she'd have wanted it that way.

I promised myself then and there that I would never attend another funeral. The words the priest spoke were meaningless dribble. I just wanted him to shut up. She wasn't there; she wasn't in that sad body. Her spirit was gone, I don't know where. I don't believe in the hereafter, but I hope I'm wrong. I hope there is a heaven, for Peggy's sake.

The words of the letter echoed in Caroline's mind as the last shovelful of dirt landed on the grave. Rosita, Ernesto's mother, threw herself onto the grave and wept loudly as the mourners turned away.

Ignacio had delivered a beautiful eulogy in Jason's stead, and if anyone thought it strange that the *patrão* was absent, Caroline had seen no sign of resentment.

How could she have forgotten? How could she have been so insensitive as to berate Jason last night? He had lived with such bitterness and pain for so long, it must be eating him up inside.

His sister Peggy haunted him still. He blamed himself for her death; he'd as much as admitted it in his letters. Not with words, but there had been as much meaning in what he hadn't said in those letters as there had been in the actual words themselves.

"Thank you for coming, *senhora*."

Caroline turned to see Ignacio standing close beside her, his brown eyes bright with sincerity and unshed tears. "It meant much to the family."

"It was the least I could do," she said, her voice quivering with emotion. "I am only sorry . . ."

"It is not your fault. It is not his fault either," he said, gesturing at something over her head.

Caroline turned slowly. Jason stood in the distance beside his horse, the reins held lightly in his hand. Her heart froze. She could feel his pain reach out to her from across the distance.

He was too far away for her to see his eyes, but she knew his gaze had found her. His body stiffened and he turned, mounting his horse and galloping away as if all the demons of hell followed after him.

She moved to follow him, but a hand on her arm stilled her. Turning, she gazed into Ignacio's eyes.

"He will punish himself."

"But why?" she asked, her heart aching for Jason.

Ignacio shrugged. "It is his way. He takes responsibility for everything that happens on the *fazenda*. He does not understand that some things are beyond his control."

"So much guilt," she murmured. The weight must be crushing, even for a man of Jason's strength.

"I see you understand him better than I had guessed," Ignacio said, and Caroline turned to gaze into his wise eyes. "Jason likes to think he is invincible, that he needs no one. He is not nearly as strong as he would like the world to believe."

"Thank you," she said past the tears in her throat.

"For what? It is I who should be thanking you. If not for you, there would be another funeral today."

"For understanding him."

"He will need you, not me," Ignacio told her. "He will not want to admit it. In fact, he may try and push you away. You understand."

Tears welled in Caroline's eyes and she turned away before she humiliated herself. If only she could reach him somehow. "No, I have to go."

Running for the wagon, she climbed on to the seat as the tears fell down her cheeks. Not only did he still carry the guilt of not being able to stop his sister from dying, he felt responsible for Ernesto's death as well.

She picked up the reins and froze. Where was she going? Back to her room to hide again? She knew that Jason wouldn't return to the house, not yet, but she didn't know where he would go. And even if she did, she wasn't sure she wanted to face him right now.

Slowly she turned toward home, urging the horses into a sedate walk. There was no need in hurrying. There was nothing waiting for her but a lonely, empty house.

Peggy was the only beautiful thing in my world. She almost made me believe there could be something else to life besides constant misery. But she couldn't shut out the world. She allowed everything to touch her, to affect her. Her skin wasn't thick enough for the Irish Channel. She wore her feelings out in the open so that anyone could see them and use them to hurt her. Even so, I didn't know how desperate she'd become.

Caroline lowered her hand to the bed beside her, allowing the letter to slip from her fingers. Tears rolled unchecked down her face.

"It wasn't your fault," she said aloud.

She'd read that letter dozens of times and it never failed to move her to tears. She'd written back to him exhorting him not to blame himself. As a result, it had taken several months of dry, pointed business letters before he opened up to her—to Derek—again.

Rolling over, Caroline dropped the letter into the medical bag beside the bed and extinguished the lamp. She wiped her eyes and settled comfortably once again.

He hadn't come home all day. He was out there somewhere, suffering, trying to deny that he could still be hurt. What was she going to do? If she could only pry that shell open and free the man inside, the man who had written those letters.

It wouldn't be easy, peeling back all those layers of protection, but Jason was worth it, worth saving. As she settled into a restless sleep, she wondered if she were equal to the task.

6

Jason entered the courtyard with a sigh of disgust. In two short weeks his home had been transformed into something that resembled a combination zoo and produce market. A jackass stood sedately drinking from his fountain as if it were a trough. Against the kitchen wall stood baskets of yellow corn, green beans, and fresh melons, gifts for the great healer, no doubt.

It had started the day after the accident. His workers and their families had begun coming to Caroline every time one of them stumped a toe or caught a chill. They paid her with produce and livestock, both of which he had in abundance. He had no idea what he was going to do with the surplus. Give it back to them when they ran out, he supposed.

Their wide-eyed adoration was almost more than he could bear. Even Ignacio, his most trusted employee and the closest thing he had to a friend, had been bewitched by her. Every morning it was, *"Bom dia, patrão*! How is *a senhora*?"

Not only that, but his own feelings were becoming more and more confused. He admired her too damned much. He was getting used to having her here, to watching her graceful movements and smelling the intoxicating fragrance that always clung to her, to imagining what it would be like to have her in his bed.

Every time he remembered that Derek's betrayal had caused this situation, a fierce rage devoured him. Derek should have known better, damn his devious soul. Jason had come here to escape the ugliness of his past. He'd wanted more than anything to start fresh, to rebuild his life and his identity. He wanted nothing that had been tainted by the outside world in any way, nothing that wasn't fresh and pure as the jungle around him.

He'd thought he could survive without female companionship. Women were so emotional, so weak. They seemed to require constant care and attention, something he couldn't provide. But they were also beautiful to look at and wonderful to touch. He'd convinced himself that if he got one young enough and innocent enough, he could cultivate her to his liking as he had the jungle. He could bring her under his control and make her what he wanted her to be, make her fit into the world he'd created for himself.

Caroline would not be molded or controlled. She had opinions and ideas and experiences. She was determined to make her own place, not to fit into the one he'd devised for her.

Experience had made her independent and given her insights that a more innocent woman would not have possessed, insights that made him wonder if she didn't see straight through his every defense, an idea he found immensely disturbing.

He had half a mind to jump on a boat himself and go all the way to New Orleans, just to wring Derek's neck personally.

Still, she was a lovely woman, a woman who stirred his deepest longings. He couldn't have her, couldn't touch her. The cost would be too dear. She would demand his heart, body and soul in return, and he couldn't give them. He couldn't be the man she wanted—a companion. Companionship meant sharing on a level that scared the hell out of him.

The donkey brayed as if mocking him. Waving his arms, Jason charged the fountain. "Go away, you bastard!" he shouted.

The beast glanced up at him with round, serene eyes. Obviously deciding he posed no real threat, it continued to drink unperturbed until Jason swatted its rump with his open hand. "Get out of here!"

"What the hell am I going to do with a donkey?" he muttered as he stepped through the open French doors into the parlor.

Sucking in his breath, he gazed around in amazement. Flowers covered every surface in the room— lavender orchids, pink bromeliads, and white lilies.

Ines stood across the room, her back to him as she arranged a vase of orchids. "What the hell's going on?" he asked.

Ines turned to face him, but it wasn't Ines at all. His eyes widened as they traveled from the bright bandanna on Caroline's head to the cotton sarong wrapped around her shapely body to her bare toes peeking out from beneath the hem of the sarong.

"Do you like it?" she asked, pirouetting.

Jason scowled, using anger as a shield against the raw desire that had been his constant companion since he'd seen her standing on the pier that first day. "You look like a serving woman," he growled, but the truth was she looked like anything but.

The cotton fabric molded to her body in a way that made his heart leap into his throat. How did she manage to appear innocent and daring at the same time? Her eyes shone with mischief, a girlish smile curving her soft, full lips. He wanted to kiss her, more than anything else in the world at that moment. He wanted to take her in his arms and taste the sweetness of her lips.

But right now, he knew that kissing her would not be enough. He closed his eyes, shaken to his core.

"You're the one who said my clothes aren't suitable for the jungle," she reminded him.

Good girl, he thought as the tension in his body eased slightly. Always ready with a good argument. He imagined he would miss the arguments. It was hard to remember what his life had been like before she'd come, and he found he didn't want to dwell on it.

"It's certainly more comfortable than anything I brought with me," she went on, oblivious to the turmoil inside him. "Women in New Orleans should dress like this."

She stepped toward him, her bare feet patting the floor.

"If women in New Orleans dressed like that, they wouldn't be safe to walk the streets. Where are your shoes?"

She blushed and he wished with all his being she had not. The knot returned to his gut, sharper than before. She was all vulnerability, all sweet femininity, though he knew well enough that she could turn into a screaming virago without warning.

"I have a pair of sandals, but they rubbed blisters on my feet, so—"

"Sandals?" He didn't give a damn about sandals. He'd been wondering what, if anything, she wore beneath that flimsy, clinging garment, and he needed a distraction, time to gather his thoughts and quell the desire that threatened to take control of his body.

"Yes, one of the women made them for me," she explained. "Oh, I can't believe her name has slipped my mind. I'll think of it."

"More gifts for the healer?" he asked, gazing around the flower-filled room.

In truth, he was proud and a little in awe of her ability to heal sickness and mend broken bodies. She'd acquired that skill in another life, in a dark, distant past that she could remember but he could not share. It added to her mystery and his torment.

He wanted to explore her uncharted wilderness. His body and soul cried out for it. But someone had been there before him. Someone had laid claim to her heart and her body, someone whose shadow still moved behind her eyes. She had a whole history he could not control because it had happened without his knowledge or consent.

Secrets. He wanted to delve into her mystery and learn all there was to learn about her—her past, her likes, her dislikes. Had she been happy as a child? What were her parents like? Her father had been a doctor, and she had respected him enough to want to follow in his footsteps. Why? Where had they lived, her family?

But he knew that he could not plumb her depths without opening himself up to her scrutiny of his past, and he would not allow it, not even if it meant losing her forever.

"What did you say?" he asked, aware that she had spoken.

"I asked how the work was coming on the dam."

She was deliberately turning the subject away from the copious bounty her medical skills had earned, but he decided to allow it—for now.

"Slowly," he said.

"I treated two more injuries today," she told him.

"I'm aware of that." Did she think he didn't even know what happened with his own men?

"They were both careless accidents." She moved to sit on the settee, taking great care in arranging herself before pulling a fan of colorful toucan feathers out of nowhere and proceeding to fan herself.

Another gift, no doubt, he thought with a scowl. The generosity and gratitude of his people were fast approaching the ridiculous. It was almost embarrassing, the bounty they had bestowed upon her. As if reading his thoughts, she drew the feathers of the fan together, running them through her hand, her mouth set in a stubborn line, though she did have the grace to appear at least a little chagrined.

"The men are tired," she said, her eyes sincere as she leaned toward him like an advocate pleading her cause. "And so are you. When's the last time you got a good night's sleep?"

"As I recall, it must have been the spring of 1870," he said caustically. What did she know about him or his men? The running of the *fazenda* was none of her business.

"I'm serious, Jason. You're pushing them and yourself too hard."

"I can't imagine that either of my men would have complained to you." He struggled to keep his temper in check. She was intruding into matters that didn't concern her; he didn't appreciate her interference in the least.

"Of course not," she said defensively, as if he'd accused her of something.

"So, in addition to being a healer of the sick, you are also gifted with second sight?"

Her chin went up and her jaw tightened and he knew he'd managed to sting her.

"Or are you speaking from your vast storehouse of knowledge about running a coffee *fazenda*?" he went on, intentionally spurring her to anger. An angry Caroline was much easier to manage than a beguiling Caroline. "Yes, let's see, you've been here, what, nineteen days? That should be quite long enough for someone with your natural talents to develop into quite an expert."

Her face reddened, and she swept the fan open again. "No, I haven't been here long, and I don't know all there is to know about growing coffee, but I have eyes. I can see what you're doing."

"I am trying to reinforce a levee so that no more lives will be lost needlessly." It was on the tip of his tongue to explain that the mud slide was just a harbinger of things to come. The rainy season would begin in a few months and there would be more slides if he didn't shore up the dam. But he didn't owe her an explanation. He didn't owe her anything.

"You blame yourself for Ernesto's death. You disappeared for two days after the funeral, and since you've been back, you've been like a demon. You're not God, Jason. You can't control the river or command the elements or—"

"Thank you for your insights," he said harshly, cutting across her words. "This plantation did quite well before you got here and it will continue to thrive after you're gone. Have you started packing yet?"

Her poise crumbled and her face became a blank mask of hurt. Pain twisted like a knife in Jason's chest, but he would not relent. He could not.

"No," she said tautly, unable to meet his gaze. "I . . . I don't have that much. It's another two weeks before the mail boat is scheduled to return. I'll be ready."

It was a moment before Jason could find his voice. She should be glad to leave him; he wanted her to be glad. At least, that was what he told himself. He didn't want to hurt her, just to keep her at arm's length. In fact, that was the reason he was sending her back. He didn't want to hurt her.

"You shouldn't encourage them." He spoke softly, as if by doing so he could ease the hurt he had caused without losing the advantage he had gained. "They will get used to running to you and you're not going to be here much longer."

"You're right of course," she said, regaining some of her equilibrium. He found himself admiring her strength. "Excuse me. I seem to have a headache. I think I'll lie down for a while."

"But lunch . . ." Ines said from the door, her eyes narrowing at Jason.

Caroline gazed from Ines to Jason and back to Ines, opening her mouth as if she would speak. Instead, she turned and fled, the sound of her bare feet hollow on the hard floor.

Jason turned toward the dining room and Ines's cold, accusing glare, and he wondered how much she had overheard. "Don't say it, Ines, I'm warning you. Just bring me my lunch."

He sat in his customary place at the table, and Ines quickly brought his plate, which she slammed down on the table with enough force to rattle his water glass.

"What the hell's the matter with you?" he asked.

"Foolish man," Ines muttered, "don't know what's good for him. Maybe you choke on your lunch!"

Jason ignored her, forcing the image of Caroline's wounded expression from his mind. He took a bite of white fish, and a searing heat filled his mouth. Swallowing quickly, he grabbed his water to wash it down.

"Damn it, Ines, are you trying to poison me?"

Ines snorted. "If I try to poison you, you be dead now. Sorry I don't think of it."

Ines left through the door into the parlor, and he knew she was going to talk to Caroline, though he had no idea what she would say to her. She would probably tell her she was lucky to be leaving, to run as fast and as far away from him as she could.

Good! he thought, stabbing at his food as if it were something hateful. All he needed was Ines encouraging her while he was trying to discourage her. Cursing under his breath, he decided that women would be the death of him yet.

Caroline threw another gown into the trunk, sniffing loudly. "Isolation is what you wanted, Jason, and isolation is what you'll get. I hope you enjoy your solitude!

If I could, I'd leave right now. I wonder how far I could get on foot?"

"He is sorry, *senhora*."

Turning at the sound of Ines's voice behind her, Caroline used her fingertips to wipe away the tears that had begun trailing down her face. "Did he tell you that? No, of course he didn't. Stop apologizing for him. Stop making excuses for him. God knows, I've done enough of that myself. No more. He's won. I'm glad to be leaving."

Cautiously, Ines entered the room, her hands clenched before her. "Please, *senhora*, do not talk that way. Master Jason is good inside."

"I don't care!" Caroline nearly shouted. "He wants me gone, and I plan to oblige him. I just wish I could do so today."

"You must—"

Caroline spun around to face Ines, cutting her off. "You were wrong, Ines. He isn't afraid of me; he dislikes me. If I haven't learned anything else in the nineteen days I've been here, I've learned that much."

"Nineteen days?" Ines asked. "You count the days?"

"No," Caroline said with a tired sigh, "it's something Jason said."

Nineteen days. Had she been here exactly nineteen days? Had Jason counted the days? A glimmer of hope lightened her heart, but she tamped it down immediately. "It doesn't mean anything just because he knows how many days I've been here. He's probably counting the days until I'll be gone now. I don't fit his perfect image of the perfect wife, so he doesn't want me in this perfect world he's trying to construct, and nothing I say or do will change that."

Turning dejectedly, Ines moved to leave. A sense

of loss tugged at Caroline's heart. She wasn't only losing Jason, she was losing Ines as well and Brazil, which she was beginning to love. She nearly halted Ines, but she wasn't sure what she would say. There was nothing to say. Jason had had the last word.

Resuming her needless packing, Caroline didn't realize that Ines was still standing at the door until she spoke. "I bring you something, *senhora*."

Caroline heaved a weary sigh, turning to face the other woman. "What is it?"

Ines dug in her pocket and pulled out a white cloth pouch about the size of a fist. Attached to it was a length of twine. "Love charm. It will make Master Jason fall in love with you."

Caroline laughed, shaking her head in wonder. "I thought you were a Christian, Ines."

"*Sim, senhora*, Jesus, he is very good, and also is *Maria a Virgem*. I pray to her for you every night. But this," she said, patting the pouch, her eyes gleaming with mischief, "this is magic powerful."

Ines stepped toward her, and Caroline stood still, fighting the urge to back away and refuse to participate in this ridiculous farce.

"See, you tie the twine around the waist like so," Ines told her. She wrapped her arms around Caroline's waist and pulled the two ends of the rope together in front. "The charm hangs down the front like this. Well, you wear it under the skirt. . . ."

Ines dropped one end of the twine and Caroline moved a safe distance away. "It's no use, Ines, I can't, I just can't keep trying. The harder I try, the more he lashes out. He has hardly said a civil word to me since I've been here."

"If you could see inside his heart, as I have. . . ."

"Please," Caroline interrupted sharply, "don't tell me any more stories." The hurt expression on Ines's face sliced through Caroline's heart, and she was immediately sorry for her harsh words.

"Just one more story, *senhora*, and I will say no more."

Caroline sat tiredly on the edge of the bed. "I'm sorry, Ines, I—"

"I owe Master Jason my life," Ines began. "My mãe, my mother, she is Indian. My father, he is Portuguese. I am *caballo*—half Indian, half Portuguese. My father does not marry mãe. So she works in the city, in a place called Manaus. You have been there, yes?"

"Yes," Caroline replied, remembering the city at the mouth of the Rio Negro, its garish wealth and grinding poverty.

"She works on the street, brings home the men. But the men who drain the rubber trees, they aren't liking the Indian. They more like *caballo*, but my mother tells them, no, that I am too young. When I am thirteen years old, mãe dies of the disease. A man, Olivais, he takes me to his mansion far up the black river. He rapes me and he lets his men rape me. I know you are thinking I am bad."

"Ines, no!" Caroline reached out toward the other woman, struggling for control of the revulsion and overwhelming horror rumbling up from her woman's heart.

Drawing Ines down to sit on the bed beside her, she asked, "Why would you think that? What could you have done?"

Ines sat beside Caroline, her gaze distant. "I could kill myself. I have a knife, and I think about it, but I am too weak."

"No one could blame you for being strong enough to live," Caroline told her sincerely. She could hardly imagine such a horror. It was every woman's nightmare, and Ines had lived it—and survived. How could she, or anyone else, ever judge Ines?

"One night, my door is unlock and I am running away. But they find me and I am brought back." Caroline felt the tremor that coursed through Ines's body. "They will do terrible punishment to runaways. You don't want to hear it. But Master Jason, he takes me away from there. He hits the big man with his fist like that." She swung out at the air for emphasis. "He takes the gun and tells them he will kill them. At the river, he put fires on their boats so they can't follow."

Jason did that? Jason had rescued her from that hellish situation. Her heart swelled with a new admiration and growing affection for her aloof husband. Ines hadn't said so, but Caroline guessed by her description that Jason must have risked his life for her. She could just imagine an enraged Jason wreaking vengeance on those despicable, brutal men. What a sight he must have been!

"Now I understand your loyalty," Caroline said, adding silently, *and the shadows behind your eyes.*

"And you understand Master Jason's heart?" Ines asked hopefully.

Caroline rose and went to the medical bag on the table across the room. "I never doubted Master Jason's heart." Reaching inside the bag, she found the bundle of letters, taking them out with loving care. "But he cares for you. Ines, you remind him of his sister."

Caroline held the letters out toward Ines.

"I am not knowing how to read," Ines told her.

"You don't have to. They're letters, letters from Jason. I brought them with me from New Orleans."

"He writes to you?" Ines asked, her brow furrowed in confusion. "But I think you aren't knowing Master Jason until you come here."

"He didn't write them to me," Caroline explained. "He wrote them to his cousin who let me read them. Listen. 'Every morning I walk out into the orchards and I am glad to be alive. I've never felt this way before. The jungle is so clean, so untouched. Its eternal newness and beauty heal me. Every day is fresh and full of promise. Peggy would have loved it here.' He wrote that. Peggy was his sister. Ines, I have seen into his heart."

Ines stared at Caroline so long and so hard that she began to feel uneasy. "What is it, Ines?"

"Master Jason, he doesn't know you have these words?"

"No." Caroline felt the same sickness in the pit of her stomach that she had felt the day she told Jason she was a widow.

"*Senhora*, Master Jason, he is very secret, *privado*. He must never know you have read these things. He will not like someone looking into his soul."

"Don't worry," Caroline said, turning away and dropping the letters back into the medical bag. "I'm not going to tell him. I'm taking that little secret back with me. I don't even know why I keep them."

"Please, *senhora*," Ines urged, "he can never know you have seen this."

Irritation began to take hold of Caroline. "Don't worry, Ines."

The expression on Ines's face as she left told Caroline that her assurances hadn't quelled Ines's anxiety. Caroline had to admit that she wasn't completely convinced herself. What if Jason did somehow find out that she was the one who had been answering his letters for the past year?

A tremor of dread shivered through her body as she bent to retrieve the talisman Ines had dropped. Love charm, she thought with a smirk. There wasn't enough magic in the world to break through the barriers around Jason Sinclair's heart.

Caroline sat up with a gasp, disoriented for a fraction of a second. She raised her hand before her eyes. Though she couldn't see in the darkness, she knew that the object she clutched was the talisman Ines had given her. The twine had become tangled around her arm, cutting off the blood flow so that her hand had gone to sleep.

The sound came again, louder this time, a knocking that seemed to come from outside. Dropping the charm to the floor, she crawled out of bed and grabbed her dressing gown as she padded into the sitting room. It came again—bang, bang, bang.

Through the window beside the door, she saw Ines standing in the darkness, gazing furtively around as if afraid of discovery. Half-alarmed, half-irritated, Caroline opened the door.

"What is it Ines?"

"Oh, *senhora*," Ines said breathlessly. The urgency in her manner and the gravity of her expression stilled Caroline's heart. "Come with me, please. Emergency."

"Jason? Is it Jason?"

"Hurry, *senhora*," Ines urged. "It is life or death matter."

7

Caroline grabbed her medical bag and followed Ines into the darkness, forgetting her feet were bare until they touched the cool, damp bricks of the courtyard. She glanced around anxiously, glad for the full moon that made it possible to keep Ines in her sights.

They crossed the patio, Ines's manner furtive as she stared at the windows and doors of the silent house. At the edge of the jungle, she halted, turning to look at Caroline warily.

"*Senhora*, I must ask a promise from you," she whispered.

"What?" Caroline asked, ready to agree to anything in order to get on with whatever they were about. She had a feeling in the pit of her stomach that something terrible had happened to Jason, and she wanted to get to him as quickly as possible. "We're wasting time, Ines. I'll do anything. Just go. Show me the way."

Ines stood her ground, ignoring the urgency in Caroline's tone. "*Senhora*, you must promise not to speak of anything you are about to see."

"I promise!" Caroline replied impatiently. "Can we go on?"

"Not even to Master Jason."

Relief flowed through Caroline like the swiftly moving river. Whatever tragedy waited for her in the darkness beyond the house, it wasn't Jason. It had nothing to do with Jason, except that Ines was asking her not to mention it to him. "But why?"

"Please, *senhora*, no one is to know of these things. Master Jason would be very angry. . . ."

"What you're saying is that whatever it is, Jason doesn't want me to know about it." Ines's silence confirmed Caroline's accusation. "What if I refuse?"

Ines hung her head in defeat. "Then I would take you there anyway. Someone will die if I don't."

Curiosity and indignation warred inside Caroline—curiosity to see what was so secret, and indignation that Jason had thought to keep something so obviously important from her.

Ines peered up at her, though she didn't lift her head. She couldn't let Ines down; whatever this was, Ines considered it extremely important. Besides, she would be leaving soon. What difference could it possibly make to her? "All right, Ines, I promise."

Ines's expression brightened instantly. "*Obrigado, senhora*. Now, follow closely, and be very quiet."

Ines turned and led the way along a path lined with wild pineapple bushes and tree ferns. The earth was damp and soft beneath Caroline's bare feet. Mud oozed between her toes, and sharp objects scratched the tender flesh. She wished fervently that she had taken the time to get her shoes. It was a selfish thought. Had she known the crisis didn't involve Jason, she would have taken the time to dress properly.

They hadn't walked far when Ines turned sharply to the left. There in front of them was a small run-down shack that Caroline had never noticed before.

"Amazing!" she said in wide-eyed astonishment. "How could I have never seen it?"

Bits of memory came back to her. Both Jason and Ines had cautioned her not to explore the *fazenda* alone, and now that she thought of it, Jason had always steered her away from this area. Something terribly important must have happened for Ines to break Jason's confidence like this.

The door groaned as Ines pushed it open, and a dim light spilled out of the shack. With one last furtive glance around, Ines entered the structure and Caroline followed.

An indistinct shadow moved against the far wall, wavering and stretching as someone stood—a woman, a gaunt-looking woman with skin as black as any African Caroline had ever seen on the street in New Orleans.

Ines and the woman exchanged words in Portuguese, while Caroline took the opportunity to inspect the space more closely. It looked like a store-house, with lanterns and blankets and mismatched china stacked against one wall. Along another were barrels, the contents of which were indiscernible. In a corner of the room, the corner the woman had vacated, stood a small makeshift cot. Straw stuffing spilled out onto the floor; a dingy white blanket covered the whole thing.

On the crude cot a fragile form lay still and silent.

Instinctively, Caroline started forward, her throat tightening at what met her gaze. The form on the bed, so still, so small, was a child.

A shriek from behind her stilled Caroline before the gnarled hand reached out and grabbed her by the arm. She turned to look into the terrified eyes of the black woman. Ines continued to talk reassuringly to her, but the woman showed no sign that the words penetrated her distrust.

Caroline had no words to give her. She didn't understand her language, and even if she did, all she could say was that she would do her best to help her child. Tentatively, she reached up and covered the woman's trembling hand with hers in a gesture of concern and confidence.

Tears started in the woman's eyes. Her grip on Caroline's arm loosened and Caroline turned back to the child. Kneeling beside the cot, she turned the small body over, unfurling it gently from its fetal position.

Despite her efforts, a gasp escaped her control at the sight of angry red spots that covered the child's exposed arms. A hand to his forehead told her he was burning up with fever. Quickly she sat on the cot and opened the medical bag, withdrawing her father's horn-shaped stethoscope. Ignoring the jerky movement behind her, she pressed one end of the instrument to the boy's chest and the other to her ear.

"Tell her I won't hurt him," Caroline said to Ines. "Tell her I'm listening to see how sick he is."

Ines spoke to the woman soothingly as Caroline continued her examination. The sound of fluid in the child's lungs confirmed her worst fears.

Caroline turned to face Ines. "Where did this child come from?"

Ines darted an anxious look at the African woman. Neither of them spoke.

"Is she the mother?" Caroline asked, moving toward the black woman who retreated in terror. "I have to examine her. Tell her."

Whatever Ines said to the woman seemed to calm her. She stood still while Caroline drew apart the folds of her garment to inspect her neck and upper chest. Red pustules dotted her ebony skin as Caroline had known they would. Reaching into the medical bag, she said to Ines, "I need to see inside her mouth."

"Inside her mouth, *senhora*?"

A flat metal tongue depressor in her hand, she turned back to the frightened woman. "Open your mouth wide," she said, opening her own as an example.

Ines translated, but the woman showed no sign of obeying.

"Ines, let me do it to you," Caroline said.

Ines backed away as Caroline moved toward her. "I am not sick, *senhora*."

"I know, but if she sees that I don't hurt you, she might let me do it to her. Be still, Ines. Have I ever hurt you?"

Ines stood before Caroline, her eyes wide, her mouth closed tightly.

"I'm going to put this stick on your tongue to hold it down so I can look into your throat. It won't hurt, I promise."

Reluctantly, Ines opened her mouth. She flinched when Caroline touched her tongue with the depressor but didn't move. Caroline withdrew the metal stick and wiped it on a clean linen cloth she kept in her bag.

"What did you see, *senhora*?" Ines asked anxiously.

Caroline smiled at her. "A very healthy set of tonsils. Now, help me convince our friend to let me do the same to her."

With Ines's help, Caroline managed to examine the woman's mouth and found the telltale white spots on the inside of her cheeks.

"Who are these people? Where did they come from?" An ugly suspicion nagged at the corner of Caroline's mind. "Jason doesn't own slaves . . . does he? Is that what he doesn't want me to know?"

"No, *senhora*!"

"Then tell me. Who are you protecting if not Jason?"

"I swore I wouldn't tell," Ines said, looking past Caroline at the child on the cot in the corner. "Can you help him?"

"I don't know, Ines. This child has measles. The disease has developed into pneumonia. Do you know what measles can do to people who have no natural immunity? I need to see everyone who has come into contact with this child."

"Please, *senhora*. . . ." Ines's words fell away in the face of Caroline's determination.

Caroline gazed at the woman, who had retreated into the shadows. Her patience was quickly running out. Somehow she had to make Ines understand the gravity of the situation. "Tell her that children will die unless they are treated properly. Some adults may die as well."

"There are no more," Ines lied; Caroline could tell by the way she refused to meet her gaze.

"They're the only ones, just this woman and this child? They live alone? Here? In the jungle? I don't believe you, Ines. Tell her what I said."

"It doesn't matter, *senhora*. Yes, there are others, but this boy, he is the sickest. Heal him and they will bother you no more."

"This child may be the sickest right now, but by tomorrow, this woman's body will be completely covered with the same red rash. If they don't get the proper treatment, others will develop pneumonia. Pneumonia almost always brings death."

"*Senhora*, I should not have brought you here. I can take you no longer."

Caroline sighed in exasperation. "I've had measles, so I'm immune. But you haven't, have you? I wonder how many people on the *fazenda* have had them."

"You cannot tell Master Jason. You gave your word."

"I know I gave my word, but this—this is something I didn't expect. If you'll tell me where these people came from and let me examine the others who have been exposed, I won't tell Jason. Adults rarely die of the disease, and there are few children on the *fazenda*. Besides, I'll be there to diagnose any outbreaks early; that's the key to treating measles. What do you say, Ines?"

Ines hesitated. Caroline could sense the battle raging inside the other woman, but even before she spoke, Caroline knew what decision Ines had reached. "It is for your own good, *senhora*. It is better for you that you don't know. I cannot."

Caroline sighed in defeat. "Damn it, Ines."

"Will you help the boy?"

"I'll try, but he is very sick." Caroline retrieved a blanket from a stack in the corner and used it to cover the boy to the chin. Compassion swelled inside her because she knew what hell he had to face before morning. "Tell her to keep him covered no matter what."

Ines repeated Caroline's words in Portuguese, and Caroline watched the boy's mother to make sure she understood.

"When the fever breaks, he will sweat and his body will grow cool." Again Caroline waited while Ines translated, her own body shivering with the memory of her childhood bout with pneumonia, an experience that had nearly taken her life. "Does she understand?"

"*Sim, senhora.*"

"If the fever doesn't break by sunrise, she must come and get me. Tell her that, Ines, exactly as I said it. She must come and get *me*."

Ines hesitated, then translated.

"If the fever does break, he'll probably have chills, then fever again. The fever shouldn't last longer than half a day. If it does, she should come and get me."

Again Ines translated, then turned to Caroline, the hope and faith in her eyes causing a catch in Caroline's throat. Closing her eyes, Caroline made a silent appeal to God for the child's recovery. There was nothing more she could do.

"You will make well, *sim, senhora*?" Ines asked anxiously.

"I'm not sure I can," Caroline admitted, coming to her feet. "It's in God's hands now."

"Will you tell Master Jason?"

"I don't know. I should," Caroline said, remembering the night of the mud slide and Jason's concern for his workers. She felt as if she were betraying him by keeping Ines's secret. What would he say if he learned that she was endangering his men and their families? Still, Ines had trusted her too. There had to be a way to keep from betraying either of them, but she was too tired to think tonight. "Let me sleep on it. We'll talk about it in the morning."

"If Jason already knows about whatever it was that I saw last night," and Caroline wasn't at all sure what that was, "why must we keep it secret from him? Ouch! Be careful!"

"Why did you not put on the shoes?" Ines asked, gazing up at Caroline from where she knelt on the floor. Her skillful hands massaged the aches and pains from Caroline's swollen feet.

"Because, you said it was a matter of life and death." Caroline sat on a stool in her sitting room, her nightgown hiked up to her knees, her bare feet soaking in a large pan of hot, soapy water.

Ines took one of Caroline's sore feet from the water and patted it dry, then gently applied an evil-smelling ointment.

"Are you sure that stuff works?" Caroline asked dubiously.

"*Sim*," Ines replied.

"What did you say those nasty little creatures were?"

"*Chigoes*—fleas," Ines told her. "They burrow in the flesh. This will kill them."

Caroline shuddered, silently calling herself every kind of fool for her recklessness. If only she'd taken the time to put on her shoes last night.

"The bandages, *senhora*?"

"They're in my medical bag," she said, motioning

with a nod of her head toward the corner where the bag stood on a small table.

Ines went to fetch the bandages, and Caroline took the opportunity to survey the damage to her feet. She couldn't see anything buried in her flesh, but the pain whenever she tried to walk and the terrible swelling were enough to confirm Ines's diagnosis.

"You are liking Master Jason more than you want to tell yourself," Ines remarked from across the room. "Last night, you think maybe Master Jason needs help, yes? So you don't stop to put on the shoes. Are you wearing the talisman?"

"Of course not!" Coloring guiltily, Caroline recalled waking last night with the object clutched in her hand, the twine wrapped tightly around her forearm. "That's voodoo nonsense. And besides, even if I believed in it, which I don't, I wouldn't want a man I had to trick into loving me. And stop trying to change the subject."

Ines knelt before Caroline again, smiling slyly up at her, then glanced away sheepishly. "Woman always has to trick the man, *senhora*. Surely you are this wise, yes?"

"Ines, how do you know so much about men?"

"*Mãe*, she tells me some." Ines grew serious, her brow furrowing with a frown of concentration. "*Senhora*, the boy, can you save him?"

Looking into Ines's hopeful face, Caroline thought she understood some of the anguish her father had suffered. He'd wanted to heal them all, but even medical science couldn't cure some things. Epidemics were the worst because there were so many, so many children.

"I'll try," Caroline told her as she had last night.

For several moments, Ines looked at her wordlessly, her expression unreadable, before nodding and rising. "I must go. Master Jason will want the lunch. I will bring a tray for you as well."

"Thank you. I've made a mess of things. How am I going to help that poor child if I can't walk?"

"Rest today. Maybe tomorrow you will walk."

"At least the mother didn't come for me. You did tell her what I said."

"Of course, yes. Rest, *senhora*," Ines said, exiting the room quickly, and Caroline couldn't help wondering if she did so intentionally to avoid further questions.

"Where is Caroline?" Jason asked crossly as Ines entered with his lunch.

"She is unwell, *patrão*," Ines replied, setting a plate of hot food on the table before him.

"What's wrong with her?"

Ines dipped her head, refusing to meet his gaze, and Jason decided it might be wise not to probe further. It was probably her monthly, something he really didn't want to discuss with Ines.

"It is not serious," Ines assured him a bit sheepishly. "She will be better tomorrow."

"I'll take your word for it," Jason said gruffly, concentrating on his meal. Scooping up a forkful of rice, he raised it to his mouth when a shrill whistle rent the morning calm. "What the hell!"

Ines went to the door, peering out. Her shoulders slumped, and Jason knew what she'd seen before she turned to stare at him with angry, accusing eyes. "It is the mail boat."

"It's early," he said. His heart settled into his stomach, and he tried desperately to deny the regret inside him. It was early, damn it! It wasn't supposed to be here for two more weeks. "Do you think she'll feel up to traveling?"

Ines shook her head. "I am not knowing, *patrão*." She stood staring at him, her eyes reproachful. Determined to ignore her, he returned to his food, lifting the fork once again, only to drop it onto the plate with a loud clatter. He'd suddenly lost his appetite. How could he eat with Ines glowering at him as if he'd drowned a litter of kittens?

"Go and find out, Ines," Jason growled. "I'll go down to the pier and ask the captain to wait." He pushed himself up from the table. "Go on. I only hope she's packed."

Caroline stood at her door, grasping the frame for support. Tears ran unchecked down her face as she strained to see the mail boat in the distance. With every second, it grew larger on the horizon. There was no escape.

She had failed. There was no place for her beside Jason, no room in his life. He didn't want her. It didn't matter that her heart was breaking, that she felt as if she were dying on the inside. He didn't want her, and nothing would ever change that.

Not only had she failed herself, she had failed Jason. She was leaving him to wallow in his loneliness and struggle for the rest of his life with the demons that drove him to hide away in this jungle. In her mind, she relived every moment she had spent here, trying to discover where she had gone wrong, what she could have done differently. The fact of the matter, as difficult as it was to swallow, was that he didn't care for her, plain and simple.

Well, Jason might not want her, but he needed her. He was just too stubborn to admit it. He would pay the price in loneliness. Would he find another wife, once the marriage was dissolved? She didn't want to think about it. She was miserable enough without adding jealousy to the emotions simmering beneath her surface calm.

He needed her, damn it! Why couldn't he see what he was doing?

In the corner of her eye, she watched Ines mount the stairs and walk slowly across the balcony toward her.

"It is the mail boat," Ines said.

"I know." Caroline wiped away the tears with the back of her hand.

"I will miss you, *senhora*."

Caroline's composure nearly broke. She managed to keep the tears at bay, though her voice trembled when she spoke. "And I'll miss you, Ines."

Taking a deep breath, Caroline gathered her dignity around her like a cloak. In a moment, Ines would embrace her, and if she did so, that would be the end of her self-control.

"Come, help me finish packing," Caroline said stiffly, turning away from the door.

8

"*What's wrong with it?*" Jason called over the unusually loud clamor of the boat's engine. He caught the end of a rope and secured it to the short post set in the pier.

"Don't know yet!" the short, burly man in the boat shouted back.

Jason turned as if he sensed her presence behind him, frowning at what she was certain must be a bewildered expression. His gaze dropped to her bandaged feet, and Caroline tugged at her skirt in an attempt to cover them.

"What's the matter with your feet?" Jason shouted to be heard over the racket made by the boat's motor. The captain cut the engine off in the middle of Jason's question, and the word *feet* reverberated up and down the jungle like an explosion.

Caroline blushed as the man in the boat gazed curiously at her half-hidden feet. Opening her parasol with as much dignity as she could summon, she tilted her chin defiantly. "You needn't concern yourself. They are sore. Ines bandaged them."

Jason scowled. "That's what you get for running around barefoot like a damned aborigine."

Ignoring his caustic comment, Caroline said, "My bags are packed and ready in my room."

"Well, you might as well go back inside," Jason told her bitterly. "There's a problem with the motor."

"How long will it take to repair?" she asked, silently cursing the hopefulness in her breast. She was a fool. How could she want to stay when he didn't want her here?

The man in the boat leaped onto the pier with more agility than she thought him capable of. It was he who answered her question, doffing his tattered brown hat in a gesture of respect. "Don't know yet, ma'am."

"I'll let you know," Jason assured her. "Go back to the house and get out of this sun."

Caroline bristled at his high-handed manner. But the relief that flowed through her outweighed her indignation. Turning back toward the house, all she could think of was that she had been given another reprieve. It might be a short one, she warned her soaring heart, and it would come to an end when the captain repaired the boat, but at least she wasn't leaving just yet.

Caroline slipped through the door into the small shack, careful not to wake the sick boy should he be sleeping. She'd been coming here for three nights now, and each time his condition had improved. He should be dead; he should have died before she even saw him the first time. The fact that he was not only clinging to life but actually improving could only be attributed to a very strong will to survive.

Caroline waited for Ines to follow her in, then closed the door behind them. Turning to face the interior of the room, she gasped aloud at what met her gaze. The boy sat up in bed, staring at her with a broad smile. His mother sat on the bed beside him, her eyes brimming with tears.

Immediately, the mother began babbling happily in Portuguese. She stood to make room for Caroline, who sat on the bed and took the boy's face in both of her hands.

"She say thank you, *senhora*. You save her son's life and she say you have great magic."

"No," Caroline said sharply. "No magic. Tell her I accept her thanks, but I did no magic. His body healed itself, with God's help."

His skin felt cool to the touch, and his breathing sounded almost completely normal. "Amazing!" she murmured, unable to believe her own eyes and hands.

Examining him, Caroline found that his lungs had cleared almost entirely and his fever was gone, as were the red pustules. She then turned to examining the mother, who had developed a full-blown case of measles.

Caroline reached into her medical bag and withdrew a bottle of quinine. She found a chipped china cup stacked in a corner of the room and poured about an ounce into it.

"Tell her to do exactly as I say," she said to Ines. "She and her son can go home, but she must rest until the rash goes away. This is quinine." She spoke to Ines as she handed the cup to the woman, and Ines translated.

"Mix a pinch," she demonstrated, taking a small amount of the powder between her thumb and index finger, "with this much water. Take it twice a day until the rash clears. Ines, the rest of her people have got to get help."

Ines stopped translating and gazed guiltily at Caroline.

"Why won't you let me help them?" Caroline asked.

"*Senhora*, what can you do? You will leave in the morning."

Pain clutched at Caroline's chest. She'd almost forgotten. The problem with the mail boat had been repaired and the captain planned to leave at first light. "You're right," she said, her shoulders slumping in abject defeat. "Let's go back to the house. You can bring them some food to take back with them."

"*Sim, senhora*," Ines agreed, and they turned to go.

When they reached the house, they saw Jason at the edge of the courtyard, surrounded by a stand of fan palms, their fronds rustling in a gentle, cooling breeze. His bewildered, forlorn expression tugged at Caroline's heart. He reminded her of a lost little boy, standing there beneath a distant moon, gazing at the house he'd built with his own hands as if he'd never seen it before.

"What will we do?" Ines whispered.

"You go around the house to the kitchen," Caroline said, pressing her medical bag into Ines's hands. "I'll distract him."

Ines gazed at her dubiously, as if she didn't

particularly like that plan, but she did as she was told, and Caroline studied Jason again.

He seemed so vulnerable, standing there in the moonlight, so fragile, despite his physical size and strength. She remembered his powerful grace, his masculine beauty as he'd showered at the *benefício*. That powerful body housed a brittle soul. How she longed to reach that soul, to mend his bruised heart.

He wouldn't allow himself to suffer, to grieve the losses he'd experienced in his lifetime. Yet he suffered for his people. He'd suffered for Ernesto's parents and for Vincente who had been injured because of his own carelessness. What a terrible weight of responsibility he bore!

What was he thinking? If she could understand that one mystery, perhaps she could find a place in his heart and his life. But she couldn't read his eyes in the darkness, and she knew that if she approached him now, his melancholy would instantly give way to anger.

Ines had been right about one thing—Jason Sinclair was the most private, withdrawn man she had ever encountered. The more she tried to break through his reserve, the more he withdrew. She could hardly blame him, after the way he'd described his early life. A child needed emotional nourishment in order to grow, and Jason's emotional growth had been stifled, his spirit all but extinguished by a life of poverty and cruelty. The only way he'd been able to survive was by burying his feelings so deeply that no one, least of all his brutal father, could dig them out.

"Who's there?"

His voice startled her so that her heart leaped into

her throat. She'd tried to be still and quiet, but something had alerted him to her presence. It was as if he possessed some special affinity for the jungle, a kinship that had allowed him to distinguish her minute noise from the usual nighttime sounds.

"Show yourself," he demanded, the threat in his voice undeniable.

Caroline stepped forward into the dim moonlight, and the tension in Jason's body evaporated before her eyes like steam from the jungle after a heavy rain.

"Damn it, woman," he growled, his voice thick with a violence that hadn't yet faded. "What do you mean sneaking up on a man like that?"

"I—I'm sorry. I didn't mean to—"

"What are you doing out and about this time of night anyway?" he asked, his gaze sweeping her from head to foot. "Haven't you been to bed at all?"

"I couldn't sleep," she explained, gaining control of her voice and her emotions. "I saw you standing there. . . . What were you looking at?"

Jason snorted, running a hand through his hair as he returned his attention to the house before them. "My home," he said bitterly, "at least what used to be my home."

Caroline followed his gaze to the stone-and-mortar structure before them. "It's the same as it always was."

"No, it's not the same at all."

Caroline turned to find him staring at her. The unmasked pain in his eyes tightened her throat. She clasped her hands in front of her before she gave in to the impulse to reach out to him. His soul ached as much as hers did. If only she could force him to admit that he was lonely here, that he needed her.

"Well," she said, trying to sound light when her

heart was being torn apart, "I've always thought it seemed more like a house than a home, actually more a building than a house."

A calm tension pulsed through the encroaching jungle. Even the night sounds seemed subdued tonight, save the insects that chirped incessantly high in the giant trees. In the distance an owl hooted a solitary song.

"Where have you been?" Jason asked, genuine curiosity and concern reflected in his ice blue eyes.

"Walking," she said, turning back toward the house.

It was a long time before he spoke, and Caroline might have thought he'd walked away. But she felt his presence as surely as the soft night air on her cheek. His strong, rhythmic breathing reached out to her, as did his scent, a unique blend of the rich, fertile soil of Brazil and a musky maleness that clung to him like moss on the cypress trees back home.

"Walking?" he asked finally, his voice coarse as gravel. "In the jungle in the middle of the night? No wonder your feet are sore."

Caroline shrugged, trying to appear casual. "I didn't go far, just to the edge of the courtyard."

He shook his head in disbelief. "You are an enigma, Caroline."

"Me?" she asked, suddenly, inexplicably close to tears. If only he truly cared about her, at least then they would have a starting point. "No, I'm the most straightforward, uncomplicated person I know. You, on the other hand—"

"What about me?"

She felt him tense across the distance that separated them. "You're the enigma. I'd daresay you know volumes more about me than I do about you."

"What do you want to know?" he asked defensive as always.

Caroline took a deep breath. What did she have to lose, after all? Why not go out fighting? "Why is it so important to you that your wife be untouched? I've never been promiscuous."

"I never accused you of anything," he insisted, refusing to look at her.

"Except being married before, as if that were a crime or a sin." Caroline stared fixedly at him, willing him to turn and face her. Before she boarded the boat that would take her away from him forever, she was determined to confront him. Maybe forthright honesty would move him, and if not, she was leaving anyway.

"You don't understand," he said, looking into her eyes as if unable to resist the force of her gaze upon him.

"No, I don't," she agreed, a terrible sadness settling on her heart. She wanted to tell him that she knew it was only an excuse to send her away. But he might walk away, and she didn't think she could bear that. Maybe if she could make him admit something, anything!

"It has nothing to do with you."

Frustration mingled with sadness inside her. He would not give way, even to the end. "It has everything to do with me. It's the reason I'm leaving in the morning."

Jason released a heavy sigh. "Caroline, this is for the best. You'll see that in a few months. You're just upset now because you came all this way only to turn around and go back. It's not—it's not you. It's about expectations."

"Why don't you try unbending a little, Jason?" she suggested, growing angry despite her determination not to do so. She longed to touch him, to relieve the rigid tension in his body. "Haven't you ever been pleasantly surprised?"

"No, I haven't," he said seriously. "Now it's my turn to ask the questions. Why did you come here?"

"I knew you needed me," she replied simply. He still needed her. Why couldn't he admit it?

Jason stiffened. "I don't need anyone."

"Everyone needs someone. There's no shame in that."

Jason turned to go.

"No, please don't go. We can talk about whatever you want," she cried out, desperate for him to stay. If he walked away now, she knew she would never see him again, and she felt as if her heart would break at the thought. Tomorrow would come soon enough.

"What do you want from me?" he asked tiredly. "What did you hope to find here?"

"I don't know. Warmth, kindness, companionship." She paused, afraid of running him off again but equally afraid of not saying what was on her mind and regretting it for the rest of her life. "Whatever is eating you up inside—maybe it would help if you talked."

"There's nothing eating me up," he insisted tautly.

"Then talk to me, Jason. I'll be leaving in the morning. What can it matter? Tell me what you're running away from." She could feel him withdrawing, fortifying the defenses that kept them apart. "When will you learn that running away doesn't solve anything? You've isolated yourself in this jungle to escape your past, to forget who you are. It won't work, don't you see? The things that happened to you, they . . . they . . ."

Her voice trailed off and she gazed away guiltily, horrified that she had almost said too much.

"What could you possibly know about anything?" he asked suspiciously. "You act as if you have some mysterious insight into my character. I've asked you before and I'll ask once again. Just what did Derek tell you about me?"

Caroline backed away from the furious accusation in his eyes. "Nothing, not really. But one tends to make certain assumptions about a man who hides away in the jungle."

"Well, perhaps you shouldn't assume," he informed her, the fury in his gaze lessening by degrees until it was gone altogether, replaced by a wary distrust. "Come, I'll walk you to your room."

Caroline approached him and he placed a hand on her elbow, steering her toward the spiral staircase she'd mounted so many times. This might be the last time she ever saw him, the last time he ever walked her to her room or touched her.

I've failed you, Jason, she thought. *You believe you failed Peggy, and I've failed you. If only I had more time.*

He followed her up the stairs to the landing above. She walked slowly, prolonging the inevitable moment when he would leave her outside her room.

"I have to go," he said huskily.

"Why? Where?" she asked, almost desperately. "I don't even know where you sleep at night."

"I don't usually," he admitted, though she could tell by the regret in his eyes that he hadn't meant to.

"Why not?" she asked eagerly, hoping for some

further revelation, hoping to keep him near for a few more minutes, long enough to think of something, anything that might make him open up to her. "Tell me. Tell me what keeps you awake at night."

"It won't work, Caroline," he whispered, remorse evident in his tone. "We won't work. You're going back to New Orleans in the morning."

"But I'm here now," she reasoned, pressing her body against his without volition, wrapping her arms around his muscled back. She offered her lips to him, her heart, her soul, her body.

"Don't," he ground out. His rasping breath undermined his struggle to appear unmoved.

And as he denied her with his words, his body responded to her with a will of its own. She recognized the turmoil in his eyes as his arms tightened around her and he drew her toward him, his lips covering hers gently at first, then harder, deepening the kiss with a fierceness that set her blood afire. A feral groan echoed inside his chest, vibrating through her body. Her lips parted beneath his, opening to his fervor. She felt the hard ridges of muscle as her hands played upon his broad back.

If I can make him desire me, maybe I can make him love me.

Then suddenly his hands grasped her arms and pulled them from around him, putting her away from him. His eyes burned with passion in the pale moonlight. Tearing his gaze from her with an effort, he moved away, stopping at the top of the stairs and looking back at her.

"Good-bye, Caroline," he said simply before continuing his descent.

Caroline stood on the balcony, gasping for breath,

gazing after Jason until he disappeared from view, feeling all the humiliation of opening herself to him and having him walk away from her without a backward glance. The taste of his lips still lingered on her mouth, the feel of his almost brutal kiss still raw on her lips.

Lifting her eyes heavenward, she whispered, "I don't want to leave. Please, make him love me by tomorrow morning."

Caroline smiled ironically. Nothing was too hard for God, she well knew, but it would take a true miracle to change Jason Sinclair's heart overnight, a miracle the likes of which mankind hadn't seen since the parting of the Red Sea.

Releasing a deep sigh, she was about to turn and go into her room when movement at the edge of the jungle caught her eye.

Ines—she was slipping away to the small shack to take the mother and her child home, wherever that was. Caroline's intention had been to follow them and find out where they'd come from so that she could try and stop this disease before it became an epidemic. The early arrival of the mail boat had changed all that.

I could still go, she thought. She could follow Ines and learn what she wanted to know. She turned, gazing toward the river and the unseen boat that waited to take her from all that she had grown to love.

Of course, if she followed Ines, she might not get back before the mail boat left in the morning. The thought stilled her, and she considered the possibility. Yes, that was one way to avoid going—be somewhere else when the boat left. Jason would be furious.

Her thoughts reeled back to the time she told Melanie how sorry she was for involving her in the scheme that had resulted in her marriage to Jason, and she remembered being concerned that Derek would be angry. But Melanie had replied, "He'll get over it."

So strong was Melanie's faith in Derek's love that she was willing to risk his fury because she knew that he would forgive her.

How Caroline longed for that kind of love.

She glanced at the place where Ines had disappeared into the jungle. If she didn't hurry, her decision would be made for her. She wouldn't be *able* to follow Ines.

He'll never forgive you, a voice inside her warned. But what did she have to lose? He was already sending her back. And if he truly wouldn't forgive her, there would be other mail boats.

Caroline drew her shawl closer around her against the surprisingly chill night air. With one last glance at the heavens, she descended the stairs and hurried across the courtyard and into the jungle.

9

The shrill blast of the mail boat's whistle broke the early morning calm. Jason straightened and wiped his face with his bare arm, fighting the rising well of pain inside him. He'd done the right thing, the only thing he could have done under the circumstances.

He felt the pressure of eyes on him before he glanced at the men who worked around him—accusing eyes, rueful eyes.

"Damn." His gaze fell on Ignacio. "What the hell are you looking at? We have work to do."

Ignacio snorted and turned away, the expression of contempt in his eyes saying more than any words could have.

All morning, Jason worked like a man possessed. He tried with all his will not to think of her, not to feel as if his own blood flowed away from him on the wide, wild Amazon, but the *fazenda* itself seemed to sag with sorrow at her absence. He'd wanted her to go, so why did he feel as if a part of him was being torn away?

When he returned to the house for lunch, he found it quiet and deserted. No lunch awaited him. It was just as well; he had no appetite and no desire to face Ines's baleful, accusing glances.

He stood for a long time, gazing out the open dining room door at the encroaching jungle, contemplating the precarious nature of his existence here. No one had believed he could make a coffee plantation work and grow in this remote region, and to be honest, there had been times when he doubted his own sanity. But somehow, with the help of dedicated men, he'd managed to carve out a place for himself.

Still, the jungle waited patiently at his doorstep for the chance to reclaim what he'd taken from it. Now and then it would send a reminder—like a plague of insects or a deadly mud slide—to remind him how insignificant he was, to remind him that he was only here, alive and thriving, because the jungle allowed it.

This was no life for a woman. A woman needed stability and comfort. The sound of the river rushing to its source, the familiar scent of rotting leaves invigorated him and made him feel attuned to the rhythm of life. A woman could never comprehend such a thing. She would have grown to hate it here before long—and she would have grown to hate him.

What could he give her here in the harsh jungle? She'd come in search of warmth and companionship, things he knew nothing about. Caroline had been duped as completely as he had.

He couldn't help admiring the willful young woman who had confronted him so defiantly that first day. She'd been his equal in every way except physical size and strength—intelligent, arrogant, bold, courageous, yet utterly feminine. Caroline was no weak hothouse flower to wither and die in the tropical heat, no delicate Irish rose unable to survive in the harshness of the real world.

Not like Peggy.

Peggy had never learned the hard lessons of life. She'd been as out of place in the slums of New Orleans's Irish Channel as a flower in a sewer. There had been something in her, something pure and beautiful. She'd had dreams, romantic dreams of finding a way out of the wretched existence they had shared. And once her dreams were killed, she'd been unable to go on living.

A faint, sweet melody floated to him on the air, the sound coming from the salon, a haunting refrain that stirred deep in his soul. He closed his eyes tightly against the pain, the hollow echo of loneliness in his deepest being.

Damn Derek to everlasting hell! It had been a mistake to trust his cousin, a mistake for which he would pay as long as he lived. Caroline would return to New Orleans and start over. She'd find someone else, someone who could give her what she wanted. But Jason knew that he would never forget, nor would the empty place she'd left in his heart ever be filled again.

He hadn't felt such a bottomless ache since Peggy's death, and he'd vowed never to feel it again, never to allow anyone to get that close to him again. And he'd succeeded—until now—until Caroline.

His boots echoed loudly on the hard tile floor as he rushed to the salon, half expecting to find her there

If you have a passion for great historical romance, here's an offer you'll love...

4 FREE NOVELS

Introducing
The Timeless Romance

Passion rising from the ashes of the Civil War...

Love blossoming against the harsh landscape of the primitive Australian outback...

Romance melting the cold walls of an 18th-century English castle —— and the heart of the handsome Earl who lives there...

Since the beginning of time, great love has held the power to change the course of history. And in Harper Monogram historical novels, you can experience that power again and again.

Free introductory offer. To introduce you to this exclusive new service, we'd like to send you the four newest Harper Monogram titles absolutely free. They're yours to keep without obligation, no matter what you decide.

Free 10-day previews. Enjoy automatic free delivery of four new titles each month —— up to four weeks before they appear in bookstores. You're never obligated to keep a book you don't want, and you can return any book, for a full credit.

Save up to 32% off the publisher's price on any shipment you choose to keep.

Don't pass up this opportunity to enjoy great romance as you have never experienced before.

Reader Service.

Yes! I want to join the Timeless Romance Reader Service. Please send me my 4 FREE HarperMonogram historical romances. Then each month send me 4 new historical romances to preview without obligation for 10 days. I'll pay the low subscription price of $4.00 for every book I choose to keep--a total savings of at least $2.00 each month--and home delivery is free! I understand that I may return any title within 10 days and receive a full credit. I may cancel this subscription at any time without obligation by simply writing "Canceled" on any invoice and mailing it to Timeless Romance. There is no minimum number of books to purchase.

NAME

ADDRESS

CITY   STATE   ZIP

TELEPHONE

SIGNATURE

(If under 18, parent or guardian must sign. Program, price, terms, and conditions subject to cancellation and change. Orders subject to acceptance by HarperMonogram.)

Indulge in passion,
adventure and romance
with your

4 FREE

Historical Romances.

TIMELESS ROMANCE
READER SERVICE

120 Brighton Road
P.O. Box 5069
Clifton, NJ 07015-5069

AFFIX
STAMP
HERE

bent over the piano, her body swaying with an abandon she seemed incapable of attaining except through
that instrument. What greeted him was an empty
room. The piano stood silent and forlorn, though the
room resonated with the memory of music, as a whisper of her scent clung to the thick air.

It was for the best; she would be better off. She'd
find a normal man without the demons that dogged
him so relentlessly that he couldn't sleep at night.

Night after night, while the rest of the world
slept, he relived the anger and fear and helplessness
of his childhood. Caroline couldn't even imagine the
kind of life he'd lived—the uncertainty of never
knowing when his father would come home drunk
and fly into a rage.

He could still hear the sickening sound of fist
against flesh as he and Peggy had huddled together
in the closet in fear and his father had pummeled his
mother until she cowered, sobbing on the floor. He
could still feel that same fist battering his own body.

And he could never forget that he was the son of
his father—the same hot temper, the same propen-
sity to drink too much, and the same tendency to
become mean and dangerous. He'd just found a way
to control it—hiding himself away in the jungle.

How had he ever thought he could risk having his
own family? He'd come here so he wouldn't have to
find out his true nature, so he couldn't get close
enough to anyone to hurt them or to be hurt by
them. He didn't think he could bear any more pain
in his life, and the fact that it frightened him so
much that he might actually grow to care for her
only added to his self-loathing.

The house seemed to close in around him. It wasn't

even his house anymore; she'd made it hers simply by living here, by moving through these rooms. How ironic that the haven he'd built with such care had become a prison. He hadn't even been able to sleep in it any more, not while she was here. Her presence awakened too many desires and fears inside him.

"Ines!" he bellowed, stomping through the house to the kitchen.

The stove was cold, the cabinets clean. Ines hadn't even prepared the noon meal. Where could she be? Had she gone with Caroline? Surely if she had, someone would have left word. Someone would have seen her leave.

Running both hands through his hair, he tried to clear his mind. Every room resounded with Caroline's memory. There were the flowers she'd arranged so carefully, her place at the table, the book left lying facedown on the table beside her chair in the salon. Sending her away might be the single greatest mistake he'd ever made in a lifetime rife with mistakes.

Perhaps she could have saved him from himself. More likely, she would have been destroyed in the effort.

One thing was certain, he couldn't stay here alone. He'd go mad for sure. As he stalked into the courtyard, he had no idea where he was going, only that he had to get away, away from the memories lurking in every corner of the house.

As soon as he stepped into the clearing, Jason was surrounded by dozens of small brown-skinned Indians. The men were naked except for a thin cotton waistband. The women wore waistbands too, with aprons of thick cotton fringe about three inches long. Many of the women wore armbands to which they had attached bird feathers and leaves.

As always, he felt like a giant among these tiny people, a large, clumsy giant. The tallest, Socrates, reached only a little above his belt.

"Man from Somewhere Else!" Socrates called in his native tongue. "We haven't seen you in a long time."

Jason smiled at the appellation, remembering the *Yanomami* custom of not addressing a person by his given name. It was just as well. Since the *Yanomami* names were unpronounceable to the Europeans who first settled Brazil, the missionaries adopted the habit of giving the natives the most absurd names—like Socrates.

"I hope that you are well, brother-in-law," Jason replied in the same language, using the honorary title that Socrates had bestowed on him when he first came to this area. They walked toward the *yano*, a huge structure made of palm thatch, about thirty feet tall and several hundred feet in diameter.

"We are very well, yes!" Socrates told him, nodding his head for emphasis. "You will join us for dinner, yes?"

Jason's stomach growled. He'd left the house early that morning to avoid seeing Caroline. Until now, he hadn't realized how hungry he was. He hadn't eaten since dinner last night.

The meal consisted of banana soup, rice, and smoked monkey. Jason ate at Socrates' hearth in the *yano*, while the other families of the community went about their business. Several of Socrates' brothers-in-law joined them.

After the meal, Socrates pulled out a long pipe to celebrate the gathering, talking animatedly as he filled the bowl with a mixture of wild tobacco and a ground leaf that produced a powerful hallucinogenic reaction. "So, Man from Somewhere Else, I have heard that you have a woman now—a tall, pale woman like you."

Jason took the proffered pipe. "I had a woman. She's gone now."

"You did not like her?"

Jason held the end of the pipe to his lips. He couldn't refuse to smoke with them without insulting his host, but he'd meant to pretend to inhale. Instead, he took a deep pull, hoping the drug would dull the pain in his heart. Perhaps it would help him forget at least for a little while that he would never see her again.

"She didn't like me," Jason replied, and the men around the circle laughed loudly.

"There is always my sister," Socrates offered, motioning toward the girl with a wave of his brown hand. "She needs a husband."

One of the brothers-in-law in the circle, a man Jason knew as Abraham, reacted by jerking his head around to stare at the woman in question. She sat in a circle of young women a short distance away, laughing and chattering, unaware that her entire life might be decided here tonight.

Abraham glared at Jason, and Jason stifled a smile. "The idea isn't unappealing," he assured Socrates. In fact, Jason had once toyed with the idea of taking an Indian bride but had decided against it. "The *Yanomami* way and the white man's way are too different. She needs a *Yanomami* husband."

Jason passed the pipe to Abraham who accepted it with a smile.

"What did you do to make her leave?" Socrates wanted to know. "Did you beat her? Did you insult her family?"

"No, nothing like that."

"Then why did she leave? Why don't you go after her and bring her back?" Jason couldn't answer that, not only because he'd been asking himself the same question ever since he'd heard the boat's whistle that morning, but because the three or four pulls he'd taken on the pipe had rendered him nearly senseless.

But instead of dulling his mind to the memory of Caroline, she was all he could seem to think about. The *Yanomami* believed that the drug made the user receptive to communication with the spirits. Jason had never put much store in such superstition, but as his mind dimmed and sensation took over, he felt as if he could actually see Caroline standing on the deck of the mail boat, gazing ahead toward the ocean that would forever separate them.

He remembered little else about that night until he climbed into his hammock much later. Their hammocks were too small, so they had designed one especially for him. Like all the other hammocks, it hung along the inside wall of the *yano*.

For a long time, Jason stared at the thatched roof, trying not to think, trying to let go and allow the hallucinogen to take control of his mind. It was no use. All he could think of was Caroline floating away from him, never to return.

With the help of the drug, his tormented mind conjured all manner of dangers for her. Sudden violent storms were common on the Amazon; the boat could be swamped and lost in the waves that sometimes rivaled the ocean's. He wondered if she could swim. Probably not.

Then there were rapids that were especially treacherous in the dry season when the river was low and fallen trees lurked beneath the surface to snag even the largest boat.

The boat could be attacked by natives. Granted, such incidents were very unusual, since most of the aborigines of the Amazon desired as little contact with whites as possible, but the drug he'd smoked dulled his reason and sharpened his imagination. When he did finally fall asleep, he even dreamed of piranha tearing the flesh from her body.

"I'm all right, Jason," she assured him, walking toward him, a long white gown flowing around her.

Bending over his hammock, her long, dark hair hanging around her lovely face like a veil, she shrugged the sleeves of the gown from her shoulders and allowed it to fall to the ground. She pressed a kiss to his forehead, smiling as sweetly as an angel.

Reaching up, he smoothed her silky hair, allowing his hand to slide down her soft, luscious flesh, lifting a heavy breast to his lips, kissing the turgid peak tenderly.

He could smell the fragrant perfume that always clung to her, taste the sweet saltiness of her skin. He felt himself grow hard with desire as blood rushed through his body, gathering and swelling between his legs. Her hands roamed over his bare shoulders, caressing, tender, a moan of pleasure escaping her parted lips.

"I love you, Jason," she murmured, her voice thick with passion. "I love you."

He awoke with a start, his body still rigid with desire, his senses still filled with Caroline. Disoriented, confused, shaken by the traces of dreams that still clung to him, he tried to rise, but the crazy rocking of the hammock, combined with the aftereffects of the drug, sent his head reeling.

When the blood finally stopped pounding in his veins and his breathing returned to normal, he rolled from the hammock. His bare feet touched the soft, sandy earth, and he realized he was naked except for a thin, irrelevant waistband similar to what the other men wore.

A groan escaped his lips as he glanced at his arms and his memory began to return, albeit hazily. His arms, chest and legs were covered with dots of red paint, and he knew, though he had no mirror, that his face had been painted as well. He also knew from past experience that the dye wouldn't wear off for at least several days.

What would Caroline think when she saw him like this?

Jason blinked his eyes at that thought, shaking his head to clear the fog. He was going after her. He must have decided sometime in the night.

He didn't know if he was doing the right thing. All he knew was that he couldn't let her go. He didn't expect to ever hear her speak the words she'd spoken in the dream. God, he wasn't even sure he wanted to. He only hoped she wouldn't someday grow to hate him for what he was about to do.

When Socrates heard of Jason's decision, he insisted that he and several men go with him. And while Jason feared that the boat's captain might open fire at sight of a band of naked, painted savages, he knew he'd never catch the steamer without help. His own boats were laden with coffee and virtually useless. He'd have to travel by canoe, and he needed help rowing.

Before they departed, Jason bathed in the river, but the dye remained, as he'd known it would. There was no help for it. All he could do was try and lessen the shock to the boat's crew by concealing as much paint as possible with his clothes and hat and by convincing the *Yanomami* to remain hidden while he talked with the captain and removed Caroline from the boat.

Overcome by gladness and an urgency to have her with him again, Jason wondered vaguely how he would ever maintain his distance emotionally once this was done. She'd know that he cared enough to go after her; she'd have that much power over him. And as they readied the boats, he worried what would happen if he ever grew to truly love her.

"What do you mean she never got on the boat?" Jason shouted. He stood on the deck of the small mail boat, acutely conscious of the anxious glances exchanged by the boat's crew of two and the half dozen Yanomami in the canoe lashed to the side of the larger vessel.

"Sorry, Mr. Sinclair," the captain said, studying the intricately painted patterns on Jason's face. "Like I said, she didn't show up that morning when we left. We gave a couple of blasts on the whistle, but I figured when she didn't show up, she must've changed her mind."

"Then where the hell can she be?" he asked no one in particular.

"Mr. Sinclair," the captain said hesitantly, "pardon me for saying so sir, but you and your . . . friends are making my crew a little nervous. I've told you all I know. . . ."

"I'm sorry for the trouble," he said, throwing a leg over the side of the boat. "We'll bother you no further."

When Jason was settled back in the canoe, he explained the situation to his companions, who thought it all quite funny. They pushed away from the mail boat and headed back up the Rio Branco the way they'd come, back to the *fazenda*.

Damn her, Jason thought, irrationally angry that she hadn't done as he'd said and gotten on the boat. The small part of him that wasn't angry feared for her safety.

Why hadn't she gotten on that boat yesterday? Why hadn't he seen her, or Ines for that matter, since? What if something had happened to her?

Grabbing a paddle, Jason caught the rhythm of the others and rowed with all his might, hoping that she was alive and safe—so he could wring her neck!

The door banged loudly against the inner wall as Jason pushed it open and stepped into Caroline's sitting room. Nothing seemed amiss or out of place there, except for a bouquet of neglected orchids that drooped over the sides of their vase.

He crossed the room and attacked the door to her bedroom with the same fervor he'd used in entering the sitting room. Her bags stood in a pile just inside the door, packed and ready to go. The bed was made, the shutters and windows closed tightly.

Jason slammed the door closed and marched out onto the balcony where Socrates and his friends stood talking and laughing animatedly, obviously enjoying Jason's distress immensely.

"What do you do now?" Socrates asked.

Jason brushed past him and his men without a word.

"Ines!" he called as he crossed the courtyard to the kitchen. "Ines!"

Ines gasped and turned to face him as he stormed into the small room, her eyes wide with surprise and fear. "*Patrão*, where have you been? I am worrying—"

Jason didn't check his pace but moved toward her like a raging beast out of control. Ines shrunk away from the anger in his eyes, but there was no place to go. He was on her in seconds, grabbing her by the arms and shaking her.

"Where is she?" he demanded.

"Please, *patrão*, I don't know what you mean!"

"Don't lie to me, Ines," he ground out. "You know exactly what I'm talking about. I want to know where Caroline is and I want to know now!"

Ines gazed past Jason at the curious natives who stood in the doorway. Her eyes widened as she recognized them as *Yanomami*, the most feared people of the Amazon. She'd known about Master Jason's friendship with them, but he rarely allowed them to come to the house.

"Ines, tell me!"

"*Patrão*, you are hurting me!"

Horror streaked through him and he released her immediately, stepping back from her, gazing in dismay at his hands. What was happening to him? He was walking a thin line, losing control more and more often.

"I'm sorry, Ines," he muttered, running his hands through his hair, struggling to still the intense anger that clung to him like a heavy morning mist. Was it Caroline's audacity that drove him toward unconstrained fury or was it only his father's legacy coming to the fore? Either way, he had to maintain the iron restraint he'd always practiced.

"There is a slave village," Ines was saying.

"Runaways?" Anger began to boil inside him once again, but this time he managed to defeat it. "Of all the reckless, irresponsible. . . . Where?"

Ines shook her head negatively, glancing past Jason at the savages who stood at the door of her kitchen, then back at Jason. "I will take you to her."

10

Jason squinted through the warm, steady rain as he used his machete to hack through the tangled verdure. He should have put her on the boat personally. At least if he'd done so, he'd know where to find her now.

A hand grabbed his arm from behind, and he turned in time to see Ines trip over the twisted branches of a fallen tree. Reacting quickly, he grabbed her by the arm, setting her back on her feet.

"How much farther?" He shouted over the roar of the storm. The urgency to see Caroline, to make sure she was all right, nearly drove him to madness. And Ines's assurances had done nothing to curb his anxiety.

"Not far!" Ines replied, slicking her wet hair off of her face.

He turned back to the trail before him, chopping through the lush jungle vegetation with a vengeance, spurred by a growing anger. Ines should have tried to stop her, and failing that, she should have come to him immediately. As for Caroline, he was beginning to realize that her daring knew no bounds. The fact that she had had the temerity to defy him was bad enough, but on top of that, she'd gone and hidden herself away in the jungle.

What he wanted to know more than anything was why. Did she have any idea what could happen to her if the slavers found them?

He shuddered at the thought and redoubled his efforts, pushing himself and those with him unmercifully.

Ines had been damned uncooperative about the whole situation. "Ask *senhora*," she'd said. "I will show you where, but you must promise not to be angry."

"I'm already angry!" he'd bellowed.

Angry? What an insufficient word to describe what he was feeling. Right now, he'd like to choke her, as soon as he was satisfied that she was all right.

The rain gave way to blue sky as the jungle opened into a slight clearing. Crude huts stood in a circle around a grassy square filled with the excited squeals of Indian children chasing a pecarry, a piglike animal with long, stiff hair, in a circle.

Slaves.

The plantations were probably in Minas Gerais or Mato Grosso hundreds of miles to the south. The runaways had come here to the Amazon jungle in hopes of eluding their masters.

Most of the structures in the tiny village were thatched huts, but two more permanent buildings stood at opposite ends of the square. Obviously this settlement had been here for some time.

"How could you have let her come here?" Jason

asked, his tone accusing as his gaze burned into Ines's guilty eyes. With the exception of murder, there was no greater crime in Brazil than aiding runaway slaves. Man or woman, the penalty was imprisonment and loss of property. He'd risked it by leaving food and supplies where they could find them, but he'd never visited their village, and he didn't like being here now.

"How could I have stopped her?" Ines asked meaningfully.

Yes, how indeed? Once Caroline made up her mind to do something, she was like a force of nature.

Slowly men and women began emerging from the huts, eyeing him and the *Yanomami* mistrustfully. Most of them seemed to relax when they saw Ines step forward, but one man remained unassured.

He walked toward Jason, his manner arrogant, his movements wary. Nearly as tall as Jason, he presented a threatening demeanor with his muscular frame and uncompromising glare.

"My name is Jason Sinclair," Jason said in Portuguese. "I believe my wife is here."

The black man gazed at Ines, who nodded almost imperceptibly. When his eyes returned to Jason, they had lost most of their fire. He appeared suddenly weary, almost vulnerable. "I am Pocedo. Follow me."

They walked toward the thatched building at the far end of the village. Jason became aware of things he hadn't noticed before—the lack of activity in the village, the sound of coughing and moaning. He could smell the sickness, and his stomach churned to think of Caroline here so close to death and disease.

There was no door, only an animal skin covering the opening. The large black man pushed it aside and allowed Jason to enter first. What met his gaze chilled him to the bone. Hammocks had been strung throughout the cavernous room, hammocks filled with suffering humanity, some so still they might have been dead.

She stood beside a hammock, whispering soothingly to its inhabitant. Her soft voice pierced his heart and set the blood pounding through his veins. Part of him wanted to shake her, to berate her for disobeying him. Another part of him wanted to rush to her, to take her in his arms and tell her how empty he'd felt inside when he'd thought he'd lost her.

Sensing their presence, she turned to stare at them with wide-eyed surprise, the signs of fatigue showing plainly on her face.

"Jason! What are you doing here? Who are these . . . these . . ."

Fear and fury and a wild joy coursed through him, causing his body to shudder with the effort to control the bombardment of emotions, to keep them from showing in his eyes lest she realize the depth of his concern, and use it against him.

This fragile woman presented a greater danger to him than any raging torrent or pestilence. The jungle could destroy his body, while Caroline and only Caroline could destroy his soul if he gave her the power to do so. It terrified him as nothing else in his life ever had.

So intent was he on his wife, Jason had forgotten the *Yanomami* were with him until Caroline averted her gaze from the naked men who had crowded into the building. Their bodies, like his, were painted with red and black dots and geometric designs.

What a shock they must present to her. He didn't know how many Indians Caroline had encountered on her trip to the *fazenda*, but he knew she would not have had any contact with the *Yanomami*. They were far too cautious for that. They stayed deep in the jungle, far from the white man. The sight of half a dozen naked, painted savages should have terrified her, but he read no fear in her expression, only embarrassment and surprise.

"Natives," he said, "*Yanomami*. And they've come with me to find my runaway wife."

He stepped closer, and Caroline's face registered further shock when she got a good look at him. He'd also forgotten the red dots that covered his own face and body. He knew they stood out much more strikingly against his white skin.

An uncertain laugh escaped her lips and she stifled it immediately. "I'm sorry. It's just that . . . What happened?"

"What are you doing here?" He cut straight to the matter at hand.

"Whoever they are, they shouldn't be here," Caroline warned, indicating the short, brown Indians with a nod of her head.

"Why? What's wrong with these people?" Jason asked with an instinctive dread.

"Measles."

The word sent a tremor through his body. Diseases had decimated some of the largest tribes in the Amazon. Because of their isolation, the *Yanomami* had been spared so far, but neither had they been exposed to European diseases enough to develop any measure of resistance.

Wheeling around, he spoke to Socrates in his native language. "These people have a disease that could be deadly to your people. Get your men out of here immediately and return to the *yano*. Thank you for your help."

Socrates nodded, smiling, "She is very plain, Man from Somewhere Else. If you decide to send her away again, remember I have many sisters."

Jason smiled at his friend's offer and his inaccurate assessment of Caroline. Beauty was indeed in the eye of the beholder. Right now, Jason didn't think he'd ever seen anything as lovely as his wife.

"What about you?" Caroline asked. She appeared uneasy, anxious, as if she wasn't sure what he might do. "Have you had the measles?"

"Yes, when I was a child," he told her, searching her face.

She wiped a stray curl from her forehead, releasing a great sigh. Upon closer inspection, he saw the dark circles beneath her eyes that marred the perfection of her skin. Her eyelids appeared puffy, her skin slightly sallow.

"You look exhausted," he said. "When's the last time you slept?"

"I don't know. What day is it?"

"You have to sleep," he scolded gently, coming to stand close beside her.

"You don't," she said weakly.

Placing his big hands on her slender shoulders, he drew her into the fold of his arms. He wanted to hold her, just hold her forever. He wanted to crush her to his chest and tell her . . . tell her. . . .

"Come on," he said gruffly, "you won't be any good to them if you don't rest."

Her weary head relaxed against his chest, and Jason felt an unaccustomed flood of affection for this courageous, determined woman who was his wife.

"I'm no good to them anyway," she murmured, her voice bitter with defeat. "I can't do anything for them. I give them quinine. It doesn't help. Nothing works."

"Now who's playing God?" he asked, trying to lessen the burden of grief he sensed inside her, trying to suppress the thrill that coursed through his body at her nearness.

"Where do you sleep?" he asked, steering her toward the door.

"I can't," she protested, trying to stop, but his momentum propelled her forward with him.

"Where?" he asked again.

"Nowhere. I haven't slept since I've been here. I don't know."

Ines stood uncertainly at the door, moving out of the way as they reached her.

"Find out, Ines," he told her, pushing the animal skin out of the way and guiding Caroline's unresisting body through the opening into the outer dampness.

Once outside, Jason surrendered Caroline to Ines's care and turned to face the man who had approached him earlier, the man he held responsible for allowing his wife to work without rest for two days.

"You bastard!" he ground out, advancing toward the other man who retreated before Jason's fury, in spite of his size.

Rage pounded in his ears and hammered through his veins. Jason drew back and punched the retreating man in the jaw, knocking him off his feet. Pain exploded in his fist, streaking up his arm, but he ignored it, stalking toward the prone man. With a feral growl, he hauled his target to his feet and drew back again.

"No! Jason, stop!"

Blinded and deafened by fury, Jason hardly noticed the voice humming in his ear. Were they willing to kill her in order to save a few of their own? A resounding yes echoed inside his brain. Yes, they would sacrifice the doctor to save the patient. She was nothing to them, no blood relation. But she was everything to him, and they were about to learn what that meant.

Once again his fist met the other man's face, the force of the blow sending him reeling backward. But this time he managed to remain standing.

"No!"

The word came again, more high-pitched this time, like a scream. A hand grabbed his arm and he shrugged it away, his every sense tuned to the man before him who seemed to have recovered and stood waiting, his own fists clenched.

Caroline stepped in front of Jason and he stopped, gazing over her head at the other man.

"Get out of my way, Caroline!" he ordered.

"No! Stop it! Please."

Grabbing her by the shoulders, Jason turned her aside, but she clutched his shirt with all her strength, clinging to him when he tried to extricate himself. Angrily, he released her shoulders and grabbed her by the arms. His large hands wrapping around her small wrists, he pried her hands from his shirt and stood staring down into her fearful eyes.

"Please," she whispered, and the blindness lifted from his mind.

Awareness returned, and he realized how tightly he held her and how violently her body quivered. Releasing her abruptly, he trembled with self-loathing, while his heart pounded in the aftermath of his anger. Had he hurt her? He didn't think so. His anger had been directed at the man who stood now staring at him, wiping blood from the corner of his mouth. But at the very least, he'd frightened her.

And he instantly regretted it. In one awful moment he realized she had never been exposed to violence, to the unremitting fear of living in a world dominated by someome larger and stronger who delighted in cruelty, a world without sanctuary. Her eyes were too clear, her face too open and trusting to have endured that kind of hell, and he didn't want to introduce her to it now.

"It's not his fault," Caroline said, her voice pleading.

"I'm sorry." Jason raised a hand to her cheek, glad that she didn't flinch from him. "I'm sorry."

"Perhaps you should tell him," Caroline said, motioning toward the injured man with a nod of her head.

Overwhelmed by relief that he hadn't inadvertently hurt her, he pulled her unresisting form into his arms, holding her tightly, his chin resting on the top of her head.

"Go with Ines," he murmured.

He held her at arm's length, gazing into her worried eyes. "I won't attack anyone, I promise. Go with Ines."

"How could you let her work like that without resting?" Jason asked bitterly in Portuguese as soon as the women were out of ear shot.

"Be careful whom you are accusing," the other man warned in the same language, massaging his throbbing jaw. "We all tried to get her to rest but she wouldn't listen. We are grateful she is here, but we want no harm to come to her."

Jason closed his eyes as the tension flowed out of his body. A thin mist rose off the warm, damp earth as the clouds parted and the sky brightened.

"I'm sorry," he murmured.

The black man smiled. "Don't be sorry. We thank you for letting us have your wife for a little while, and we are glad to see that you take good care of her. And now you are here, the gods will smile on us all the more. Come, there is *cachaca*. We will drink to your wife."

Jason groaned, his head still not quite clear from the drug he'd smoked the night before. What he really wanted was to go with Caroline, to hold her until she fell asleep, to be with her when she awoke.

But it would be impolite to refuse to drink with the man, especially after attacking him, so he followed him to a small table made of two tree stumps with a smooth slab of wood laid on top of them, thinking that politeness would do him in yet.

Caroline awoke to the sound of cicadas chirping so loudly she thought at first she must have fallen asleep in the open. Sitting up, she gazed around her at the profound darkness, swatting ineffectually at a noisy mosquito that hummed close to her face.

"Are you well, *senhora*?" Ines's voice reached out to her from the darkness, and she knew she hadn't dreamed Jason into existence. He had really been there that afternoon. Was he still somewhere in the village?

"I'm fine," Caroline assured her, rising from the low, crude cot.

Ines struck a match to a lantern and the room brightened to a degree, shadows flickering and growing long against the rough walls. "You should stay in bed."

"Why?" Caroline asked. "I feel rested. Where is Jason?"

"I am not knowing," Ines replied. "Will I find him?"

"No!" Caroline gasped, crossing her arms over her breasts, aware suddenly that she wore nothing but her thinnest chemise. "No, I just wondered. I can't sleep another minute, Ines. I think it will be morning soon."

Caroline moved to the crude table in the corner where a pitcher and bowl stood.

"The water is fresh," Ines told her. "I draw it while you sleep. But it will be not hot."

"Oh." Caroline almost sighed, running her hand through the silky, tepid water. "It's too warm for hot water anyway. I'll just wash up and then go and check on the patients."

"You'll be sick yourself. . . ."

"Please, Ines, Jason already pointed that out to me. I know what I'm doing."

Jason. What was he doing here? How did he learn that she hadn't boarded the mail steamer? However he had gained that information, he had evidently forced Ines into bringing him here. How angry he must be to realize that he had to wait another month or more before he could finally be rid of her.

"Have you slept at all?" she asked Ines.

"Some, yes."

"I'm sorry Jason dragged you through the jungle like this. It's my fault." Her voice broke with emotion, fear coalescing in her throat as she imagined her next encounter with Jason.

"Do not apologize, *senhora*. I am glad he finds you so he can maybe keep you from killing yourself with work."

Caroline ignored the comment, her mind and body absorbed with visions of how wonderful the cool water would feel on her skin as she tried to push the picture of an enraged Jason from her mind. She would not cower before him; she would face him defiantly and calmly.

"I will find some food, yes?" Ines said, exiting quickly.

Caroline closed her eyes, slipping the sleeves of her chemise over her shoulders and allowing it to hang down from the waist. He would berate her for disobeying him and for causing him to lose valuable time away from the *fazenda*. But she hadn't asked him to come after her. She would have been just fine had he not.

The water felt as wonderful to her deprived skin as she'd imagined. Dipping the edge of her chemise into the water, she used it like a washcloth, smoothing it over her face, her throat, her bare breasts, careful to keep her back to the door in case someone accidentally stumbled into this room.

The thought had barely left her mind when she felt the prickling of a presence behind her. She wasn't sure if she'd heard something or simply sensed movement, but she knew with a desperate kind of fear that there was someone else in the room, someone between her and the door.

She turned with a start to find Jason standing in the doorway. Her arms went up automatically to cover her exposed breasts, and she stood there, half-naked and trembling.

Instead of relief that the intruder was Jason, Caroline's body resounded with a primeval fear. It coursed through her and set her heart to hammering as he stepped further into the room, his large body filling the small space. She took a step back. Spotting her discarded shirt on the floor, she bent and picked it up, wrapping it around her.

"What—what do you want?" she managed to ask. "Why are you here?"

If only she could read his expression, but she couldn't bear the intensity of those slate blue eyes long enough. Never had she felt so vulnerable, so incredibly aware of her own body. The air crackled with male vitality as he stepped farther into the room, stopping at the tiny gasp that welled up from her throat.

"Ines," he murmured, his heated gaze moving slowly over her exposed flesh, "she said the hut was empty. I'm sorry."

Ines. Why had she lied? She'd known Caroline was still inside the hut—bathing. That little schemer. She'd deliberately misled Jason, deliberately thrown them together.

Caroline watched him turn to go, knowing in her deepest heart that if she didn't stop him now, she might never have another chance to try and reach him. They'd be returning to the house soon, and Jason would disappear again. If she couldn't find him, how could she get through that impenetrable shell of his?

"Wait!" she cried desperately.

He turned to face her, and her mouth went dry. She felt terribly foolish, standing there trembling like a virgin, afraid for him to stay, afraid for him to go.

The bright red paint on his face brought to mind the Indians who had accompanied him here. Had he taken part in some savage ritual? He'd seemed so at ease with the natives; he'd even spoken their language.

Her mind catapulted her back to the day she'd encountered Jason bathing at the *benefício*. The image set her blood on fire.

"I have something that might take that off," she murmured. "The dye, I mean."

She turned away, quickly donning her shirt, her fingers fumbling on the buttons as she struggled to calm her body's violent trembling. Opening her medical bag, she found a large bottle of witch hazel and a clean cloth.

"Sit," she said, motioning to the cot with a nod of her head.

Jason moved to obey her command, eyeing her warily as he removed his shirt. She hesitated, surprised by his action. "It's everywhere, I'm afraid," he told her.

Caroline felt her face turn furiously red but tried to act casual as she thought of red dots *everywhere*. She stood before him, the top of his head level with her chin. He lifted his face and she dampened the cloth with the witch hazel, willing herself not to think of how her shirt gaped open, to forget that she wore nothing beneath the thin material, to ignore the fire in his light blue eyes that turned her legs to rubber and caused her heart to hammer against the wall of her chest.

Concentrating on his face, she tried not to notice the naked expanse of his chest. Whenever she allowed herself to think of it, a dizzying ripple rose up from her knotted stomach, devouring her, threatening her fragile control.

"I'm sorry I spoiled your plans by not getting on the mail boat," she said, trying to make conversation, to fill the silence with sound, any sound but the fierce drumming of her heart. She massaged the cloth against his skin and the dye dissolved. "But these people need me. There will be another mail boat."

Wiping the rest of the dye from his face, Caroline stood uncertainly, trying to decide how best to approach his chest, how to tame the trembling of her hand. She decided to start at the top, applying her ministrations to a dot of dye on his collarbone.

It was a chest, after all, just flesh and bone, part of a man's body. She'd seen a chest before—many times in medical school or when she would assist her father. But Jason was not a patient or a medical specimen to be dissected and studied.

And he most certainly was not Wade Marshall. Her first husband had been only a few inches taller than she, always carefully manicured, always fashionably dressed. There had been nothing threatening or unsettling about Wade, nothing overwhelming. Still, the marriage bed had been a shock, even with the medical knowledge she'd acquired beforehand— the intimacy of it, the invasion of body and soul, the terrible vulnerability. She had never known another man, but then, could there be that much difference?

Yes, she thought immediately, yes, there could be a world of difference.

"Do you want to leave Brazil?" he asked huskily, his chest vibrating beneath the cloth that separated her flesh from his.

Anger stiffened her spine and blinded her raging senses. "Why do you ask?" she nearly spat, moving her efforts to another circle of dye. "You never have before. I think my feelings have been abundantly clear from the start. Are you trying to humiliate me by making me admit something? What I want or don't want has no bearing on this situation."

"Ouch! Be careful!" he growled, his voice heavy with desire. "You'll rub the skin off."

Comprehension flooded her and Caroline realized she'd been wiping viciously at a dot near his small, flat nipple. She drew back and doused the cloth again, acutely aware of his body and the intimacy of what she was doing. His unwavering gaze searched her face, unnerving her further.

Pressing the cloth against his breastbone, she felt the hard ridge of muscle through the material. Her rapid breathing sounded loud to her ears in the raw silence that connected them, and she wondered if he could hear it, too.

"You're so beautiful," he murmured, reaching underneath her gaping blouse, his big hand rough and gentle as he caressed the underside of her breast. The breath caught in her throat at the explosion of sensation along her every nerve ending. Her nipple grew painfully taut, aching for his touch.

She knew she should pull away. He might desire her physically, but he did not love her, and she wasn't sure any longer that the gulf between their hearts could be bridged by their bodies. Still, her body leaned toward him. She braced herself with her hands on his broad shoulders because a terrible weakness had begun to insinuate itself into her marrow and she didn't think she could stand upright under her own power.

"Please don't," she managed to gasp, "not if you don't want me . . . want me to stay."

A low moan rolled up from Caroline's throat as his thumb teased a taut nipple. Currents of sensation flashed from his hands through her body with the force of a violent thunderstorm. Wade had never made her feel this yearning fervor, this all-consuming hunger.

While his one hand stroked her breast, his other undid the tiny buttons she'd fastened so ineptly, pushing the shirt sleeves down her arms. She gasped, the thought of covering herself gleaming in her mind for an instant. But the feel of his breath, warm and pulsing against her flesh as he bent and kissed a swollen nipple, stole her thoughts and the last of her resistance.

"Stay," he whispered against her burning skin, his tongue light and wet on her tumescent flesh. "Stay, Caroline."

His words filled her foolish heart with joy. She seemed to be melting into him, surrendering control of her own body to him as his hand cupped her buttocks and he pulled her close so that she was standing between his legs. He lifted her off the floor, turning her so that she lay on her back on the cot, the swiftness of his actions startling her.

He covered her with his body, his elbows on either side of her shoulders holding his weight off her. His hands cupped her face, massaging her scalp, her temples, her lips, as he planted kisses on her nose and eyelids, filling her with a wild fire, a sweet longing that forced her body toward a swirling tempest.

He stood to finish undressing, and she watched him because she wanted to and he wanted her to, and there was no one to tell her it was wrong. She studied him as she'd longed to do that day at the *beneficio*, memorizing every muscle, every contour of his magnificent body. The thought of unleashing all that male power made her weak inside, her body almost fluid. The raw intensity in his gaze stole her breath.

The reality of Jason Sinclair bore hardly any resemblance to the man she'd expected from his letters. And yet, she would not trade the reality for the fantasy if given the chance. She remembered fearing what he would be like after so long without social contact—savage, coarse, barely human. Now she found that the very wildness she'd feared was the thing that set her heart to pounding and caused the raw yearning deep inside her.

Her mind stopped functioning as she surrendered to passion, swept away by his ardor. He was all over her . . . his hands . . . his mouth, touching her, tasting her, robbing her will. His hardness huge and full against her sent jolts of fear and desire pulsing through her body. His profound maleness overpowered her and left her trembling like a maiden. Three years of marriage might never have happened.

One hand cupped her face as he kissed her deeply, possessively. His other caressed its way over her shoulder to her breast, his finger and thumb tugging and teasing her nipple, then moving lower, lower until he found the moist heat between her thighs.

His fingers slid into her and she cried out, arching her hips toward him, panting now with a sweet madness as his lips trailed a path of fire down her neck. He demanded nothing less than total surrender, and her body obeyed, trembling with a fervency deeper than anything she'd ever experienced or imagined.

He raised his head to look at her, his back bowed so that their faces touched, his rasping breath warm and sweet on her lips. His fingers were gone now, replaced by the velvet hardness that touched the opening to her center.

He whispered her name, his soft, strong voice quivering down her spine as his legs forced hers wider apart.

A ragged gasp rumbled up from inside her, and he hesitated, gauging the cause—pain, fear, passion? When her body arched toward his, it took every ounce of restraint in his being not to take her quickly, forcefully, and end the agony in his loins. But he remembered her reaction to his earlier violence and felt the delicacy of her small, soft body. She seemed so fragile he feared he might crush her if he weren't careful.

He hadn't meant for this to happen when he'd come looking for her, but from the moment he'd walked into the hut and seen her standing there, her breasts barely covered by her crossed arms, he'd sensed a frightening inevitability about everything that had led them to this moment. Still, he would have stopped had she reacted in fear or revulsion, had she denied him in any way. She had not.

He sensed her body opening beneath him, even before he began to press gently into her yielding flesh. Soft moaning sounds rumbled up from her throat as he pushed himself deeper into her, sounds she could not control any more than she could control the way her body clung to his or the way the pulse in her throat beat fitfully beneath his lips.

He wanted to absorb her into himself and make her a part of him forever. He needed to feel her arms, soft and firm, holding him against her warm, willing body. For just a little while, he needed to believe that she was his completely, that nothing could ever drive them apart, that the darkness of the past could be conquered.

She gave a sharp cry as he penetrated her depths, and he went still, though the urge to thrust pounded in his blood. He wanted to savor the feel of her body soft and warm around him, beneath him. Her delicate arms around his back drew him closer, urging him with a longing that shone clearly in her passion-darkened eyes.

She lay still beneath him, connected to his motionless body, perfectly filled with him, fearful of the fire that raged inside her as her body and her soul opened and opened to him.

Finally he moved, pressing deeper into her arched, panting body. A ragged groan escaped his lips as he withdrew, then pushed into her again and again, filling her completely, only to withdraw again.

It was a violent, tender thing, their lovemaking. She clung to him, her body responding to his mounting ardor. His fierce strength and unbearable gentleness sent her spinning toward an infinite abyss as he thrust into her, slowly at first, the tempo building to a shattering climax.

11

A warm hand covered her naked breast. The heat of a man's body pressed against her back, as she lay enfolded in his large, sinewy form. A long, muscled leg lay over hers, his thigh wrapped intimately around her hips, his supple sex resting against her buttocks. The sound of his rhythmic breathing sent currents of sweet contentment through her languid body.

A sense of peace washed over her as she lay there, cradled against her husband's strong body. She closed her eyes, and the memory of their lovemaking filled her senses and turned her blood thick. He'd been passionate and tender, loving her with a fervor she'd never known.

The fact that women considered sex an unpleasant duty bewildered her. With Wade she had found the act not unpleasant, if a bit monotonous. But Jason was not Wade, not by any means. Making love with Jason was like opening a dam and allowing a torrent of floodwaters through, riding the crest until the powerful tide ebbed.

He hadn't told her he loved her, but he wanted her to stay. That was a start. And before long, he would confide everything about his past, everything that kept him awake at night. Once he faced the ghosts, they would leave him, and the two of them would be able to have a normal, wonderful life together. Think of it—a lifetime of Jason. Truly she must be the luckiest woman in the world.

She moved slightly, her body unfurling, and the flesh against her buttocks responded before his hand tightened on her breast. Desire coiled inside her, her heart thundering in sweet anticipation as the bed shifted under his weight. Groaning low in his throat, he moved to place a kiss on the sensitive place behind her ear.

How had he known? How did he find out that she hadn't gotten on the mail boat? The questions leaped unbidden to her mind and she quieted them immediately. It didn't matter, not now, not while she could feel his ardor building like storm clouds before a hurricane.

Caroline shivered with pleasure, a smile curving her lips as she imagined waking up next to Jason every morning for the rest of her life. If only he loved her as much as he desired her. It would come in time, she told herself, giving herself over to sensation, surrendering her body and her will to him.

Kneading her breast softly, he nuzzled her neck, his lips trailing down to the hollow that connected her neck to her collarbone. His hand slid underneath her breast and down her ribcage, and she gasped at the fiery sensations evoked by his touch.

Those hands possessed so much strength, yet he caressed her with such gentleness. Gentle yet demanding. Always demanding. Always urgent.

How had she ever thought him inelegant or unrefined? The elegance of his touch took her breath away, and at the moment, she didn't give a whit for refinement.

A low animal growl rumbled up from deep in his chest, vibrating where his lips touched her shoulder, his teeth gently grazing her flesh, sending threads of desire pulsing through her pliant body. Her breathing turned shallow, her heart hammering erratically as his hand moved beyond her ribcage, over the slope of her hip, downward into the nest of curls between her thighs.

Her body convulsed beneath his burning caress. The heat of his loins against her backside, the terrible agony of passion evoked by his hands, the sensation of being surrounded, devoured by masculine strength, pushed her beyond reason, beyond anything she'd ever experienced.

He controlled her body, there was no denying it. Her powerlessness frightened her, exhilarated her. His strong, gentle hands molded her into a mindless animal she didn't recognize, a needful beast that only he could satisfy.

By the time he turned her gently onto her back, her body had given way completely to a fierce ardor. He took her quickly, his thrusts deep and powerful, his body demanding an explosive response from hers. A bottomless eruption racked her in spasm after spasm of exquisite madness that left her physically drained and emotionally raw.

Slowly his rapid breathing returned to normal. Rolling onto his back, he carried her with him. She lay her head on his broad chest, his heart strong and steady beneath her ear. His arm around her made her feel cherished, and she wished she could stay like this forever, wrapped in the safe haven of his arms and his body.

Had she cried out? She thought that she had. Loudly. Embarrassment suffused her body as the lingering effects of euphoria wore off.

She had responded like a wanton. Nice women weren't supposed to cry out, were they? She hoped that he had been too absorbed in his own passion to notice, but she remembered how he'd skillfully played her body like a master musician, and she knew that he had been aware of her every gasp, her every reaction.

Trembling, she nuzzled even closer to him, wanting to absorb him. He'd mastered her body, made her utterly his in a way that Wade never could have.

Compared to Jason, Wade had been nothing but a boy, a soft, pouty boy without the slightest idea how to please a woman. But then, pleasing a woman in bed, especially a man's wife, was not something to be sought after or admired in polite society. She wondered vaguely if Wade had been different with the prostitutes he'd frequented.

And to think, she might have died not knowing the heights of pleasure to be found with a man, not knowing the great disparity that could exist between men. What a pity that would have been, she thought drowsily as sleep reclaimed her.

*   *   *

"You know, it just occurred to me," Caroline said later that morning as they dressed, trying to sound casual when her blood ran cold in anticipation of what she was about to do. "We've never really talked."

They'd argued, they'd fought, they'd made love, but they'd never talked, really talked beyond the casual conversation one might have with a stranger. It was time, whether he realized it or not. The time had come when he would have to unbend a little and let her at least glimpse the man inside his defenses.

"Of course we have," he insisted, facing her with a guileless, open expression she'd thought never to see on his handsome face. She cherished it, whispering a silent prayer that she would see it more often.

"I mean really talked." Though she warned herself to proceed cautiously, Jason's inviting, almost carefree attitude heartened her. Maybe today, maybe now he would talk to her, tell her about his past, his feelings, his secret soul.

"What do you want to talk about?" He stood close by, shrugging into his shirt. Caroline repressed the urge to run her hand over the hard planes of his chest, experiencing a twinge of regret when he buttoned his shirt.

"You."

The word brought him up short. Tension radiated from his body, his demeanor no longer open but carefully guarded. Normally the glint in his eyes would have been enough to quell her curiosity, but if they were to have any kind of relationship, he was going to have to let her inside that carefully guarded heart of his.

"Why did you leave New Orleans?" she asked, starting with something relatively safe.

With a false casualness, he bent down and placed a tender kiss on her lips. Her body sprang to life under the firm, gentle touch of his mouth. For a moment, she forgot what she'd been saying, diverted from her purpose by a spontaneous sexual hunger that stunned her with its power.

"I wanted to go to a place where I could build something with my own hands and not have to work for someone else all my life."

"Why Brazil?" she asked, struggling for control of her senses when every fiber of her woman's body ached to rekindle the passion of a few hours ago.

He released an impatient sigh. "Coffee. I worked for the coffee company and most of our coffee came from Brazil and Colombia. I decided I wanted to be on the production end instead of the distribution end. It was a logical decision."

"Derek says that your father died under somewhat mysterious circumstances." She spoke the words quickly, as if by doing so she could soften their impact. *I think you killed your father*, she wanted to say, but of course she could not. That was something he would have to admit on his own, and she wasn't sure if he ever would.

"We have to get back to the *fazenda*," Jason said sharply, putting an end to the conversation. His closed expression and rigid stance convinced her not to push him further.

"But what about these people?" she asked. He appeared calmer now that he knew she wasn't going to pursue her questioning.

He didn't have to touch her; she only had to stand

next to him to feel her body melting, her heart thundering so loudly she was sure he could hear it. He only had to look at her with those slate blue eyes to start a fire smoldering inside her.

"I can't stay here, you know that," he said, lifting her chin with a gentle finger so he could look into her eyes, "and I'm not leaving you behind. We'll arrange something. You have no idea how dangerous it is for you to come here. These are slaves, runaway slaves. Aiding them is a serious crime. We could lose everything."

"Well, it's a stupid law," she argued, her mind registering the fact that he had said "we."

"You said that your treatment wasn't working. Why not show Ines how to do what you've been doing. She can stay a day or two until she's convinced they know how to administer whatever treatment you recommend. Maybe in a week or two you can come back and check on them."

"Maybe?" Caroline asked with a wry smile.

Jason smiled in return, and Caroline couldn't remember ever having seen a genuine, guileless smile on his handsome face before. It transformed him and touched a tender place in her heart. The Jason she longed to reach shone through clearly in that candid, almost angelic expression. If only she could reach him, pull him out from behind the emotional wall that always surrounded him.

"All right," he conceded, "you can come back. But I want you to bring several armed men with you next time. Now, let's get your things together."

"I need to check on my patients first," she insisted. Several of them were very ill, and she wanted to assure herself that she had done all she could before heading back to the *fazenda*.

Jason glanced around the small room. "There doesn't seem to be much. I'll pack while you see to them." He lifted the bottle of witch hazel from the table beside the cot. "I hope we don't run out of this stuff," he said with a lascivious grin.

Caroline smiled in return, her face growing crimson as she turned to go, wanting more than anything to stay with Jason for the rest of the day, but knowing that there were people who needed her desperately.

A sweet soreness lingered between her thighs as she moved through the morning. It was hard to concentrate when her every thought was filled with her husband. The wanting never dimmed.

Vaguely she wondered how he had become such a consummate lover, locked away in the Amazon jungle as he had been for most of his adulthood. She didn't want to think of him with another woman, other women. Had he been as tender, as passionate with them as he had been with her?

Closing her eyes tightly, she forced herself not to dwell on the past. They were together now, she and Jason. No matter what had come before, they were man and wife, bound together for all time.

They would be all right, she and Jason. He hadn't said he loved her yet, but that would come in time. He desired her; he'd asked her to stay. She had an inkling what that one request had cost him. To admit that he wanted someone in his life must have taken a great toll on him emotionally.

Every time he'd ever expressed a need or desire or affection for anything, his father had taken it away from him or found a way to use it against him to manipulate him. Jason had grown up believing that the best solution to the problem of not knowing whom to trust was to trust no one. He had just taken one small step toward trusting her. That, in itself, was a miracle.

Jason carried the bottle of witch hazel to the medical bag on a table in a corner of the room. Caroline had been right when she said she hadn't brought much with her. He could well imagine that she had acted on impulse, on the whim of a moment, running off into the jungle without regard for the dangers she might encounter.

He should be furious at her for defying him. But to his astonishment he found that her willful independence delighted him. It was so much a part of who she was. Would he ever get used to her capricious, headstrong nature? He doubted it, but he didn't doubt that he'd enjoy the effort.

He smiled to himself, then frowned as fear rocked his composure. When had he lost the restraint he always exercised over his emotions? She made him happy, made him glad to be alive, and there was nothing he could do about it.

He hadn't let another human being into his heart since Peggy. He'd vowed never to do so, and he'd kept that promise for twenty years—until now, until Caroline.

In truth, he hadn't let Caroline into his heart. She'd burrowed through his defenses, despite all his efforts to prevent it. Now he found himself thinking about her when he wasn't with her, craving her touch, yearning to tell her that he loved her and hear her say that she loved him, as she had in the dream. But the risk was too great. What if he opened his heart to her and she rejected him? If he admitted he cared, she would want to delve deeply into his soul, and he could never allow that.

Yes, he wanted to be near her. Yes, he wanted to hear her laugh and smell her perfume and make love to her. He wanted to know her deepest thoughts, the desires of her heart, but he couldn't do that and keep her at arm's length at the same time.

She stirred his blood like no woman he had ever known. Her outer confidence housed a deep well of vulnerability, along with the core of strength that made her who she was. The combination of the two—vulnerability and strength—made her feminine and independent at the same time. He wondered if she needed him nearly as much as he needed her, and the thought stilled him.

When had he come to need her? How? He had to stop this, stop it now before she betrayed him, as she was bound to do.

He opened the medical bag to put the bottle of witch hazel away. A bundle of papers caught his eye—letters. He hesitated, a twinge of guilt piercing his conscience. These were private, none of his business, but whatever they were, whomever they were from, they meant enough to Caroline that she'd brought them all the way from New Orleans. She kept them in her precious medical bag, of all places.

Curiosity stirred inside him. These letters might hold the key to knowing her as deeply as he desired without having to reveal anything about himself. Glancing furtively around the small room, he fought a moral battle within himself. She wouldn't be back for some time; she'd never know.

No, he wouldn't. He couldn't read someone else's mail.

But he couldn't help lifting the bundle of papers out. They were letters all right, but they weren't addressed to her. Without warning, his heart began to pound as a chill crawled over his body.

They were addressed to Derek. What in hell was she doing with letters addressed to Derek? As shocking as that discovery was, there was something else, something just beneath his consciousness.

The writing, the script. It was his own handwriting.

Realization dawned. Somehow Caroline had acquired private letters he'd written to Derek. But how? Anger and confusion suffused his brain, both giving way to humiliation as he realized that she must have read them, and he remembered some of the things he'd told Derek in those letters.

For reasons he didn't understand any more now than he had at the time, he'd written those letters with more candor than he'd shared with any other person in his life. He'd written of things he hadn't meant for anyone else to know, certainly not his curious, meddling wife who thought she could come into his world and change it and him.

Of all the emotions vying for dominance in his soul, fury won out, a blinding, boiling fury that coursed through every nerve in his body.

How, damn it? How had she come by these private letters? The question rolled over and over in his mind, pushing all other thoughts out. A part of him realized that the *how* didn't matter, not really. No matter how she acquired them, she'd read them, and in doing so, she'd glimpsed a part of his soul he never meant to share with another human being. Still, it gave him something to focus on, something other than the humiliation of having all the layers of his soul peeled away. It gave him a target for his anger.

The medical bag in one hand, the letters clasped tightly in the other, he stalked from the room, intent on finding his deceitful wife and wringing her neck.

12

By *the time he found her* in the large hut at
the other end of the village where she'd been yesterday,
his rage roared out of control. Moving among the hammocks, Caroline talked soothingly to the occupants and
administered medicine. A small child followed her
every step, his eyes gleaming up at her with adoration.

Treacherous, lying woman! She'd managed to
win them all over, including himself. How pathetic
they all were!

Words eluded him. He stood staring at her with
such unremitting force that she finally turned to
glance at him. Her soft lips curved upward in an art-
less smile that reminded him forcibly of all that had
passed between them last night and this morning,
reminded him of her supple body moving against
his, the clarity of her trusting gaze, the cries that had
slipped past her control as he'd made love to her.

Lust and fury shuddered through his body in
equal parts.

"Some of them seem better," she said. "Maybe the quinine is helping after all."

A jolt set her heart pounding. Something was wrong, terribly wrong. She could see it in his face. Her hand trembled as she placed it on the child in the hammock. Maybe she was mistaken; maybe if she ignored it, ignored him. . . .

She jumped at the sound of something hitting the dirt floor behind her. Turning around, her gaze fell on the packet of papers between them before lifting to his rage-contorted face, only to return to the papers.

Letters.

"Oh, dear God!" she muttered, her throat tightening as she recognized Jason's letters to Derek. "Jason, I can explain."

She started toward him, but the glint in his hard, cold eyes halted her. His chest rose and fell with the force of his furious breathing.

This should never have happened. How could she have been so careless? Tears clogged her throat, but she managed to speak past them. "Please listen."

"That's my handwriting," he said, pointing to the letters on the floor. "They're my letters, letters I sent to my cousin."

"I know. I know. I'm sorry. I should have told you. . . ."

He moved closer to her, and Caroline backed away from the steely, uncompromising hatred that burned in his pale eyes.

"Please let me explain," she pleaded.

In two steps, he was on her. Paulo, the child she'd treated in the cabin, moved between them, but Jason ignored the small boy.

Grabbing Caroline by the arm with such force that she cried out in pain, he dragged her toward the door, stopping to retrieve the bundle of letters. Outside in the glaring light of day, he hauled her along, unaffected by her attempts to pull free. Paulo trailed behind them, shrieking in agitated Portuguese.

Activity came to a standstill as all eyes turned to the *doutora* and the tall, angry man who dragged her so forcefully through the village. Pocedo, the man Jason had attacked yesterday, the leader of the village, stepped forward, but Jason glared a warning at the other man. Pocedo might wield ultimate power in the village, but Caroline sensed that Jason made it clear to the other man that his authority did not extend to his wife.

Pocedo seemed to understand. He stopped where he was, his countenance every bit as angry and threatening as Jason's. No one in the village liked the idea of this stranger attacking their *doutora*, but no one dared challenge him.

Nearby, a woman bent over a cooking fire. Jason stopped before her and tossed the letters onto the flame.

"No!" Caroline shrieked. She rushed toward the fire, taking Jason by surprise and breaking free. But before she could reach the fire, he'd grabbed her by the arm again and wheeled her around, forcing her up against his hard body.

"We will not speak of anything in those letters— ever!" he said through clenched teeth, his tone indomitable. "I've packed your belongings. We're leaving now."

*   *   *

The cold, slate blue sky sizzled with lightning as the first huge drops of rain began to fall. Caroline walked behind Jason, unsure whether she was more afraid of the storm brewing overhead or the one brewing inside her husband. She struggled to keep up with his long, angry strides, gasping in shock when a loud peal of thunder rent the eerily silent jungle air and a wall of water fell upon them in a rush.

For the first time since they'd left the village, Jason stopped to wait for her, his face a mask of impatience as she labored toward him, squinting to see through the pelting rain. The muddy earth sucked at the hem of her wet skirt, impeded her progress, reminding her of the day she'd arrived, the way Jason had cut her skirt away when she'd stumbled.

When he'd walked toward her with that lethal looking blade in his hand, she'd wondered in that brief, heart-stopping moment if he were deranged, if he had sent for her only to kill her. She knew now that he was no maniac, but the fury roiling inside him frightened her nevertheless.

Without a word, he grabbed her by the wrist, hauling her along behind him, heedless of the effort it took for her to keep up or the pain that radiated from his crushing grip. She tried to twist her arm free, but he only tightened his hold, jerking her so viciously that tears spilled down her cheeks, mingling with the rain. By the time they reached a cabin tucked away in the jungle, Caroline was near hysterics, her wrist and hand nearly numb.

He flung her inside, slamming the door behind them, enveloping them in darkness and oppressive heat. The sound of scurrying along the floor filled her heart with dread, but an unnamed fear kept her from speaking or moving in the absolute darkness.

She couldn't see him, but she could feel the heat of his presence and hear the fast, shallow cadence of his breathing close by.

"Jason?" she said finally, struggling to keep from sobbing, to keep the panic welling in her heart from devouring her.

A blinding flash of lightning illuminated the room for an instant. She caught a glimpse of his angry countenance as if it had been captured on a daguerreotype, before darkness swallowed them again.

An unreasoning terror gripped her at the sound of his boot heel striking the dirt floor. Breathlessly she waited for a response from him, but he refused to speak. The unbearable silence choked her, stretching her nerves to the breaking point.

"Jason, where are you? What are you doing?" She couldn't control the trembling of her voice any more than she could stop the trembling in her body as she wondered if he could see more clearly than she. The thought unsettled her and sent a chill crawling over her flesh.

"Please speak to me, Jason," she pleaded. "Say something, anything!"

Caroline jerked and gasped at a loud, popping noise, and then shutters were thrown back from a window, filling the cabin with light.

A quick survey of her surroundings convinced her that darkness suited the small structure much better than light. There was nothing inviting or comforting about the crude hovel, but it would provide shelter from the storm that sent limbs crashing around them.

However, there was no escaping the tempest inside

the man who glared at her with contempt and a growing lust. His gaze raked her from head to foot in a manner that made her feel naked and vulnerable. Her nipples hardened as his searing gaze lingered on her breasts. She could well imagine how the rain must have molded the material of her gown to her wet skin.

His jaw muscle worked back and forth as if he would speak, but instead he turned away and went to stand at the window, pulling the shutters back to see outside, leaving her trembling with a deep disquiet.

She backed away, out of reach of his fury. Something ran across her foot, and she gasped, jerking her skirt out of the way. She jumped away from the hairy creature on the floor, her heart hammering in terror.

"It's just a tarantula," Jason said impatiently, his deep masculine voice echoing in the empty room.

He walked toward her, drawing the machete from the leather sheath at his side, and Caroline backed away in shock.

He graced her with a disgusted scowl before turning his attention to the creature on the floor, using the blunt edge of the weapon to urge it out the door. She'd thought he was going to kill it; she'd expected it. Had she had a weapon, she certainly would have. The gentleness of his action surprised her, though it shouldn't have.

"He's probably more afraid of you than you are of him," he told her, but Caroline seriously doubted that was possible. "Tarantulas won't bite unless they're backed into a corner, but their sting can be painful."

She mused that the same thing could be said of the man who was now closing the cabin door and turning to face her with eyes as hard as glass. Was that what she'd done to Jason? Had she charged in and tried to force Jason to respond to her instead of coaxing him gently as he had the spider?

"Aren't you going to talk to me?" she asked unsteadily as he returned to the window. She didn't want to press him and possibly anger him further, but she had to reach him somehow. "If you'll only listen to me. Derek was very busy. When I first started working for him—"

"You never bothered to mention that you worked for Derek," he said, turning around to glare at her in surprise.

Oh, dear, this was going to be difficult. "You never asked," she replied defiantly.

His incendiary gaze scorched her flesh in a way that stole her breath and set her heart pounding. He didn't want to talk to her or listen to her, but he desired her. At least he wasn't able to shut her out completely, but the combination of anger and desire stirred a powerful fear deep in her soul.

More than anything, she wanted to withdraw into a corner of the room and wait out the storm in silence. The last thing she wanted to do was stir his ire, but she had no choice. She had to try and make him understand, or she would lose him forever.

"After Wade died I had to support myself. Derek hired me to handle his appointments and filing and correspondence. My intelligence amused him," she continued, struggling against the unshed tears that burned behind her eyes. "Most of the men he dealt with took me for granted. His competitors would say things in front of me. . . ."

"I'll just bet they did," he said, his glare blistering her flesh again.

The heat of his gaze on her breasts sent a shudder of apprehension through her body. Her mouth went dry as the sultry heat in the cabin intensified. She fought the urge to bolt through the door and weather the storm outside.

And then he broke the contact, turning to the window again with an air of indifference belied by the tremor that ran through his body. "I'll bet you were good at convincing them to lower their guard."

"That was petty and unfair, Jason," she said unsteadily. "I don't deserve that."

The quiet stretched interminably, accentuated by the pounding of rain on the roof of the small cabin. Finally she had to say something to keep from going mad.

"At first your letters were very businesslike and to the point. Once when your letter came, he was too busy to reply, so he gave it to me and told me what to tell you. I wrote the letter. He proofed it and signed it, and I posted it. Well, as time passed I answered more and more of your correspondence until he finally stopped proofing my replies and—"

"Damn!" Jason exploded, pounding his fist against the wall with enough force to rattle the shutters at the window and tear a cry of alarm from Caroline's throat.

"I said we would not speak of it ever and I meant it," he growled, the fury in his eyes destroying her composure.

"How can we not speak of it, Jason?" She tried to quell the fear that trembled through her body at the violence reflected clearly in his eyes. "It will always be between us."

"What will always be between us is your treachery!"

Caroline turned her head aside, unable to bear the intensity of his accusing, hate-filled glare.

"I never meant to deceive you. I wanted to tell you—"

"Then why didn't you? Why the hell didn't you?"

"Would it have made any difference? No. You wanted to send me back almost as soon as I arrived. What could I possibly have gained by telling you?"

"*I don't know anything about you, Jason,*" he mocked her, flinging the words at her like stones. "*Tell me about yourself, Jason.* Playing me for a fool."

"No! No, I only wanted you to talk to me, to tell me who you are—inside."

"You already know who I am. Jesus, you know more about me than anyone on earth. What more do you want? My soul? Do you want my soul, Caroline?"

The words seemed ripped from deep inside him, and for the first time since he'd confronted her with the letters that morning, she sensed a softness in him. He was as frightened as he was angry—frightened of her.

Her throat tightened with compassion for this powerful man who could be reduced to terror by the thought of caring for someone or having someone care for him.

"I never meant to hurt you," she said, her voice soft and thin.

"Hurt me?" He laughed shortly. "You can't hurt me! I don't care enough about anything to be hurt!"

If only it were so, Jason, she thought, realizing for the first time that the barriers he'd built to keep the world out had failed to do so. Instead, they had become a prison, trapping him in a world of isolation and pain.

"All I want is you, Jason, your love—"

"Maybe you don't know me as well as you think," he said bitterly, his gaze fixed on something beyond the window. "I am incapable of love. Love is just a word to me, a meaningless word."

"This morning and last night . . ."

A smile curved his lips as he turned to face her, his gaze traveling the length of her body in a slow caress that sent hot color up her throat to her face. "I loved your body, Caroline," he said, moving toward her, his eyes burning with a hunger she recognized all too readily.

She backed away, aware of her precarious position. She was alone in the jungle with a man who desired her despite the rage that still pulsed through him, a man against whom she was utterly defenseless.

"Surely you know the difference," he went on, advancing as she retreated, his tall, broad frame blocking the scant light from the window. "I love your body now. That kind of love I understand. Is that enough for you? Will you prostitute yourself to me? Will you share my bed whenever I want and leave me the hell alone?"

He touched her cheek, his fingers warm and gentle on her skin. Swallowing hard against the fear and desire inside her, she stepped back out of his reach, and his hand fell away.

"No," she said breathlessly.

"Well, it's all I have to offer," he said. "It's all I've ever had to offer. You just never understood that. The rain's letting up, let's go."

Caroline stood her ground, folding her arms in front of her. "I don't believe that you sent for a wife just for . . . for . . ."

"Sexual fulfillment? God, you are naive, aren't you? Believe whatever you like. I'm going back to the *fazenda*."

"I know I'm not exactly what you asked for, but. . . ."

Turning abruptly, he glared at her, his face reflecting comprehension and fury. "Derek never saw my request for a wife, did he?"

"He—he was in Europe and I. . . ."

Jason turned as if he couldn't stand the sight of her, walking through the door and leaving her to gape after him.

"Jason!" she called, running after him. This time her hand on his arm halted him, but he stared straight ahead, refusing to look at her.

"I'd like to strangle you right now," he said.

Caroline backed away from the threat in his voice.

"You disgust me with your righteous indignation and treachery, pretending to be wounded by my reaction when all the while you've lied—lied about everything!"

"Please, Jason." She spoke rapidly before he could interrupt her. "I'm sorry I didn't tell you sooner. I'm sorry I continued to write as Derek. But I sensed your loneliness, your need for someone to talk to. If I had revealed my true identity—"

"I'd have known to whom I was writing and I would have told you what I wanted you to know, not what I wanted Derek to know. You took that choice away from me. Have you no shame?"

Tears streamed freely down her face now. "I'm sorry," she choked out.

"Stay away from me, Caroline," he warned. "You'll be leaving when the mail boat returns. This time I mean it. I'll put you on board personally. In fact, I may send Ignacio with you all the way to Belem. The marriage can't be annulled now, you saw to that!"

Caroline flushed indignantly. "What? Are you accusing me of seducing you? How dare—"

Jason turned on her, grabbing her by the shoulders in a viselike grip that tore a cry of pain from her throat. She leaned away from him, trying to pull out of his hold, but her struggles were useless.

"The marriage can't be annulled," he ground out, shaking her violently, his face trembling with barely suppressed rage, "but I'll arrange for a divorce. By God, I'll be rid of you once and for all."

He released her abruptly and her own momentum propelled her backward. Surprise and horror flashed across Jason's face as he tried unsuccessfully to save her from falling, but she landed on her rump in the mud with a jarring thud. He extended a hand to her, but Caroline struggled to her feet unaided, not knowing whether she was angrier at herself or him.

"Are you hurt?" he asked, a frown of concern marring his brow.

Good, she thought, let him worry, the brute. A thought occurred to her and she smiled inwardly at her own cunning.

"What if I'm pregnant?" She lifted her chin with her last vestiges of pride and courage. "Did you think of that?"

His eyes widened and she knew he hadn't. Neither had she, to be honest, not until that moment. In three years of marriage to Wade, she'd failed to become pregnant. She'd suspected there might be something wrong with her, but Jason didn't have to know that.

"No," he said, "I didn't think of that, but I'm sure you did. I guess we'll know by the time the mail boat returns, won't we? In the meantime, I want you to stay away from the slave village."

Shock tore through Caroline. "But you said I could go back and—"

"That was before I realized that your condition might be so delicate. You're endangering your life, and perhaps my child's, to say nothing of my liberty. Aiding runaway slaves is punishable by imprisonment, and they won't care that you're a woman or that I forbade you to go there. Besides, I don't want my pregnant wife exposed to sickness."

"But I've already had the measles," she reasoned.

"My word is final, Caroline! For as long as you remain here, you will do exactly as I say or I swear I'll lock you in your room. Is that clear?"

Caroline jerked free of his hold and drew herself up to her full height, glaring at him. "Quite," she said, her heart in tatters as she watched him turn and walk away from her.

13

Jason sat at the bar in the small, crowded room, nursing a glass of whiskey and lamenting his decision to come to Manaus. He hated the city, any city, but Manaus in particular. It reminded him of the Irish Channel and the life he'd been running from all these years.

So many things about Manaus touched the chord of memory inside him—the stench of the sewers, the sight of barefoot children playing in the streets, the sound of steam whistles from the river. He could imagine what life must be like for those barefoot children running back to their tenement homes in a part of Manaus that the city fathers tried with some success to hide behind a facade of prosperity. In his mind, he could see inside those unpainted eyesores to the sparse, crude interiors devoid of ornamentation, devoid of tenderness.

He'd been right about one thing. Manaus had

come of age since last he'd been here. The seedy
underbelly still existed, but it had been carefully covered with a veneer of civilization. A city built on the
blood and flesh of slave labor, Manaus, like New
Orleans, possessed an inbred decadence that no
amount of culture could disguise.

He coughed, squinting in the dark smoke-filled
room. More than anything, he wanted to leave this
place, to wash the dirt and corruption of Manaus
from his soul.

For ten years, he'd been sending coffee to market
in Manaus, and for ten years, he'd avoided the city by
sending Ignacio to conduct his business—until now.

Jason closed his eyes and the vision of lush green
vegetation and the scent of fertile earth filled his
senses. He yearned to get back to the *fazenda*, but
he couldn't go back for the same reason he'd left in
the first place. Caroline. Every time he thought of his
home, there was Caroline to be reckoned with. What
a coward he'd become, hiding from a woman. Her
power and strength confounded him.

She'd disrupted his life, taken over his house, his
last refuge, and now she'd forced him to flee to the
city, the one place he'd been trying to escape for fifteen years. He couldn't bear to face her every day, to
look into her eyes and know that she might discover
the worst about him.

What he couldn't understand for the life of him
was why she was still here, why she'd come at all,
knowing what she did know about him.

That was the heart of his agony. She knew the very
worst about him—the truth. He'd come to Brazil and
built his own world, a world he controlled absolutely,
from the orchards to the *benefício* to the handpicked

servants who ran his household. Nothing happened on the *fazenda* without his approval.

A thousand miles of jungle and as much water separated him from anyone who might challenge his authority, from anyone who knew that he was Cullen Sinclair's son and what that meant. Caroline had changed that. Caroline challenged him at every turn.

He tried to close his mind to the surge of memories that crowded his consciousness—Caroline playing the grand piano with an abandon that made his blood run hot; Caroline working like a mad woman to save a wounded boy, unmindful of the mud and muck and blood; Caroline soft and alluring in a sarong, her toes peeking out from beneath the hem; Caroline holding an orchid bloom close and inhaling its essence as if it were the elixir of life; Caroline moaning, warm and yielding beneath him, her eyes half-closed in passion.

It would be just like her to be pregnant. If he were dealing with any other woman but Caroline, he might have to concede that she could hardly control something so capricious. But he wasn't sure that Caroline didn't command the sun to rise and the stars to twinkle at her pleasure. If she didn't, it was surely not for lack of trying!

"Pregnant," he snorted, downing the watery whiskey in his glass. The very word awakened a dark terror inside him, while it caused his foolish heart to yearn for something unattainable—for love, for belonging.

"What did you say, *patrão*?" Ignacio asked.

Jason scowled. "Damn and hell, I said I need another drink." He slammed his empty glass down on the bar for emphasis.

"*Patrão*, surely you've had enough to. . . ."

"What do you mean enough? Don't you know I'm full blooded Irish?" he asked, affecting an Irish brogue. "There's no such thing as enough to an Irishman!"

Ignacio frowned as the bartender filled Jason's glass again. "*Patrão*, when will we start for home? The men are getting restless."

"The men are old women!" Jason growled, raising his glass and draining half its contents. If he drank enough whiskey, maybe he could forget the softness of her smile and the sweetness of her perfume.

"You have never been away so long," Ignacio pointed out. "Don't you wonder what is happening?"

"Mr. Baur will take care of things."

"He is the overseer," Ignacio reasoned. "If the jungle overtakes the coffee and the river runs dry and the *benefício* burns to the ground, he will move to another *fazenda*."

Jason frowned at his irritating companion. "Aren't you being a little dramatic, Ignacio?"

"I've never seen you like this, *patrão*. Don't you care?"

Ignacio's question hit its mark. Of course he cared. He cared too damned much. Worry about the *fazenda* kept him awake all night. Worry about Caroline robbed him of his appetite. So he drank to forget them both, only it didn't work.

Maybe she wasn't even there any more. The idea left him feeling as empty and lost as when he'd thought she'd sailed away on the mail boat.

Oh, he was a man trapped in a hell of his own making—wanting her to stay, wanting her to go.

"The coffee has been sold," Ignacio pointed out reasonably. "Some of the men have families."

"Families? What the hell is a family?"

"You know what a family is, *patrão*. How should I answer that?"

"I'm dead serious, Ignacio." Jason squinted at the double image of the other man. "Is it a house, or is it two people who decide to have children so they can bully them and mistreat them? Oh, no, I suppose we're talking about happy families, right? Happy." He lifted his glass and pronounced in a loud roar, "To happy families!"

"Please, *patrão*, you will attract attention."

"Do you think I care?" Jason asked with a snort.

"Maybe you should, unless you want to end up in jail for fighting again."

Jason flexed his right hand, the pain in his knuckles reminding him of last night's brawl, which had landed him in jail for the night. He could hardly remember the face of the man he'd beaten to a bloody pulp, nor could he remember the insult that had provoked him. He was losing control more and more often. It was a good thing he was away from Caroline.

Of course, she'd been unable to resist prodding and probing. She couldn't just leave well enough alone. Given the chance, Caroline would challenge the patience of Job and spit in the eye of the devil himself!

No, that didn't excuse his actions. He'd pushed her. His chest tightened as he remembered her falling—just like his father had.

Clenching his fist, he silently commanded the visions to leave him in peace, but they would not. He'd been in a towering rage that day, too. Until then, he'd been too small and too afraid to stand up to his father, but on that last day, it hadn't mattered. The fury inside him had tripled his strength.

"We've been here three months, *patrão*," Ignacio was saying, pulling him back to the present. "It's a long time since we sold the coffee, and it will take at least three weeks to get home. Before long, the rainy season will set in, and the journey will be much more dangerous."

"You're right!" Jason declared, banging his glass on the bar for emphasis. Whiskey sloshed over the sides and onto his hand. "There's no point endangering the men just because I have nothing to go back to."

"Nothing?" Ignacio laughed. "You have what you have always had—the *fazenda*, the jungle. And now you have a beautiful wife waiting for you."

Jason turned his glass up and drained it. "Have you ever thought you wanted something, and when you got it you found out it wasn't what you wanted at all? I want things back the way they were before she came."

"Why? Nothing is so very different."

"Everything is *so* very different," Jason contradicted emphatically.

"What is different is better! Besides, you sent her away once and you only ended up going after her."

"She defied me!" Jason shouted. "She didn't even get on the bloody boat!"

Ignacio smiled wryly. "In all the years I have known you, I always believed you to be an intelligent, fair-minded man—until now."

"Well, maybe you don't know me as well as you think." He seemed to be pointing that out often lately. He'd said the same thing to Caroline.

"I know you better than you know yourself. You sit here in a filthy saloon feeling sorry for yourself—"

"Feeling sorry . . ."

"I may be overstepping my place, *patrão*, but someone has to talk some sense into you. I am speaking to you now as someone who has known you for a long time and can't stand by and let you destroy yourself. You sit here night after night drinking in order to dull your mind when you have a beautiful wife waiting for you in the house you built and furnished so that you could have a family, a wife who cares for you for some reason that I can't understand."

"Neither can I, Ignacio, neither can I."

"If she'd gotten on the boat, you'd have taken her off. You want her to stay but you do everything in your power to run her off!"

Ignacio was right. Fool that he was, he'd gone after her. Fool that he was, he'd allowed himself to be seduced by her beauty and her grace and her charm.

"It's the principle of the thing, Ignacio," he said with all the passion he could muster, "the principle! No matter! Tell the men we leave for home tomorrow morning. The boats should be ready in a matter of days."

With that, Jason stood on wobbly legs. The room swam around him, but he managed to right himself.

"Are you all right, *patrão*?" Ignacio asked, grabbing Jason by the shoulder to help steady him.

"I'll be fine as soon as I find my room."

"We'll walk together," Ignacio offered, groaning under Jason's weight.

Ignacio steered Jason toward the door and into the damp night air.

*   *   *

Caroline placed her pen in the ink stand and went still. Brilliant sunlight poured through the window across the study, spilling bright patterns of light on the terracotta tile floor. She listened intently, the only sound in the cluttered study the loud ticking of the clock on the white stucco wall behind her.

It came again, a sound like no other. Shriller than a train whistle, the steamboat whistle had been a part of her life since her first recollection. In New Orleans, they came so frequently one hardly noticed them. But in the remote Amazon, any man-made noise caught the attention immediately.

Standing, Caroline straightened her skirt, hurrying around the desk to the open window. From here she could see the river for several miles, until it made a sharp curve on the horizon.

The first time she stood at this window and gazed down at the river and the orchards beyond it, she realized that this was the view from Jason's study that he'd described so poignantly in his letters—*"the coffee trees heavy with berries and bright with blooms . . . the river pulsing through the very heart of a boundless wilderness . . . nature and man in perfect harmony. . . . This is what the Garden of Eden must have been like. I have reclaimed paradise."*

How could a man with such depth of feeling live in the emotional isolation that Jason had fashioned for himself?

She spotted a boat as it rounded the bend and steamed toward her, and her heart leaped into her throat. It was too far away to see any markings, but

Caroline was almost certain it couldn't be the mail boat. It had just left going south with Senhor Aveiro aboard five days ago.

How would Jason react when he learned that his trusted bookkeeper had resigned and returned to Portugal and that she had taken over his plantation books? Well, that was easy enough to predict. He'd be furious. He'd be angry enough to find that she hadn't left in his absence.

When Senhor Aveiro made the announcement that he would be returning to Portugal, Caroline had been thrust into a dilemma. She had to get word to Jason in Manaus, but how? Mr. Baur had informed her that with so many men away in Manaus, the plantation needed every hand just to keep running. She couldn't take even one away from his work to make the two month trip to Manaus and back.

The smartest solution seemed to be to have Senhor Aveiro find Jason in Manaus and give him the sad news. But a third option occurred to her almost immediately. She'd kept books for Derek. She knew about balance sheets and accounts payable and accounts receivable, debits and credits. Why not do the job herself? When Jason saw how useful she could be, that she could be a partner as well as a wife, maybe he would realize that he needed her. At the very least, her keeping the books would force him to deal with her. If she held the purse strings of the *fazenda*, he would not be able to ignore her as he had done in the past.

Was he still angry about the letters? Would he finally talk to her or would he push her away again?

The doubt and fear that tugged at her soul weren't enough to keep her from bounding out the door and racing to the pier. She arrived in time to see the first boat dock and the occupants disembark.

Most of the men who stepped onto the pier were familiar to her. She'd treated many of them for everything from minor scrapes to serious contusions. They appeared tired and travel-worn, but glad to be home. Many of them had families who greeted them joyfully. Tears flowed freely, and it was only then that Caroline was able to look past her own loneliness and realize that not only had Jason kept himself away from her far longer than necessary, he had also forced his men to stay away from their loving families. Everyone had suffered because of Jason's stubborn pride.

As man after man left the boat, Caroline realized that Jason was not aboard and her attention turned to the second boat which arrived a few minutes after the first.

Again men disembarked one after the other and were greeted by elated family members. Ignacio stepped ashore, and his wife and son embraced him immediately. His expression when he pulled away from them and spotted her made her breath catch. She glanced up the river for the last boat, only to find the river empty.

Her pleading gaze followed Ignacio as he walked wearily toward her, his hat in his hand, his head bowed.

"I am sorry, *senhora*," he said as he came to stand before her, his eyes reflecting some of the pain in her heart. "He would not come."

"Where is he?" she asked, struggling to keep her voice from shaking.

"We left him in Manaus," Ignacio told her.

"But what . . . ?" A faintness washed over her; her body swayed slightly, trembling with dread that he might never come back as long as she remained here. "Why? When?"

"He will come home," Ignacio assured her as if reading her thoughts. "He cannot bear the city. He will grow weary of it and return soon."

Caroline lifted her chin high, her lower lip trembling with the tears that threatened to humiliate her. There was nothing left to say. A persistent pain burned inside her soul, but she beat it down, substituting anger for the hurt that she could not, would not allow to devour her. She walked slowly back to the house with all the dignity at her command.

"What are you doing, *senhora*?"

Caroline gazed up from the papers spread on top of the mahogany desk to see Ignacio staring at her from the doorway in openmouthed astonishment.

"What does it look like?" she asked, smiling in order to cushion the harshness of her words.

What she'd been doing was staring at stacks of papers and ledger books without comprehension. She'd hoped keeping busy would take her mind off of Jason, but all she could think of was Jason sending his men back and remaining in Manaus. She had half a mind to jump on a boat and go after him herself.

Ignacio's brow furrowed in suspicion. "What have you done with Senhor Aveiro?"

Caroline laughed softly past the persistent pain in her heart. "What do you think, Ignacio? How could you think I would do anything to that kind old man?"

"I didn't mean. . . ." he began, removing his hat and stepping cautiously into the room.

"He received word on the last mail boat that his father is ill, so he left immediately for Portugal. Judging by Senhor Aveiro's advanced age, I can only imagine that his father must be over a hundred years old."

"But, *senhora*," Ignacio said, twisting his hat nervously. "What are you doing?"

"I'm keeping the books," she replied impatiently. He acted as if he'd caught her with her hand in the till.

"You can't!" he insisted vehemently.

"Why not?"

"Because . . . because . . ."

"Because I'm a woman?" she asked angrily.

She'd received the same reaction from men in New Orleans when they learned that her position at the Sinclair Coffee Company entailed a little more than smiling and looking pretty. Filling her lungs with air, Caroline launched into her defense. "I kept the books for the Sinclair Coffee Company for a year. I paid the bills, placed the orders—"

"No, *senhora*," Ignacio managed to interrupt. "Because . . . well, you know the *patrão*, how he is. He likes to make all the decisions."

Caroline settled back into the comfortable leather chair. "Well, then he shouldn't stay away so long."

"I told him the same thing," Ignacio assured her. "When he finds out what you've done, he will—"

"He will be angry, I know!" Caroline rolled her eyes and gazed toward the ceiling as if beseeching heaven. "Everything I do or say or even think about doing or saying makes the *patrão* angry. I don't care! He's not here and I'm not as confident as you are that he will ever come back as long as—"

She cut her speech short before she blurted *as long as I'm here*.

"I must write to the *patrão* and tell him so he can hire another man while he is in Manaus," Ignacio told her, turning to leave.

"Wait!" Caroline cried, coming to her feet once again. How could she explain her need to keep busy? The opportunity to keep the books had come at a time when she desperately needed something to occupy her mind.

"Ignacio, please," she pleaded, trying to keep the urgency from her voice, "let me do it. Give me a month. If I don't do a good job, you can take a boat and go to Manaus to find someone yourself."

Ignacio scratched his head in indecision. "I don't like it. You should not anger the *patrão*."

"I only have to breathe to anger the *patrão*. Please, Ignacio. Maybe he won't be angry. Maybe he'll be glad I'm so resourceful. Besides, it'll save him money. He'll be happy about that, especially since I had to order a new water pump for the *benefício*."

"You did what?"

Stunned by the horror on Ignacio's face, Caroline felt a prickling of apprehension and prepared to defend her position once again. "It stopped working, so I sent an order back with the last mail boat. In the meantime, they've had to use a hand pump."

"Oh, *senhora*, you shouldn't have done that!" Ignacio said, making the sign of the cross in front of his chest.

"Stop it!" Caroline snapped, anger pushing the momentary fear from her mind. "I had to. The *fazenda* can't operate without water power."

"*Senhora*, it is an old pump."

"Yes, I know," Caroline said, settling in her chair once again. "High time it was replaced."

"It breaks all the time."

Caroline nodded agreement. "My point exactly."

"It breaks, Luis fixes it. Master Jason isn't a man who spends money freely. He has had that pump for nine years."

"Freely? Surely he knows there are things he has to spend money on to keep the *fazenda* running?" Stony silence met her words. Gazing at the horrified Ignacio, her temper rose steadily. "Luis wasn't here to fix it this time!"

Caroline watched Ignacio's inner struggle as the clock on the study wall ticked away the seconds. Surely he could see her point. Why continue to fix a piece of equipment that broke regularly? It took time away from harvesting the coffee, which was the main occupation of the *fazenda*. There was plenty of money in the plantation account to cover a new pump.

"Maybe you're right," Ignacio said unconvincingly. "That pump was old and worn out."

"Of course I'm right," Caroline said with a smile of relief. If Ignacio agreed with her, it must have been the right thing to do. "We had no choice."

Swallowing the nagging doubt in the back of her mind, Caroline added, "Besides, I'll take full responsibility."

"The boat, *senhora*!" Ines called. "It is coming!"

Caroline stopped in the motion of snipping a parsley stem and came to her feet, lifting her head to listen as the sound of a steam whistle rent the air.

Her whole being trembled as she walked slowly along the narrow path between the well-defined rows of Ines's herb garden, the handle of a wicker basket draped over her arm.

Finally, he'd come home. Finally, the waiting was over, the wondering, the frustration. Her heart faint with dread, she remembered how they'd parted more than five months ago. Was he still angry about the letters? Was he ready to face his past and the fact that she knew much of it so that they could get on with their lives?

An uneasiness settled in her chest every time she considered that Jason, who had built his life in such a way that he could completely avoid contact with civilization, had spent so much time in the city. No matter how much he hated the city, he'd chosen it over her. How would he react when he found her still here? The thought filled her with dread.

At the edge of the garden nearest the kitchen, she stopped in indecision. Should she rush down to the pier to greet her husband with open arms or ignore his arrival and continue with the day as she'd planned it? She'd made a fool of herself once, running down to meet him, only to find that he hadn't returned with his men.

How dare he just float home on a Tuesday morning and expect her to be waiting eagerly?

Her bottom lip quivered and she cursed herself for allowing the pain of rejection to seep through her control. She took a ragged breath as another whistle blast sounded.

"Come, *senhora*!" Ines called, running across the patio, her face beaming with delight. "Master Jason is back! Let's go meet the boat!"

Ines grabbed her arm, but Caroline remained immobile. "No. You go on."

"But, *senhora*! Master Jason—don't you want to see him after so long?"

"Not particularly." If only it were true, Caroline mused, trying not to meet Ines's gaze for fear the other woman would read something in her eyes.

"But why not?"

"Go, Ines! Meet the boat. I have a garden to tend."

Ines called after Caroline as she turned to go. "But you can do that later! I will help."

"Ines! I am not going to run down to the pier like some silly girl! Go if you like. I'm staying here."

Her face a twisted mask of confusion and hurt, Ines tried to reason with her. "Maybe he will not be still angry."

"I don't care," Caroline said tiredly.

"But—"

Caroline walked away, back down the garden path to the place she'd left when the steam whistle had sounded. There were herbs to be cut and weeds to be pulled. Life went on, in spite of Jason Sinclair.

Three mail boats had come and gone in Jason's absence, and Caroline had come close to boarding each and just sailing away from this place and her unreasonable, heartless husband. He didn't want her; he would never want her. Even if his anger had cooled during his prolonged visit to Manaus, he would never forgive her for the letters. Those damned letters!

She snipped a sprig of basil and placed it neatly in her basket, careful not to mix the herbs together.

He'd arrived for the final battle, she knew, the

last skirmish in the war they'd been waging since the day she stepped off the mail boat. They'd each had ample time to assemble their resources and formulate a plan of attack. Now all that remained was for one or the other of them to open fire.

Pushing with the back of her hand at an errant curl that had slipped out from under her wide hat, she settled back on her heels, listening for another whistle blast in spite of her resolve.

With a determined sigh, Caroline deposited her small scissors in the basket and stood up, wiping her dirty hands on her skirt. She'd take the herbs to the kitchen and then occupy herself elsewhere. This time, she would not be the one to seek him out.

None of the arguments mattered. No matter how fiercely he tried to convince himself to do otherwise, he could think of nothing but seeking her out. He didn't want to face her. He'd spent the last five months hiding from her and the unwanted emotions she stirred in him. He didn't want to wonder if she'd look the same, if her skin would be as clear and sweet as he remembered it.

And yet somehow, without making a conscious decision, he found himself in Ines's herb garden. Caroline was there, as Ines had said she would be, bending over the plants that had pushed their way through the earth. Her light dress of pale rose cotton swathed her body in a way that made it evident she'd forgone corset and petticoats.

A wide straw hat shielded her face and head from him, but he heard her sigh before she straightened wearily and wiped her hands on her skirt.

He couldn't help marveling at her ethereal beauty, her fragile grace, her sensual power. She stood for a moment, her face lifted, her eyes straining toward the distant dock, and his foolish heart quickened at the thought that she was looking for him, thinking of him.

Oh, Caroline, how I've missed you. The thought leaped to mind before he could crush it.

Why was she still here? Why hadn't she left while he was gone. It would have made it so much easier all the way around. Unless. . . .

His gaze followed her hand as it moved caressingly over her gently rounded abdomen.

"Hell and damn," he muttered under his breath, shock vibrating through his being. He'd known it was possible, but somehow he hadn't really believed it would happen.

He couldn't take his gaze away from her belly. He couldn't stop thinking about his seed growing inside her, his child. It filled him with joy and terror.

Stepping back so that the shadows of the jungle concealed him, he watched her walk away toward the house. He'd gotten what he'd wanted, what he thought he'd wanted. A child. His own child. The very thought scared the hell out of him.

14

The door to the study flew open and Caroline glanced up from the ledger with a gasp. Jason stood in the doorway, his face registering shock as he stared at her in wide-eyed confusion.

Her heart hammering in her chest, Caroline tried to still the trembling that had overtaken her at the sight of him. He looked the same but not the same. Lines of fatigue creased the flesh around his eyes. His hair had grown longer and hung nearly to his shoulders. A day's growth of stubble shadowed the lower half of his face. His wrinkled clothes appeared as worn as he did.

Anger and joy mingled in her chest. How she'd missed him, even if he was perpetually angry. They had parted so bitterly. The months of waiting, waiting for another chance to reach him, to make him love her, had seemed interminable.

"What are you doing in here?" he asked as he

moved toward her like a jaguar stalking its next meal.

Swallowing hard, Caroline managed to find her voice. She would not be intimidated by him. "Senhor Aveiro received word that his father was ill."

He placed his hands on the desk and leaned across it toward her. She'd forgotten how tall he was. Even when she stood before him, his size dwarfed her, made her feel small and helpless. But seated as she was now, he towered over her like a tall Amazon canopy tree over a palm.

Fighting the urge to recoil from the cold anger in his eyes, she continued, "He—he had to leave immediately for Portugal. There was no one else. . . ."

Jason slammed his fist on the desk and Caroline jumped. The force of the blow set everything on the desk to trembling.

"Why didn't you send word?" he asked between clenched teeth.

"I knew I could do the job," she replied, unable to keep her voice from shaking. "I kept the books for Derek."

Jason seemed not to hear her. Reaching into his shirt pocket, he withdrew a piece of paper that he flung onto the desk. "Are you responsible for this?"

Caroline's heart grew cold as she recognized the purchase requisition she'd drafted for the new water pump.

"I can explain," she muttered past the lump in her throat.

"I might have known," Jason said, his voice soft and full of loathing. "You forged Senhor Aveiro's signature."

"It—it was the easiest thing. . . ."

Caroline fell silent as Jason's booming laughter filled the room. "God, you amaze me!"

"I knew that the companies in Manaus were accustomed to dealing with Senhor Aveiro," she hurried to explain, though she doubted he was listening to her. "Instead of writing and trying to explain the situation, it made more sense to handle it that way."

"You had no right! What the hell were you thinking?"

"Please do not swear at me, Jason!" She came to her feet, facing his irrational fury with calm poise—on the outside at least. On the inside, her heart quaked and her body trembled with apprehension.

"I should do more than that! I should wring your neck!"

Trying to remain calm in the face of his fury, Caroline said, "The water pump was broken and—"

"It breaks regularly."

"I know. That's my point."

After her talk with Ignacio, Caroline had expected some initial resistance from Jason, but not this unreasonable fury. It was only natural that he be frugal after living in poverty for the first part of his life, but how many times had he repaired a worn-out piece of machinery to keep from spending a little money? "The pump needed replacing months—perhaps years—ago."

"Who gave you the authority to make a decision like that? To spend my money? It breaks and Luis repairs it and it works again. You had no right!" He slammed his fist on the desk again for emphasis.

"Luis was with you!" She took great pride in reminding him and watching the color rise to his throat and the fury flame in his eyes. "Besides, have you ever stopped to think about how much time you waste repairing an old, worn-out pump? Time that you could use more productively?"

"That is none of your concern! I thought I'd made myself clear that I didn't want you sticking your nose into my business!"

"I was only trying to help," she said, forcing the tears from her eyes. "You know, with a new pump, you could harvest the coffee much more quickly. The faster you can wash it and dry it and get it off the patios, the sooner you can harvest more. In fact," she went on, lifting a book from the edge of the desk and riffling through it, "the man who wrote this book says that you can increase the drying time twofold by—"

She released a cry of surprise as the book went flying from her hands and Jason's booming voice shuddered through her.

"Stop it! Stop it!" he bellowed, his voice echoing in the suddenly small room. "I don't want to hear about your theories on coffee cultivation. I don't care that you decided the pump needed replacing. I want you to stop. . . ." He paused, a growl of rage rumbling up from his chest and trembling through his body. "Stop interfering with my life!"

Movement in the hallway behind Jason caught her attention. Glad for the time to gather her composure, she called, "What is it, Vincente?"

Jason released a sigh and moved away, standing in a corner against the wall, his arms crossed in front of him. Vincente entered the room cautiously.

"Are you all right, *senhora*?" he asked, darting a warning glare at Jason, despite his apparent unease.

From his corner, Jason snorted and returned the boy's stare with an expression that Vincente evidently understood, though its meaning was lost on Caroline. The boy stiffened, his face and throat reddening as he turned away from Jason and gazed at her sheepishly.

"We have unloaded the water pump," Vincente said, standing before her, twisting his hat in his hand. "What should we do with it?"

Caroline gazed at Jason, wondering what had passed between the two of them. Vincente was just a boy, a boy who felt obligated to protect her because she'd saved his life. Now she was the one who felt protective.

"Senhora," Vincente prompted, drawing Caroline back from her musings, "the pump. What shall we do with it?"

Caroline glared at Jason. "I suppose you should ask the *patrão*, now that he's back."

"It's your pump," Jason grumbled from the corner.

"Very well," Caroline said stiffly, lifting her chin in defiance. "Have it taken to the *benefício*. The *patrão* will decide what to do with it after that."

With a nod and a last frightened glance at Jason, Vincente quickly exited the room.

"You frightened Vincente," Caroline accused as soon as they were alone.

Jason shrugged. "He presumes too much. You may have every man on the *fazenda* under your spell, but there are some things I will not abide."

"Vincente is just a boy," she reasoned.

"Boy or not, I will not tolerate anyone interfering between me and my wife."

A thrill raced up her spine at the possessiveness in his words. Perhaps he cared more than he was willing to admit, or was he only protecting his property as he would have done with anything else he owned?

"Why didn't you just have them take the pump off the boat before you left Manaus?" she asked, steering the conversation onto safer ground.

"How could I?" Jason reasoned, pushing away from the wall. "I'd have damaged Senhor Aveiro's credibility. The next time he ordered something from that company, I'd have to vouch for him. And word would get around to the other merchants I deal with. You put me in an untenable position."

"I'm sorry." But she wasn't sorry, not really. She was right. Why couldn't he admit it? And why did she get the impression that he was only using the water pump as a diversion from whatever was really bothering him? "This isn't about the pump at all, is it?"

"How long did it take you to master Aveiro's signature?" he asked, ignoring her question. "You're really good at forgery. Maybe you should become a criminal."

"I thought I was doing the right thing. I still believe so. Why are you so angry? I'm the one who should be angry. You were gone far longer than necessary. When the pump quit, Luis wasn't here to repair it. It took two men to operate the hand pump. We were already short workers because of the men you'd taken with you to Manaus, men who should have been back more than a month before they finally returned. There was coffee ready to be picked and no way to keep it from ruining once it was in the *benefício*. If I'd waited for you to return, we would have lost half of this year's crop."

"We? There is no we. This is my *fazenda*, not ours. I don't need your help. I don't want your help. Your meddling has cost me a fortune."

Again his cruel words hit their mark, causing tears to well behind her eyes. Again she fought them down and faced him squarely. "You cannot expect to be successful if you hoard every penny you make. Surely you realize that you have to reinvest some of your money in the plantation or it cannot operate. Why don't you tell me why you're really so angry? It's me, it's not the pump at all."

"I don't spend money unnecessarily. And I don't need you telling me how to run my business. I did quite well before you came and I can continue to do so without any interference from you."

He stalked away toward the open door. He'd just arrived, and already he was running away from her, and he hadn't even asked why she was still there or if she was pregnant.

"What are you going to do? You don't have a bookkeeper," she asked, even though it was the last thing she wanted to talk about.

"I'll send Ignacio to Manaus to find someone."

"And in the meantime?"

"That's not your concern. I'll deal with it."

"Jason!" she called desperately.

"What now?" he snapped, turning with a scowl of absolute annoyance.

Caroline opened her mouth, but the words wouldn't come out. Two simple words—*I'm pregnant*—two words that would alter their lives forever, and she couldn't say them.

"Nothing," she said, dropping her gaze to the desk before her.

Just go, she thought, run away again. Leave me alone.

She glanced up and her breath caught, her chest

tightening. He was still there, staring at her with such an expression of longing and fear that she knew in that instant that somehow he'd guessed the truth.

His eyes met hers and her legs went weak before he disguised his yearning with anger and turned to go, slamming the door resoundingly behind him.

Sinking into the soft leather chair, Caroline buried her head in her hands and gave in to the torrent of tears she'd held at bay for so long.

Caroline allowed the notes of the étude to float softly away until the parlor settled into silence. The sound of rain falling gently beyond the open window slowly insinuated itself into the stillness of the empty room.

She closed her eyes and her mind took her to the orchards where no doubt Jason worked alongside his men. Or perhaps they had taken refuge from the rain beneath the red-tiled roof of the *benefício*. She couldn't help remembering the first time she'd seen it—Jason standing naked on one of the patios, water pummeling his body and running over his muscled torso in rivulets.

With a low growl, she came to her feet, walking angrily to the open door and peering out. He was back to his old games, avoiding her by staying away from the house. What was he waiting for? Was this a new tactic? If his strategy was to wear down her nerves, it was working brilliantly.

Five months! He'd been away for five months.

She'd made the trip from Manaus, and she knew how long it took. In good weather like they'd had lately, it took less than three weeks. Even allowing two weeks to transact business, he should have been back three months ago.

She almost wished she weren't carrying his child. Almost. In the beginning, she'd wished it fervently. She'd been violently ill every morning and queasy for the rest of the day. She'd actually lost weight. Her clothes had begun to hang on her. Only now was she beginning to fill them out again, and shortly they would be too small for her.

And she didn't even want to think about what waited for her at the end, the pain. Whenever she thought about her crude surroundings, her heart grew faint. There were no facilities, no help at all for a pregnant woman, not even a midwife. She tried to shore up her courage by reminding herself that women had children in the jungle every day.

How she needed Jason now. She needed the strength and comfort of his arms around her. She needed to feel that he wanted this child as much as she did, that it wasn't just her baby. She needed to talk to him about her anxiety and to hear him say that everything would be all right.

That was the root of the problem, she decided. She still cared for him. She still wanted him to love her, wanted it even more now. She didn't want to bring a child into a house where a constant state of open warfare existed. She wanted to be a family, the three of them.

But when she thought of the way Jason had been raised, the kind of family life he'd described in his letters, she wondered if he were capable of that kind of bond.

A terrible sickness settled in the pit of her stomach every time she allowed herself to think of the life he and his sister must have lived. Home was the one place in all the world where one should feel completely safe, especially a child. Jason had never experienced that kind of home. Perhaps he had no concept of it, but even so, she knew from his letters that his heart yearned for it.

Was he still angry at her over the stupid water pump? Despite his harsh words, she had continued to handle the plantation books and he'd left her alone to do so. Evidently she'd proven her competence, but he wasn't about to admit it. Instead he ignored her while Ignacio traveled to Manaus to hire a new bookkeeper.

But something more powerful, much deeper than anger kept him away from her. A huge chasm had opened between them, a wide emptiness that she wasn't sure could ever be spanned. Why? Why had he withdrawn from her completely? Surely it couldn't still be the letters. It was worse than with Wade. Never had she felt this way about Wade, or any other man, for that matter. She told herself it was because she could feel his child growing inside her day by day, but she suspected there was more to it than that.

She wanted desperately to recall the intimacy they'd shared so long ago at the slave village. She'd thought, hoped, that a closeness was beginning to form between them. Now that had been destroyed, perhaps forever.

Sensing someone behind her, Caroline turned to see Ines standing in the doorway, her expression as forlorn as Caroline's own heart.

"What am I to do, Ines?" she asked, turning to gaze into the impenetrable jungle once again.

"I am not knowing, *senhora*. It is as I said, you should not have kept the letters."

"I know!" Anger and impatience pushed Caroline toward an emotional explosion which she tried with all her might to curb. It wasn't Ines's fault, none of it. "I can't undo it and he won't forgive me."

"Be patient."

Caroline laughed mirthlessly. "Patient? It's been two weeks. Two weeks and he hasn't spoken a word to me. In the mornings, he rises early and he's gone by the time I arrive at the table for breakfast. In the evenings, he disappears completely."

"When he went after you to bring you back—"

"What do you mean?" Caroline asked, turning to face Ines again. "When he found me at the slave village? He came after me then to put me on the mail boat."

"Oh, no, *senhora*, he thinks you are on the mail boat and goes after you to take you off and bring you back."

"Are you sure?" Caroline asked, her heart soaring at the thought that he hadn't wanted her to leave, that there might be another reason for his allowing her to stay besides her pregnancy. Maybe he did care about her but was afraid to admit it, even to himself.

Even so, if he intended to ignore her and scorn her for the rest of her life, what had she really gained?

"I've been here nearly six months, and I don't even know where he sleeps," Caroline mused aloud, turning to face Ines, who came to stand close behind her. "But you do, don't you?"

Ines's eyes filled with terror. "Oh, no, *senhora*, I couldn't! He would be so angry if I told you."

"All right, fine," Caroline said with an exaggerated shrug. "I'll just open every door in the house until I find his rooms. I don't know why I didn't think of it before."

"Rooms, *senhora*?"

Sudden insight illuminated Caroline's mind. "He doesn't sleep in the house, does he? Where then?" But a better question was why. Why had he gone to all the trouble to build this mansion and not even sleep in it?

"I—I can't, *senhora*. Please don't ask me to."

Caroline's shoulders sagged. "You're right. It wouldn't be fair of me to ask you to betray Jason that way. I'm sorry for trying to force you to defy him." Turning, she grasped Ines by the shoulders and hugged her, then said with all the emotion she could gather, "I suppose I should be packing."

Caroline walked past a dumbfounded Ines, taking her time in reaching the door, certain that Ines would stop her.

"Packing?"

Suppressing a smile at her own cleverness and at the ease with which Ines had fallen into her snare, Caroline turned to face Ines with a dejected expression. "I can't stay here. I can't live like this, with a husband who won't speak to me. If I can't even find him, how can I convince him to forgive me? The rain has stopped. I'm going to my room to start packing."

"No!" Ines called as Caroline reached the door. "*Senhora*, you cannot go. Master Jason, he cares for you. Once the baby is born, he will forget his anger. I know it."

"I'm not as certain as you are, Ines. I'd rather my baby be raised without a father than with one who resents him and his mother."

"Wait, *senhora*!" Ines cried in panic. She took a deep breath, the struggle with her conscience and her loyalties apparent in her eyes. "When Master Jason is here first, he builds a hut in the jungle to live in until his house is finishing. There is where he sleeps now."

"The hut where I nursed the child with measles?"

"No, that is storehouse. Master Jason puts food and supply there for the runaways."

"What?" Caroline asked in stunned disbelief, remembering the blankets and barrels of supplies she'd noticed in the hut. "Jason provides supplies for the runaways?"

"He can do no more," Ines explained.

Tears formed in Caroline's eyes as she thought about Jason's generosity and sacrifice. The storehouse was on his property. If the slaves were discovered there, he could lose everything, including his freedom.

"Please, *senhora*," Ines pleaded, "do not go there—to his place. He will be unpleased."

"I can't go there unless you tell me where it is."

"Master Jason, he comes to the house very lately, when you are in sleep. He will eat and then goes to his place in the jungle. If you waited for him. . . ."

"Yes! Ines, why didn't you tell me this before?"

Ines hung her head. "He'll be even angry to me for this."

"He cares about you, Ines," Caroline assured her, gripping her by the shoulders again. "He will forgive you. Besides, he doesn't have to know you told me."

15

Jason ran the coarse brush over the bay stallion's glossy coat, trying not to think of anything beyond the animal that nickered contentedly under his ministrations.

Bad blood, his father's voice rang clearly in his ear. *Me da' passed it to me and I'm passing it to you. You'll never amount to nothing, you worthless, ungrateful wretch!*

Closing his eyes and his mind against the memory, he stroked the animal on the muzzle and moved to the stall door. The stallion tossed his head, snorting in protest that Jason had stopped the daily grooming ritual too soon.

"That's enough for tonight," Jason said with a half-smile. "You're spoiled, that's what's wrong with you."

Jason fastened the stall door as the stallion began to munch on his feed, once more content.

If only he were an animal. . . . If only he didn't have to think or remember or feel pain. His father's beatings hadn't been the worst of it. There were hundreds of more subtle injuries. Emotional wounds took far longer to heal and left much deeper scars.

He paused on the patio, staring up at the door on the second floor. Closing his eyes, he tried to head off the surge of tenderness that suffused his heart.

He'd thought having a family of his own would blot out the past and give him a chance to start over. Now that his goal was within his grasp, he wasn't so sure.

Was he capable of harming a helpless child or a woman? Was there a monster sleeping inside him, waiting for the right moment to awaken? His father had battered his own family, the people he was honor-bound to protect and nurture, physically and emotionally until they loathed and feared him. To this day, he couldn't use a razor strop without being reminded of cowering in the dark with Peggy, terrified that their father would come after them.

He'd learned early to withdraw into himself, to dull his mind so that he didn't feel anything, physically or emotionally. But those tactics didn't work with Caroline. Intimidation didn't frighten her, perhaps because he hadn't pushed hard enough. What if he pushed her and she pushed back? Would he be able to control himself, to keep things from escalating too far?

More than anything, he wanted to go to Caroline, to talk to her, to make her understand. But how could he when she knew the very worst about him—his secret fears, his bitter failures. He should have done something to stop his father. Instead he'd stood by and watched his family being destroyed.

"At first your letters were very businesslike," she'd said. Had there been something in her letters, something so subtle he hadn't been aware of it consciously, that prompted him to pour out his heart to her? To Derek?

Christ! He didn't know anything anymore except that he could never face her again. Every time she looked at him with those deep hazel eyes, he felt as if his soul had been stripped bare.

Turning with a heartsick sigh, Jason made his way to the dining room where, as usual, Ines had left a plate of food and a lighted candle.

He didn't even taste his food as he ate in silent solitude, trying not to think, not to wonder what the future held. Trapped in a life that had become a living hell, he found himself constantly yearning for his wife but unable to touch her, to even talk to her, wondering when he would become a brute like his father.

The right thing to do would be to put her on a boat for New Orleans. He knew exactly how far along she was; how could he not? She still had nearly four months, ample time to reach New Orleans. He'd provide for her and the baby financially; it was the least he could do.

But selfish man that he was, he couldn't bring himself to send her away. His position was intolerable. He couldn't bear having her near, and he couldn't bear the thought of sending her away.

Downing a glass of warm wine in one gulp, he stood and, taking the candle with him, stepped into the parlor. The shadowed figure of the grand piano mocked him from the corner. He hadn't heard her play since he returned, but then he'd spent as much time as possible away from the house. He missed it, missed the beautiful sounds she could evoke from the instrument.

Softly he ran a finger over the ivory keys, his touch so light that no sound came from the instrument. How recently had she played? Perhaps tonight while he was away hiding in the jungle, he thought, imagining that he could feel the warmth of her touch lingering on the silent keys.

In a way, it was as if she'd gone and he was alone again. He had to get a grip on himself. He'd gotten along fine before Caroline had come into his life. As long as she stayed out of his way, he would be able to control his violent nature—or so he hoped. All he had to do was convince her to stay inside the boundaries he'd established for her.

Jason laughed softly in the quiet darkness. He'd have better success convincing the Amazon to flow upstream! He struck a white key and a clear, dulcet note filled the room. A soft moaning sound behind him startled him. Jerking around, he found Caroline lying on the sofa, her eyes closed in sleep, her brow furrowed.

Momentarily dazed, Jason could only stare at her, his little forger. He should be furious with her for what she'd done. It didn't matter that she'd been right. She'd acted without his authority. She'd forced her way into every facet of his life.

But despite all his efforts to hang on to the anger, he couldn't prevent his heart from twisting with a deep longing that took his breath away. She lay on her side, her dark hair draped over her shoulder, her hands crossed underneath her chin to serve as a pillow. How innocent she appeared, how vulnerable, how sweet. He wanted to touch her soft, white skin, to kiss her awake, to make love to her. He wanted to tell her about his demons and to hear her say it didn't matter.

Instead, he stood immobilized by this vision, this woman, his wife. He still didn't understand why she'd left everything behind and traveled to this remote, uncivilized jungle.

Placing the candle on the piano and extinguishing the flame, he moved toward her slowly, quietly, so as not to wake her. She'd probably been waiting up for him; it would be just like her. Having allowed him to retreat for several days now, it was about time for her to take action.

He drew a deep, ragged breath, stunned by the depth of his knowledge of her. He could predict her reaction to nearly any situation with alarming accuracy. When had she become so much a part of him?

Leaning over her sleeping form, he reached out and smoothed tendrils of hair from her forehead. His hand trembled as a surge of affection engulfed him. He didn't want to feel anything for her; he'd fought the feelings she evoked in him since the first moment she'd swept into his life and his heart.

Though she appeared comfortable enough right now, he couldn't leave her there to sleep the night away on the sofa. In her condition, she needed plenty of rest, and she didn't need to be cramped.

Carefully, he wedged his arms underneath her limp body. She groaned but didn't open her eyes as he lifted her off the sofa and straightened, twining an arm around his shoulders and nestling her head against his chest.

"Jason," she murmured.

His throat tightened as he felt a tiny chip form in the armor around his heart. Steeling himself against the swell of longing that rose in his chest, he carried her through the open doorway.

Her eyes fluttered open as the cool night air touched her skin. "Jason," she repeated, "what are you doing?"

"I'm putting you to bed," he informed her caustically, unaccountably angry.

"That sounds wonderful." She smiled languidly, pressing her soft body against his in a way that made his breath catch and his heart pound.

By the time they reached the foot of the stairs, Caroline was asleep again, and Jason was painfully aroused. Her feminine essence called out to his male body. The softness of her body in his arms and the absolute trust with which she nestled against him disarmed him and left him defenseless against her hypnotic spell.

Gazing up the precarious staircase without enthusiasm, he shifted her weight so that he could hold on to the rail before starting up. At the top, he paused, catching his breath before approaching his next obstacle—the door. He considered waking her and making her walk the rest of the way to bed, but he knew that if he did, she'd want to talk, and he wasn't in the mood. They would end up arguing or making love on her bed. He didn't have the strength for the former, and he didn't want to face the consequences of the latter.

He turned the doorknob and entered the dark sitting room, making his way through that room and into the adjoining bedchamber. He was lowering her to the bed when she gasped and opened her eyes.

He tried to rise, but she clung to him, pulling herself up, pressing her soft lips against his. His body responded with a will of its own. He wrapped a hand in her loose hair, deepening the kiss despite the alarm that sounded in his fevered mind.

Drawing herself up with her arms around his neck, she brushed her breasts against his chest. Her soft, pliant body beneath him awakened a sleeping torrent of desire that rushed through him with the force of a rain-swollen river.

He rose slightly, trying to remove himself from her embrace, but she only tightened her hold. Unsure whether he could extricate himself without hurting her, he relented.

"Caroline," he whispered against her parted lips. "No."

Releasing his neck, she ran a small hand down his chest in a seductive caress that ended at the waistband of his trousers and left him shaken to his core and painfully aroused. He tried to pull away, but she held him fast with a dark sorcery against which he had no defense.

In the netherworld between sleep and waking, she seemed to give herself over unreservedly to the demands of her body. She held him in thrall, her fingers working almost frantically on the buttons that ran down the front of his shirt.

He hadn't meant for this to happen. He'd meant to carry her to bed and leave quickly. But it had been too long, too long since he'd touched her, tasted her. His body remembered and urged him toward the inevitable culmination.

Cupping a tender breast, he realized on some elemental level that the soft, swollen flesh he felt through the thin fabric of her gown was heavier than before. He ran his hand downward, over the softly rounded curve of her abdomen.

Under his hand beat the heart of his child. The thought filled him with a primal joy and stark terror. Jerking upright, he sprang agilely away from her, his chest heaving, his heart pounding, his arousal still painful and demanding release. The very idea of touching her sickened him, as if by doing so he would be defiling her and the promise of life growing inside her.

"Jason," she murmured, reaching a hand toward him imploringly, like a siren luring an unwary fisherman to his death.

Why couldn't she let him go? Couldn't she see what being near her did to him? He wanted her—God, how he wanted her—wanted her in every way a man could want a woman.

It was all mixed up in his mind—Caroline, the child in her womb, his demons. Inside her body pulsed every mystery of the universe, of creation and life itself. He wanted to grasp it, to hold it and never let it go—never let her go. He wanted to watch his baby grow inside her body and know that they had created something good and perfect—he and Caroline together.

"Jason," she whispered again, her voice soft as silk and deep with desire.

The passion in her wafted around him like her scent. It showed plainly in the labored rise and fall of her breasts, the soft, dazed quality in her eyes. Closing his eyes, he tried not to remember the way her body had opened to his when they made love, the feel of her, soft and aroused beneath him, the way she'd cried out as he drove into her over and over.

Gazing down at her passion-heavy eyes, her swollen, parted lips, her flushed face, he gave in to the hunger surging through his blood. Quickly he slipped out of his clothes and covered her with his body, kissing her deeply, his tongue emulating what he wanted to do with his body.

He pushed her gown up over her hips, and his hand lingered on the moist flesh between her thighs. A terrible tremor ripped through his body as he struggled to control his growing urgency. He pressed her legs apart, and her soft, warm body opened eagerly to him, too eagerly.

All thought of control fled as his need overpowered his mind and he plunged into her, filling her with one unrestrained thrust that tore a gasp from her throat. Arching her body toward his to take him in fully, she moaned low in her throat. Already he could feel the waves of ecstasy swelling inside her as she writhed beneath him.

There was no holding back, no gentleness in the way he took her. Her body responded to his with a wildness that stirred his blood to the point that he forgot everything but the flesh around his flesh and the body clinging to his. He wanted to be inside her . . . inside her forever, to absorb her into himself and to be absorbed into her at the same time.

She cried his name as a shattering release trembled through her. The uncontrollable pulsing flowed into his body until her tremors became his, the pressure building toward an explosion that tore an animal growl from his throat as he spilled himself inside her.

A precarious silence filled the room, like the lull in a violent storm. Spent and exhausted, he lay on top of her, still inside her, not wanting to pull away and feel the consuming desolation of loneliness. As his labored breathing slowly quieted, his pulse calming to a degree, he felt her jerk sporadically beneath him, and he knew she was crying.

Fear and guilt sliced through him like a knife. Quickly he withdrew from her, rolling onto his back and taking her with him. He cradled her against him as if she were a child, smoothing the damp hair from her face, near to tears himself, tears of self-loathing.

"I'm sorry," he murmured. "I didn't mean to hurt you. I'm sorry."

She sniffed loudly, taking a quivering breath. "You didn't hurt me."

He kissed her cheek, her mouth, her tears salty on his lips. "Don't cry, Caroline. I'm sorry."

"Jason," she said, her voice shaky, lifting her head to look into his eyes, "you didn't hurt me."

The sincerity in her voice did nothing to allay his fears. He touched her cheek with his thumb, wiping away the tears that clung there. "The baby. . . ."

"The baby is fine," she assured him with a tremulous smile.

She kissed him lightly on the lips, and he wrapped a hand around her head in an automatic gesture, instinctively eager to deepen the kiss, damning himself for wanting her again. She pulled away and he released her.

"Then why are you crying?" he asked.

She settled beside him, her fingers burrowing in the hairs on his chest, her breasts soft and full against his side. The pressure began to build between his legs again as his breath grew thick.

"Why?" he asked, fighting the desire awakened

by her feminine form pressed so intimately against him.

"I don't know," she said with a sigh that he could only interpret as contentment. "It was so . . . perfect, so devastating. Besides, I'm always on the verge of tears these days. I can't explain."

Her hand on his chest became more demanding, massaging him in a way that stirred him to renewed hunger. Grabbing her hand, he brought it to his lips, kissing it softly. "Caroline, don't. . . ."

His voice fled him as she moved her leg over his, pressing her womanly curves against him. She wanted him again, and he wanted nothing more than to oblige her, but the fear congealed inside him, now that he could think clearly again. "I might hurt you, Caroline."

"You won't hurt me, Jason. It's all right," she assured him, kissing the hollow at the base of his throat, rubbing her hand over his sensitized nipple.

"The baby," he said thickly, running a hand caressingly down her back, over her hip, between her legs.

Caroline gasped at the fire that blazed through her body at his touch. She'd never wanted anything as badly as she wanted Jason right now, and she knew that he wanted her as well, even before he rolled her onto her back and pinned her to the bed.

"You make me crazy," he murmured, his voice and his face hard with passion, his hands all over her, eliciting the sweetest responses from her willing body.

This time he held back, controlling himself with an iron restraint until she'd reached fulfillment, before finding his own release.

Caroline fell asleep with a smile of contentment on her lips, knowing they had crossed an important threshold. A closeness, an intimacy that went beyond the physical, had fused them together. Tomorrow they would start anew. Tomorrow he would tell her he loved her, and they would begin to build the kind of home their child needed and deserved. Tomorrow. . . .

But in the morning when she awoke, he was gone and the room echoed with an empty longing that reduced her to tears once again.

16

Jason's shoulder throbbed from swinging the ax. He'd been at it since sunrise today, as he had every day for the last four weeks, working frantically beside his men to build a fire break between the good trees and those overrun by fungus. But at least physical strain blocked the mental anguish of seeing his dreams destroyed.

Every day more infected coffee trees, sometimes whole groves, were discovered and had to be isolated and then destroyed. He'd have to sacrifice at least two hundred acres of trees in order to save the rest, and even then there was no way to be sure his efforts would stop the fungus from spreading.

Fungus needed two things in order to grow—a damp, warm environment and plant life to use as a host. It couldn't spread across charred earth, unless, of course, it did so through the air.

Then there was the chance that other trees had

already been infected but hadn't been discovered yet, in which case his efforts might well be for naught. The only thing he knew with any certainty was that if he did nothing, he would lose his entire *fazenda*—everything.

Damn! If only he'd returned from Manaus when he should have. He'd been so preoccupied with Caroline and her treachery that he neglected the *fazenda*, something he could never afford to do with the jungle lying in wait to regain anything it could of its lost territory.

Wiping his brow with his bare arm, Jason choked on the smoke that filled his lungs. It added to the misery of the sweltering afternoon. A brief shower earlier had done nothing to lessen the oppressive heat. Instead, it had intensified it by adding even more moisture to the already sodden jungle. Three of his men had succumbed to the heat, and he'd taken them to the house to be treated by Caroline.

His mood suddenly grim at the thought of his wife, he attacked his task with renewed vigor. Taking a deep breath, he suppressed the bitterness boiling inside him with a supreme effort. In less charitable moments, he blamed Caroline for his own folly. If not for her, he never would have gone to Manaus in the first place, much less stayed there for two months. But it wasn't her fault, not really. He should have known better than to allow anyone into his life. If he'd learned nothing else, he should have learned that lesson well.

"We need to talk," she'd said that morning.

"Not now, Caroline, I don't have time," he'd told her harshly before fleeing back to the orchards.

After nearly four weeks of allowing him to hide,

she was suddenly eager to talk. What had been going through that devious, intelligent brain of hers? Caroline with something on her mind was a daunting prospect.

"*Patrão.*" Ignacio's voice penetrated Jason's thoughts. "What are you doing?"

Jason looked down at the sapling he'd hacked into mulch. Blood roared through his veins, and his chest heaved with suppressed anger.

"It's time to rest. The men are already taking the siesta."

"I suppose you're right." He'd been so preoccupied he hadn't noticed when the men left the orchard to return to their homes for the noon rest.

He waited for Ignacio to walk away, now that he'd delivered his message, but the other man didn't move. He stood nervously by, and Jason sensed that there was more.

"Out with it, Ignacio," he said gruffly.

"The *senhora* is here to see you," Ignacio announced.

"Here?" Jason asked in total disbelief. "Where?"

"At the *benefício*. I told her to wait there."

"Damn! You should have told her to go back to the house!" Jason groaned, realizing how irrational it was to blame Ignacio for his wife's impetuousness. But if he'd wanted to see her, damn it, he would have gone to the house. How dare she invade his domain.

With a violent curse, Jason hurled the ax, embedding it into the trunk of a nearby tree.

Without a word, he stalked away in the direction of the *benefício* where the one person in the world he didn't want to face waited for him. He hadn't set foot inside the house in four weeks, partly because of the frenzy of activity in the orchards, but also because he didn't want to face her and the inevitable recriminations.

He tried to close his mind against the memory of their lovemaking, but it was no use. He thought of it—of her—day and night, especially when he wasn't so exhausted that he fell into an immediate, deep sleep. And when he did manage to drive himself to exhaustion, she invaded his dreams with her eager sensuality.

It had meant nothing, their lovemaking, at least that was what he'd been trying to tell himself since that night. She'd been so soft, so alluring, so willing, beguiling him with her ardor. Her need had matched his that night. He had needed her; she had wanted him. Purely physical.

His heart thundering in his chest, he stepped into the open near the *benefício*. His blood turned thick, pounding with involuntary gladness at sight of her. Vincente helped her step out of that damned two-wheeled cart his men had built for her while he was in town. The two-seater was low enough to the ground that she could easily get into and out of the contraption despite the awkwardness of her ever-expanding belly.

The short, narrowly spaced wheels made it easy to steer the vehicle through the jungle. And the fringed cover kept the blistering sun off her head when she wasn't protected by the jungle cover.

He had to admire her ingenuity, while he cursed her independence and his men for bringing her design to reality so eagerly—anything for *a senhora*.

As soon as her feet touched the ground, she turned and retrieved a large basket from the rear compartment.

Just looking at her made him feel things he'd vowed never to feel—tenderness, possessiveness, and a passion that went far beyond pure lust. She wore a brown cotton garment that Ines had constructed for her—a sort of shift with a white apron over it, wide enough around the middle to accommodate her widening waistline.

A wide straw hat shielded her face from the glaring noon-day sun and concealed her dark hair, but soft tendrils had come loose to frame her face in a way that made his throat catch as he walked slowly toward her. Her skin glowed with healthy color, and the rounded shape of her middle added to the alluring picture because he knew that his child grew inside her.

The emotions that assaulted him took him by surprise. He wanted to hold them fast, his wife and child, to protect them, but perhaps the best way he could protect them was to stay away from them, though the thought left him empty and desolate. If only he were a normal man who could give his family the loving devotion they deserved.

And then her gaze found him, and he thought he saw her face brighten before she blushed and glanced away, waiting for him to come to her. Her small, pink tongue flicked over her lips, and a jolt of desire surged through him, surprising him with its intensity.

Caroline noticed the darkly sexual expression that moved across his features for an instant, and her pulse raced in reaction. Perhaps she had only imagined it. How could he desire her when she looked like a cow that had been fattened all winter for the slaughter?

He looked tired, tired and angry and filthy from working in the orchards all day. He wore no shirt, and she found it difficult, if not impossible, to keep her gaze on his face, to keep herself from remembering the feel of that chest beneath her hand, against her breasts.

Of course, she knew the crisis in the orchards occupied most of his time and his attention at present. The smell of coffee burning permeated everything in her world. Smoke veiled the house in a constant gloom that suited her mood.

Never had she been so hot, so miserable, physically and emotionally.

Constantly close to tears and easily wounded, she felt the sting of his rejection more strongly than ever. She needed him to want her and the baby. They should be making plans, deciding on names. Next week she would enter her seventh month, and Jason still hadn't faced the issue of her pregnancy. She could understand his rejection of her, but how could he completely shut his child out of his life?

For four weeks, she'd been trying to reach him, to corner him so that she could talk to him. But he defeated her at every turn. She'd even thought of waiting for him in the hut where he slept, but she wasn't quite desperate enough yet to compromise Ines. Instead, she decided to come to the one place where he was sure to be—the orchards.

He stopped close before her, and Caroline had to fight her uneasiness in order to look into his eyes. She attempted a smile, but she knew it must look as artificial as it felt.

"I brought you something for lunch," she said, trying to sound casual, when all she could think about was their lovemaking—the power in his body, the gentleness in his hands, the concern he'd shown when he thought he'd hurt her.

"You shouldn't be here," he said gruffly, breaking the spell of desire that had consumed her. "Go back to the house."

"No." She would not be dismissed without a fight.

He had already started to walk away when her single word halted him. Turning, he glared at her as if she were some alien species he'd never seen before.

"You need to eat," she said, trying to deflect the incredulous anger in his expression. "Ines says you never eat lunch and—"

"Ines should mind her own business. It's hot and smoky here. You know my men are collapsing in this heat. You have no business here in your condition."

The baby chose that instant to change positions, and a sensation like tiny fingers poking at her stomach from the inside surprised a gasp from her lips.

Jason lurched forward, shock and fear contorting his face. "What's the matter? Are you all right?"

In the fraction of a second it took him to reach her and take the basket from her hand, Caroline made a decision. Sighing, she acted as if she might sink to her knees at any moment from whatever malady Jason imagined she might be suffering. She wasn't proud of herself, playing on his concern and fear, but desperate situations demanded desperate measures.

"I do feel a little weak," she murmured, holding her hand to her forehead.

"I told you to go back to the house." Now he was angry.

"If I could just . . . sit down for a minute."

In the blink of an eye, he swept her into his arms. Quickly Caroline recovered from the initial shock and twined an arm around his neck, smiling inwardly at the warmth of his masculine body and the security of his strong arms.

He didn't look at her, his expression intent on his task. Carrying her to the one empty patio of the *benefício*, he settled her gently into a worn wicker chair she'd had placed there while he was in Manaus so she could sit here in the shade of the *benefício* and oversee the harvest.

Glancing up, she found Jason watching her closely and feigned a wan smile. "I feel much better now."

"You look pale," Jason told her crossly. "I'm sending you back to the house right now. You shouldn't be running all over the countryside in that contraption. Where is Vincente?"

"Jason, I feel much better. Really. Besides, the cart was built for me. Vincente is far too tall to fit comfortably. And I think the wagon ride would make me sick right now." She gestured toward the basket hooked over his arm with a nod of her head. "You might as well eat while I recover."

Jason studied her, his expression revealing nothing. He was weighing his options—trying to decide between two evils.

Reaching for the basket, she placed it on what was left of her lap and withdrew a clean linen napkin, holding it out to him. Smiling crookedly, he took the cloth and wiped as much grime as possible from his hands.

"The fish is still a little warm," she told him, waiting expectantly for him to react. What choice did he have? His invalid wife couldn't be moved at present, and the food must smell delicious to a man who hadn't eaten since morning.

Finally, he dropped the soiled cloth to the floor beside her chair and took the plate, helping himself to the fish.

"I hate for you to eat standing up," she said. "Maybe you could find another chair or—"

"This is fine." His blunt voice cut her off.

"It's been nearly four weeks," Caroline said, referring to the last time they'd made love or even spoken more than a few polite, meaningless words to each other. "Are you ever going to talk to me again?"

"I have nothing to say," he said, brushing his arm across his mouth. "As you can see, I've been busy."

"What about the baby?" she asked, determined to force some kind of response from him and succeeding. She could feel the tremor that coursed through him as he handed the plate back to her and turned away.

"You seem to be better," he said over his shoulder. "Wait here until you feel like moving, then go back to the house. I've got work to do."

He didn't want to hear what she had to say, she knew, didn't want to face the truth. "It won't go away!" she called after him, placing the plate in the basket and the basket on the ground.

Paralyzed with apprehension, Caroline waited. He stood at the edge of the patio, his back rigid, his hands clenching into fists at his sides.

"I'm going to have a baby soon—your baby, Jason!"

"Go back to the house," he said, his stance unbending.

In desperation, Caroline went to him, grasping him by the arm so that he stopped and turned to face her. Taking his hand, she placed it on her belly. Instantly, he recoiled, jerking away and putting a safe distance between them.

"Leave me alone!" His voice shook with suppressed emotion. In his eyes she saw fear and fury.

He was like a rain cloud about to burst. Pressure built inside him so that an explosion seemed unavoidable. And as much as she wanted to be anywhere else when he finally erupted, she couldn't let him go, not like this. He wanted the baby; she knew he wanted it more than he'd ever wanted anything in his life. So why did he deny it? Why couldn't he be glad?

"It's our child, Jason," she told him, tears clouding her eyes and causing her voice to tremble. "Isn't that what you wanted? A child? I read your letters. *If I could undo it, I would.* Can't we get past that?"

"I don't think so." He walked away from her, and again her words halted him.

"I know your sister killed herself!" she cried, knowing she might regret bringing into the light something he'd tried so desperately to keep in the shadows.

"No!" he shouted, turning and stalking toward her with such vehemence that it was all she could do not to back away. He stopped an arm's length from her, the fury inside him causing his body to tremble with suppressed violence. "You see, I don't want to discuss this with you. With Derek, maybe, but not with you. It never happened. Or it happened to someone else a long time ago. It has nothing to do with me, with now. I came all the way to Brazil to start over."

"It has everything to do with you," Caroline argued, though the urge to flee from the anger and anguish in his eyes resounded inside her. "Can't you see how it's tearing you up inside? You and I can't have a future until you deal with your past."

"I don't need or want you telling me that. I don't need you trying to fix me, the great healer, Mother Earth personified! You're like a whirlwind, you know? You whirl around and suck up everyone and everything in your path. If you don't like the way something is, you just tear it down and rebuild it to suit you. You and I are stuck with each other, but I don't have to like it."

His words pierced her soul like arrows. She tried to remind herself that it was his anger talking, but it did little good. He was trapped inside a prison of guilt and regret, and she didn't know if she had the strength or the courage to release him, to cross that moat of cold fury and free the man inside.

"I am your wife," she reminded him, struggling in vain to keep her voice from quivering. "Why won't you talk about it? Tell me about your past."

Jason laughed without humor. "You read my letters. Why don't you tell me about my past? You know, this is exactly why I asked for a young, inexperienced wife. I didn't want to have to be answering a lot of questions about my past, and I didn't want to always be wondering about my wife's past."

"I'll tell you anything you want to know," Caroline said, though she knew he was trying to change the subject.

"Did you love him?" he asked with an uncompromising glare.

The unexpected question hit her like a blow. She

could only stare at him in openmouthed amazement. Finally, she shook her head wearily. "We've been over this before, Jason. Why is it so important to you?"

His lips twisted in a smug half smile. "Anything, you said. It's a simple question requiring a yes or no answer. Did you love him or not?"

Glancing away from the blue intensity of his eyes, Caroline murmured, "It's not that simple. . . ."

"Admit it, Caroline, you loved him. Why is it so hard for you to say it? You never would have married him if you hadn't cared for him. I know you well enough to know that."

"I was infatuated with him," she conceded, searching her heart and mind for some link with that part of her life. She couldn't conjure any emotion for Wade. It was as if he'd never been a part of her life. She honestly couldn't say whether she'd loved him or not.

"Infatuated?" he asked sharply. "He charmed you, is that it? You found him attractive and he courted you patiently. Did you think of him when you weren't with him? What did you talk about, the two of you? Did you cry out when you made love?"

"Stop it!" Her face flushed at the memory of Jason's lovemaking. No, she'd never cried out with Wade, but she wasn't sure she should admit it. It would only give him an opening to steer the conversation down a road she didn't want to travel and away from himself. Angry and yet somehow thrilled that he cared enough to interrogate her, she asked, "Why are you doing this? Wade is dead! Dead! What does it matter whether I loved him or not?"

"My past is dead. Why is it that you think you have the right to dig up the corpses of my past but I shouldn't even be curious about yours?"

"Because it's irrelevant here. I've buried my corpses. You dug yours up and brought them here with you."

His jaw tightened, the only sign of reaction in his otherwise stoic expression. "I disagree," he said tautly, "I think your past is very relevant. What's the worst thing that ever happened to you?"

"My father's death," she replied without hesitation. She didn't have to think about it. Her father's death was the single most devastating event in her life.

"Your—your father's death?" he asked as if stunned by her unexpected response. "Not your husband's?"

"By then I didn't love him, if I ever did." In her mind, she relived the disillusionment she'd experienced so long ago, when she'd learned that Wade had lost all the money her father had left them and with it their future. "I can't answer your question because I don't know. I don't know if I loved him. I was so young, so . . ."

"So what?"

"So vulnerable." She felt suddenly, inexplicably cold. "He was handsome and witty and so aloof. I chased him shamelessly. When my father died, he was there, waiting to step in and take over. I thought he was so strong. It was only after two years of marriage and his squandering of not only his own money but mine as well that I began to see things—to see him as he really was. So, now you know as much about me as I do about you."

"The difference is you knew who you were talking to," he said obstinately, turning and walking away once again.

"All right! I'm sorry!" Caroline cried, trembling with rage. "How many times do I have to apologize? You're not angry because I read your letters, Jason. You're angry because of what was in them, because I know—"

"Know? What the bloody hell do you know, Caroline?" he thundered.

Caroline looked away, unable to bear the intensity of his glare, yet unwilling to back down. They were very much alone here, she realized thankfully. The workers had abandoned the orchards for the siesta. The fires kept the animals and insects at bay, so the only sound that reached them was the relentless lapping of smoldering fires. A strong breeze swept through the *benefício*, bringing the promise of rain with it. Far overhead a soaring condor cawed loudly, breaking the unnatural silence.

"I know about your father—what your relationship with him was like. I know that he beat you and you hated him. Of course you did, he brutalized you and your family."

Jason laughed, the bitterest sound Caroline had ever heard. "You said the worst thing that ever happened to you was your father's death. The day my father died was like a liberation for me. That was the day my life began."

"I'm sorry," she choked out. She wanted with all her heart to touch him, to comfort him, but she knew he would only push her away.

"Just so you know what kind of man you've married, Caroline, I have a terrible rage inside me, a gift from my father. It boils up now and then and I lash out at whatever or whoever's closest to me." He studied his hands, turning them over in front of his eyes. "These hands have already killed."

"What are you talking about?" The blood seemed to drain from her body, and she waited in breathless silence.

"Yeah, now you're afraid. Maybe you're smarter than I gave you credit for."

"Who . . . who did you kill?"

"He was always bigger than me," Jason murmured, his gaze distant as if he'd left her and traveled back through time to his boyhood, "even to the last. I was a tall kid, but I was very skinny. It didn't matter. He was drunk. I pushed him. He fell and hit his head on the edge of an ax I'd been using earlier in the day. For a long time, I kept searching my memory, wondering if somehow subconsciously I'd put that ax there on purpose. I killed my own father."

"It was an accident," she said, her voice trembling.

"It doesn't matter. He's no less dead than he would have been had I killed him intentionally. My rage got control of me. That's why I came here, don't you understand? So I couldn't hurt anyone else!"

"No!" Caroline cried sharply. "You can lie to yourself, Jason, but not to me. You've hidden yourself away in this jungle to escape a world you don't understand. It's not hurting someone else that frightens you so much, it's being hurt."

"I don't have to listen to this!" He moved to leave again.

"Then run away again, Jason, it's what you do best!" He continued to walk away from her as if her words had no effect on him. Driven by desperation, she shouted, "You're a coward, Jason Sinclair!

You're afraid to care about anyone because you could be hurt."

"What do you know, really know, about me?" he asked, turning to glare at her. "Do you know what it's like to be hated by someone who's supposed to love and protect you? Do you know what it's like when even the place you live isn't safe? He'd come home drunk and fly into a rage about nothing—something I'd done or hadn't done or the way I looked at him. I never knew what would set him off. He'd beat me until I nearly blacked out. Sometimes I was afraid he'd never stop. If I tried to defend myself, it only made him madder."

She tried to touch him, but he shrugged her away.

"He hired me out to work in a sugar factory when I was eleven so I could supply him with money to buy whiskey and women. I didn't go to school. I'd work in that boiler room for fourteen hours a day, stoking the fires under the kettles or turning the handle so the sugar wouldn't stick and burn. If I got home later than he thought I should, he'd beat me. If I didn't bring home enough money, he'd beat me."

The beginnings of tears burned behind Caroline's eyes at the image his words evoked. "Jason, I wish I could take away your pain."

"Well, you can't," he said with a great sigh that seemed torn from his very soul. "You never could. It's my own hell."

"What did your mother do?"

"Do?" he asked with a laugh. "She hid and hoped he wouldn't get tired of beating me and turn on her."

"She didn't try to stop him?"

"Like I said, you don't understand. My father was

a very big man, big and mean. No one messed with
Cullen Sinclair. What could my mother have done to
stop him?"

"I don't know, Jason," she said, absently caressing
her swollen stomach. "I only know that if anyone did
that to my child, I'd have to try and stop them."

Without warning, Jason grabbed her by the shoulders, his hands biting painfully into her flesh, his
eyes glowing with fury. "Don't you dare judge my
mother! You don't know what it's like to be terror-
ized night and day. I tried to fight back once when I
was thirteen and he broke my nose. Look at this," he
said, releasing her and pulling his shirt sleeve back
to reveal a small circular scar on his wrist. "See, my
father smoked a cigar, and one night he got really
mad and. . . ."

Caroline felt as if she might faint or be physically
ill. Her head reeled and nausea rose in her throat.
"Stop, please."

"Damn it!" he growled between clenched teeth,
shaking her roughly. "That's not the worst he did,
Caroline. Should I describe the scars he put on my
mother or what he did to my sister?"

The pain caused by his grip on her shoulders
receded, replaced by a hollow, agonizing ache deep
inside her. Tears rolled unchecked down her cheeks
as she tried to pull away, tried to flee from the bitter
hurt in his voice and his uncompromising words.
Finally he released her and she fell away, sobbing
brokenly.

"You feel guilty because your sister killed herself
and you couldn't stop her."

"Shut up," he snarled, but Caroline couldn't stop
herself.

"You blame yourself," she went on, despite the mounting fury so plain in his features. "You couldn't even stop your father from hurting you."

"Shut up!"

"You hate yourself because you knew what was going on, and you were too afraid to try and stop him."

"Shut up!"

Caroline flinched, a gasp of horror welling up inside her as he drew back his hand and she closed her eyes, expecting to be struck, expecting the blow to knock her off her feet. Fear convulsed in her chest as she tried to brace herself for the pain. When it didn't come, she opened her eyes and saw her own horror reflected in his stunned eyes.

Jerking out of his grip, she backed away to the edge of the patio, then hurried as best she could toward her waiting cart.

She couldn't think straight, couldn't even contemplate what had just happened, not yet. She had to get away, that was all she knew. She had to get back to the house and . . . and . . .

Once settled into the cart, she shook out the reins and the horse bolted forward, jarring her, and the baby protested vehemently. A sob tore from her throat as she thought of the baby, her child. Was Jason like his father after all? Was he capable not only of harming her but of hurting their child as well?

For the first time she understood something of the unremitting terror that had been a part of Jason's childhood. She could flee back to the house, but there was no place to hide, no protector to run to because the one who was supposed to protect her had threatened her.

The pain Jason had carried in his heart all these years opened to her and she understood. And she also knew that she could not expose her child to that kind of life. She would not!

Rounding a curve in the path, Caroline drew back on the reins, slowing the horse to a walk. She was out of sight of the *benefício*, and Jason hadn't come after her. Her body ached from the bouncing, jolting ride she'd just experienced, and she knew she couldn't keep it up all the way back to the house. For the sake of the baby, if not her own, she had to take her time. Besides, there were things to think about, decisions to be made. Whatever else happened, no matter how badly it hurt, she had to get away from this place.

17

Caroline watched as the muddy riverbank littered with the corpses of trees moved slowly past. A lone heron searched the shallows for food, while tiny surface fish churned the water in the middle of the river, their silver bodies flickering brightly in the sunlight.

She gasped and ran a hand over her distended stomach. Bracing herself, she waited for the next movement, but the child inside her grew still once again. Smiling into the brilliant sunlight, she remembered the first time she'd felt the fluttering. Then it had been as faint as the butterflies she experienced as a child whenever she rode the train from New Orleans to Memphis with her father. But over the months, the movements had grown stronger, more unsettling.

She knew from her medical training that an active baby in the womb meant a better chance that it would be born healthy, and she prayed that would be the case. She couldn't even contemplate the possibility that the baby she carried so close to her heart might not be perfect.

Something primitive and a bit frightening had taken control of her body. And as disturbing as the idea might be, it was also incredibly thrilling. Changes took place inside her every day, changes in her shape, her appetite, her energy reserves—changes over which she had no control, no choice. And the ultimate change would come when her body, acting on its own volition, expelled this child from her womb and into the world. What a terrifyingly savage thing!

"We'll get through it, you and I," Caroline whispered, caressing her rounded abdomen, pushing the stark fear out of her mind.

Tears threatened her control as the weight of loneliness crashed in upon her. She'd had no one to talk to about her joys and fears, no one but Ines, who had never experienced pregnancy. The other women on the *fazenda* had given advice and gifts, but for the most part they were strangers to her, acquaintances at best.

At first, she'd wanted to share her growing awareness of the life inside her with Jason, to make plans, to wonder together what their child would be like. Their child—hers and Jason's. But Jason had been so aloof, so distant, as if by ignoring her condition he could make it disappear.

Now she understood so many things. Jason was right. She hadn't considered the depths of the emotional scars such a childhood would leave—until that day at the *beneficio*.

For more than a month now, she'd been reliving their last argument over and over in her mind. She'd contemplated Jason's revelations and considered how the things that had happened to him had shaped him into the man he was today.

She released a wretched sigh. He'd become a wraith during the past month, a phantom. From time to time she'd feel a prickling of sensation that told her he was nearby, but she never actually saw him.

Not sure what to say to him, she'd allowed him to withdraw. They both needed some time to sort out all the things that had passed between them. Perhaps they just couldn't live together.

He wanted this child; she'd seen the yearning in his eyes when he'd let down his guard. And yet, when she'd taken his hand and placed it on her stomach, he'd pulled away from her as if he couldn't bear to touch her, as if the very thought terrified him.

What did it matter now? She would not live the fearful life Jason and his family had endured, and she would not allow her child to do so either. She'd tried to reach him, tried every way she knew, and she'd failed. He had finally won. And so today she had boarded the mail boat as it docked at Jason's pier and sailed away, removing herself and her baby to safety.

Sniffing loudly, she went over her plan again in her mind. Within three weeks, she would be safely in Manaus. She'd wire Melanie for money. She hated to do so, but Melanie was her only hope, her only friend. She had enough money to survive in Manaus for a while, but time was not her ally. She would be able to go no farther before the baby was born.

Perhaps it had all worked out for the best, in

some strange, unexpected way, she thought, as she watched the shore move swiftly past, the mail boat carrying her farther and farther away from her heart. She'd been so afraid of having this baby alone in the wilderness, now at least she would be in a city. Surely she would be able to locate a doctor.

If only . . .

Oh, she could go mad dwelling on the if onlys. If only she'd had more time. . . . If only she hadn't forced him into a corner time and again. . . . If only she'd allowed Jason to be Jason instead of trying to mold him into what she wanted him to be.

Caroline gazed around in dismay. She'd been so intent on her musings that she hadn't noticed how dark the hazy afternoon sky had become. On all sides, the walls of vegetation receded into shadows. The cold slate-blue sky went suddenly purple and the boat's captain steered the craft toward the almost indiscernible bank to their left.

One crew member walked toward her across the deck as the rain began to fall, slowly at first, the violence of the storm increasing with every passing second. She reached the cover of the striped canopy just in time, just as the man she knew only as Juao reached her.

"The captain knows of a cabin where we can wait out the storm," he told her in impeccable English, his tone apologetic, his dark, bushy brows drawing together in a frown of regret.

As Juao bowed to her and moved toward the front of the boat, Caroline clung to one of the poles that held the awning in place. The boat pitched in the suddenly violent river. She could barely see in front of her now, and the savage pounding of the rain and the stench of sodden leaves and earth ravaged her senses, causing her to yearn for the safety of her rooms at the *fazenda*.

A fierce shudder ripped through the small boat, and to Caroline's horror, it began listing to the left, leaning so far in that direction that she nearly fell over the side.

She screamed as the pole she'd been clinging to snapped in half, but the sound died unheard in the roaring tempest. The deck fell away, vanishing from beneath her feet, and she was falling, tumbling through an infinite void just before a blow to her head rendered her senseless and the world went black.

Jason pushed the door to Caroline's sitting room open and gazed around with a deep, ragged sigh. He didn't even have to cross the threshold to know that she'd gone. He could feel it in the stillness of the room. It was worse than the first time because his feelings for her had grown tenfold.

He'd miss her, damn how he'd miss her. He'd even miss the arguments, her constant probing, her infuriating belief that she could fix every problem, right every wrong. He'd miss her every day of his life.

Walking through the doorway, he gazed around him at the wilted orchids on the table across the room, the windows left open, the tidiness of the room. It was almost as if she hadn't been here at all, but his heart knew better.

Sadness tightened his throat and he swallowed against it, running a hand through his hair as he tried to convince himself that it was for the best, that it was what he'd wanted all along. He'd kept his privacy intact, his damned secrets undiscovered. Now they were all he had to keep him company, and his heart ached at the prospect of a lifetime of regret.

He couldn't forget the day at the *beneficio*, the day she'd finally encountered his true nature. In the weeks that followed, she'd avoided him, staying in her room as much as possible, even taking her meals there in order not to have to look at him or be in the same room with him.

She'd thought she understood him and the life he'd led, but she was terribly innocent in some ways. She'd been shielded from much of the ugliness of life. There were things she couldn't even imagine, things he'd wanted to protect her from. But how could he protect her from anything when she needed protection from him most of all?

Closing his eyes, he shuddered as a torrent of self-loathing swept over him. He'd almost hit her. He'd raised his hand to her, and he'd seen the stark fear in her eyes. It still sickened him. In that instant, he'd felt the rush of power his father must have experienced. A savage satisfaction had permeated his being—he could make her shut up. In an instant, he could put an end to her infernal crusade to find a human heart inside him. He'd felt her helplessness, and he'd been unable to take advantage of it. But what about next time?

She'd done the only thing she could do under the circumstances. She'd taken herself and her child out of his presence. She'd run away. He just prayed God she'd stay in Manaus until the baby was born instead of trying to make it all the way back to New Orleans. Time was running out.

His gut twisted as he realized he'd never see his own child, his own flesh and blood. And though he knew it was better this way, the pain persisted. Caroline would take care of him. She'd provide a loving home. He would provide financial support for them through Derek. It was the least he could do and the only thing he had to offer anyway.

The loud, piercing blast of a steam whistle rent the still afternoon air, and a thrill trembled through Jason's body, his first thought that the mail boat had turned around and come back. But as soon as his rational mind asserted itself, he realized that it must be Ignacio returning from his mission to Manaus. The mail boat had stopped only briefly yesterday afternoon. It would be miles downriver by now.

Steeling himself against the pain that pierced his heart, he left the empty sitting room, closing the door behind him.

"This is Senhor Deiras," Ignacio said, and Jason shook hands with the slight, bespectacled man who stepped from the boat.

The smaller man's hand trembled noticeably, and Jason wondered at the cause of his unease. "Welcome," he said with a smile, trying to reassure the nervous little man who clasped his battered hat to his chest as if it were a lifeline.

Ignacio smiled. "I'm afraid he's still a little shaken by the storm we went through yesterday afternoon. Traveling the river in the rainy season can be deadly, as you know."

A shudder of apprehension sliced through Jason as he thought of Caroline on the river. He hadn't allowed himself to dwell on the dangers of traveling at this time of year, but they were very real. Sudden, violent storms could produce ten foot swells and near gale force winds.

"We had to wait the storm out in an Indian hut," Ignacio went on. "I thought the wind would blow the roof off."

"Well," Jason said, forcing a smile, "at least no one was hurt."

"No," Ignacio agreed, "but I'm afraid the mail boat wasn't so fortunate."

The blood pounded loudly in Jason's head as he stood stiff as a statue, listening to Ignacio's news. Panic, raw and bitter, rose in his throat. "What happened?"

"For several miles, we passed the debris. And as we reached a bend in the river, we saw the rescue party drag the captain and his mate out of the river." Ignacio finished by making the sign of the cross over his chest.

"Two bodies?" Jason asked, barely able to speak past his rasping breath.

"*Sim, patrão,*" Ignacio replied, his brow furrowing in concern. "You are very pale, *patrão*, is anything wrong?"

"Survivors?" he choked out.

Ignacio shook his head negatively. "You know *Capitão* Polonia seldom took passengers. I suspect there was no. . . . *Patrão*, where are you going?"

Jason leaped onto the small steamboat as his men unloaded the last of the cargo and luggage from its hold. "Untie the ropes!" he shouted.

"But *patrão*. . . ."

"Do as I say, damn you!" Jason bellowed, ignoring Ignacio's confusion. His men obeyed and the boat floated free of the pier. Thank God, they hadn't cut the engines yet or it might have taken an hour to get them hot again.

"*Patrão*!" Ignacio shouted from the quickly receding shore, "where are you going?"

"Where did they find the bodies?" Jason asked, trying to quell the paroxysm of terror inside him. Caroline's life might well depend on it—on him.

"About thirty miles downriver! But where . . . !"

"Caroline was on that boat!" The words, spoken aloud, made the terror all too real.

Ignacio ran to the edge of the pier. "Come back! I will go with you!"

"There's no time!" Jason called. "I need you here! If I'm not back by morning, send a party after me!"

"Be careful!" Ignacio shouted, his words carried away by the breeze that ruffled Jason's damp hair.

Caroline, Caroline, he thought desperately. Please be all right. Maybe she hadn't gotten on the mail boat. She'd tricked him before. Maybe she was hiding somewhere in the jungle. Maybe she'd gone back to the slave village. Dear God, she had to be all right.

Caroline tried to move her left arm, and a numbing pain shot through her body. Broken. Useless. Tears sprang to her eyes as she stretched out her right arm and grabbed hold of a sturdy-looking root just above her head. She'd given up wondering how she'd come to be here on the muddy bank, and now all her thoughts were concentrated on getting to safety. She could feel the river lapping steadily at her ankles and knew she had to get to higher ground before another storm crashed down on her.

She tried not to think of the snakes and alligators and flesh-eating fish that populated the Amazon, lest she give in to the consuming fear that lurked close to the edge of her mind, waiting for the chance to devour her.

The soft, cloying bank beneath her clung to her skirt, dragging her down, making it nearly impossible to move in her weakened state. She wanted to cry, to lie there and give up. She had no idea how badly injured she might be, only that her head throbbed and her left arm was broken—and the baby hadn't moved since she'd regained consciousness.

A sob tore from her throat as she pulled desperately at the root, moving slightly up the bank and settling in a new position only inches higher than she'd started out. The effort drained her strength and cost her dearly in terms of pain.

Gasping for air, she lay there for a minute. Just a minute. She had to rest, to regather her strength and her will to go on. Closing her eyes, she'd almost succumbed to the weariness that enveloped her like a heavy cloak when a tearing, searing pain exploded deep inside her belly, wrenching a groan from her and leaving her even more breathless in its wake.

"Not now," she murmured. "Please God, not now. It's too early. I . . . I can't. . . ."

Grasping at the soft earth, Caroline tried again to pull herself up the bank, but there was nothing solid to hold on to, nothing but soft, loose mud. She tried to crawl, but that only caused her more pain when she fell helplessly onto her injured arm.

Exhausted, she lay still, her head reeling, nausea rising in her throat. It was so hot, so humid, she could hardly breathe. Life pulsed through the jungle around her. Bird songs and the chattering of monkeys in the trees filled her ears, as hungry insects whirred around her. She didn't even have the strength to swat at them but endured their frequent bites. At least the stinging sensation affirmed that she was alive and not in hell.

Without volition, she began to pant rapidly, deeply, as another pain swelled inside her, gathering strength before breaking over her brittle body with a vengeance.

How far apart had they been? She strained to concentrate, to calculate, but every minute seemed an eternity here in this isolated, savage place. How could she be sure of anything?

"Not now. Please, not now," she gasped as a silken darkness overwhelmed her and she surrendered to a painless nothingness.

"Caroline!" Jason called, cupping his hands over his mouth.

His frantic gaze swept the banks of the river for any sign of her, but nothing met his eyes, nothing but green and brown jungle. On his journey down the river, he'd passed pieces of floating debris left by the wrecked mail boat, and his urgency had increased to the point of unremitting panic.

She had to be all right. If anything had happened to her, he'd never forgive himself. It was all his fault, his fault. Where could she be?

In his desperate search of the shoreline, he'd refused to allow himself to search the river itself, refused to entertain the idea that what he might find instead of his frightened, bruised but indomitable wife was a lifeless body skimming the surface of the river. He couldn't even allow himself to contemplate it or he would go mad.

"Caroline!" he called again, desperation raising his voice.

The engines chugged softly. He'd cut them as low as he dared so that he could hear any response, but none came. Gazing at the heavens, he realized that he didn't have much daylight left. He had to find her before nightfall. If she had survived last night, she would be frightened and hungry and possibly injured. Could she endure another?

"Caroline!" he called again.

Maybe she was afraid of him. Maybe she heard his voice but feared him more than she did being alone in the jungle.

"Please answer me," he murmured. "I . . . I'm sorry."

Jason's ears perked at a chilling sound, a shiver trembling down his spine at its stark, piercing quality. At first he thought it must be a monkey. They could sound amazingly human, but the scream came again, inhuman yet somehow human at the same time. A scream of agony.

"Caroline!" he called, steering the boat toward the sound, toward the right bank.

Desperately he searched the shadows for a sign of life. How could he find her when he could hardly make out the shore at all? In the last few minutes, the sun had dipped dramatically, lengthening and deepening the shadows that clung to the bank. The way voices carried on the river, she could be anywhere within a five-mile radius, but she was alive!

His heart raced with jubilation and alarm. She

was alive, but if he couldn't find her. . . . Something had caused that blood-curdling scream. Whether a scream of pain or terror, something had caused that agonized, terrified cry.

"Caroline!" he called frantically. "Answer me!"

Something moved, something white, brilliant in the waning sunlight. Quickly he turned the wheel, intent on returning to that spot, but the current carried him several yards downriver before he could turn the vessel. Hugging the bank, he moved slowly back upriver in the direction of the apparition. Maybe it had been nothing more than a shadow or an animal approaching the river to drink.

There it was again!

Jason rammed the boat into the bank. Cutting the engines, he jumped from the deck and quickly secured a rope to a sturdy-looking tree. His every sense urged him to rush to her, to forget about the boat and find her, but he knew that if the boat floated free of the bank, they'd be trapped here, and from the sound of her scream, she might need immediate medical attention.

The boat secure, he ran toward the place where he'd seen movement. His heart froze in his throat. "Caroline!"

She lay on her side, her body covered with mud— still, silent. He rushed to her, silently praying that she was still alive as he knelt beside her and rolled her gently onto her back.

She screamed and Jason released her, a cold terror crawling up his spine. It was then that he noticed her twisted left arm and tried again, careful to avoid the injured appendage. She was panting, her eyes only half-open.

"Jason!" she breathed. "Jason!"

"I'm here."

He nearly gasped aloud at the sight of blood covering the front of her soiled skirt. His pulse racing in alarm, he pulled her against him, cradling her head and shoulders in his arms. How badly was she hurt? Had she survived the boat wreck and what must have been a harrowing night alone, injured and terrified in the jungle, only to bleed to death in his arms?

"Where else are you hurt?" he asked, forcing the raw emotion from his voice, not wanting to frighten her. She was in shock, he knew, and she might not realize how badly she was bleeding.

"The baby," she murmured. "The baby, Jason."

Her body stiffened and she began to pant, groaning low in her throat. When she was able to speak again, she gasped, "Jason, oh, Jason, my water broke! Oh, Jason, I'm so afraid!"

That explained the blood, he realized with short-lived relief. She wasn't cut anywhere; she wouldn't bleed to death, but the baby was coming—now.

"I'm here," he said soothingly, trying to sound calm when an overwhelming urgency pounded inside him. He had to get her to safety. He had to . . . to . . . God, he was going to have to deliver the baby. "How long has it been since your water broke?"

"Oh Jason, I don't know!" Her head rolled from side to side as she tried to do something, anything, to distract herself from the pain that would envelop her again in a few minutes—or was it seconds? She wasn't sure. She wasn't sure of anything right now except that if Jason let go of her, the pain and darkness would devour her.

"Try to think," he said gently. They were a long

way from the *fazenda*. He had no way of knowing if there was shelter close by. The boat would have to do.

"I don't know!" she cried. "I'm sorry, I'm so sorry, Jason. It's my fault. The baby . . . the baby . . . it's too soon. I shouldn't have left. I'm sorry."

Careful to hold her injured arm steady, Jason pulled her limp body into his arms and stood. She gasped, clinging to him with her right arm wrapped tightly around his neck.

"What are you sorry for, Caroline?" he asked as he carried her toward the boat. "I'm the one who drove you away. Don't talk foolishness. I'm the one who's sorry."

"I'm sorry," she murmured, resting her head against his shoulder, sending a sharp, painful surge of protectiveness through him.

Blinking his eyes against unexpected tears, he whispered, "I won't let anything happen to you, Caroline. I swear it before God. I won't let anything happen to you or the baby."

18

Jason's hands trembled as he wrapped his son in a small square of material he'd cut from one of the blankets he found below deck. Gazing at the small, reddened body, he could hardly comprehend the fact that he had guided his own son into the world, that he'd watched him take his first breath, that he held him in his hands now.

His own blood flowed inside that small body, his and Caroline's, mingled together to form a new life that hadn't existed before.

Everything seemed changed—the jungle, the night-darkened river, his own heart. All his hopes and fears converged in the miracle he held so carefully.

A boy. He'd known all along it would be a boy. What he'd never anticipated was the overwhelming surge of love and pride that racked his exhausted body. He knew, with a certainty more powerful than anything he'd ever experienced, that he would die for this child, if need be—and for Caroline.

Walking toward his wife where she lay in the bed he'd brought up from below deck, Jason felt his heart skip a beat. He'd almost lost her—both of them. Because of him, she'd run away. If he hadn't found her when he had, they would have both almost surely died. How could he have ever lived with that?

Carefully, Jason slipped the child into the crook of Caroline's good arm, and she received him with a weary smile.

"He's so beautiful," she said, her gaze caressing the infant as she fumbled with the buttons on the front of her blouse. "Jason, I think you're going to have to help me," she said as the baby began to fuss.

Awkwardly, Jason stepped forward and began unbuttoning her blouse. A raw, elemental desire shuddered through his body, mingling with another emotion he could not name, though its power nearly drove him to his knees. By the time her breast was free, he could hardly breathe.

Caroline guided the baby to her breast, gasping in shock as his tiny mouth closed over her nipple and he began to suckle.

Exhausted but radiant, she gazed at Jason, a soft smile curving her lips. "He has your eyes," she said.

Jason backed away, swallowing convulsively. He'd noticed right away, of course. They were clear blue, *as blue as an Irish sky in springtime*, his mother would have said. Of course, they might change when the child got older. The thatch of snow white curls almost certainly would.

"Where are you going?" Caroline called.

Jason stopped, realizing that he'd reached the edge of the boat and had been about to jump out onto the bank. Why, he couldn't say. All he knew was that he needed to get away from them, from the emotions tearing at his heart.

"Please don't leave me," she pleaded. "I need you. I can't care for him alone with this broken arm."

"I—I can't," he murmured without facing her, the admission torn from his very soul.

He'd held the babe, bathed him, wrapped him against the elements, because he'd had no choice. But when he surrendered him to his mother, he'd meant for it to be a final relinquishing.

As he secured a hammock to the boat's walls near where Caroline lay, he thought about how tiny and helpless his son was. He'd made himself a solemn vow to protect them, and the best way to do that was to keep himself a safe distance from them. But there was only so much a man could endure.

"Where will he sleep?" Caroline asked.

Jason turned to gaze at them, his wife and son. The babe still clung to his mother's breast, though he had dozed off. His tiny fist lay against her soft flesh, his head resting on her white shoulder.

"He can sleep with you," he suggested.

"Jason, this cot is too narrow," she reasoned. "I can't support him with one arm. And if he needs attention in the middle of the night, there's nothing I can do."

How could he make her understand? He needed to distance himself from this child—from both of them—now, before the attachment he'd already begun to feel devoured him and pulling away was no longer a possibility.

"Jason!" she called. "You held him before. What are you afraid of?"

"Myself," he murmured.

"He's your son," she reminded him.

A tremor flashed through his body and he closed his eyes, his hands clenching into fists at his sides as he struggled against the hunger in his chest.

"I'm a coward, Caroline. You were right. I'm afraid I'll—I'll care too much."

There, he said it. He admitted his deepest weakness. He was afraid that he would lose anything he cared too much about and he couldn't bear the pain. If he didn't care so much, maybe pulling away wouldn't destroy him.

"I'm afraid you can't control that, Jason," she was saying as if she'd read his thoughts. "Haven't you learned as much yet? You ran away from the world because you couldn't control it. You thought that if you isolated yourself, you could stop feeling. Now you believe that if you distance yourself from your son, you can make yourself not care about him either. Don't you see? You can't control your heart."

Was she right? He wondered. He'd always believed he could control anything, everything, once he escaped the iron fist of his father's rule. But he hadn't been able to control Caroline or the fungus that had decimated his orchards or the overwhelming emotions that had devoured him at the moment of his son's birth.

The realization that there were so many things beyond his power should have terrified him, but it didn't. There was a strange comfort in letting go of some of the weight of responsibility.

Gingerly he reached for his son, and Caroline lifted him with her arm as best she could.

"Watch his head," she urged.

"Caroline, I can't do this," he said, fear flashing through him without warning as he wrapped his arms around the baby.

"You did it before," she reminded him. "I'm so tired, Jason, and my arm is throbbing. Please . . ."

Her words trailed off, and Jason had the uncomfortable feeling she'd fallen asleep. Now what was he supposed to do?

He stood, gazing down at her sleeping form, his son cradled in his arms. If he allowed himself to, he could feel a swell of contentment as pure and joyous as anything he'd ever known.

A son. A wife. A family. They embodied everything he'd ever truly wanted.

Tears welled in his eyes as he realized he'd surely die if they were ever taken from him.

Caroline was right. She'd been right about so many things. He could not head off the surge of affection for his new son, any more than he could hold back his feelings for her. They were part of the fiber that made him who he was. From this day forward, he would never be the same again; he knew it as surely as he'd ever known anything in his life.

Glancing one last time at his sleeping wife, Jason carried his son to the hammock in the corner. Carefully he climbed in and lay on his back, the baby resting on his chest. Both hands securely around the infant, he closed his eyes, dreaming of the years to come, years of watching his son grow and teaching him the things his own father had never taught him. Before long he settled into a peaceful sleep, the first he had known in seventeen years.

*   *   *

Jason steered the small boat through the early morning quiet. The river spread before it, as smooth and benign as silk. Peaceful, serene.

Caroline lay sleeping in the bed he'd left on deck, her left arm in a sling lying beneath her breasts. Her strong, rhythmic breathing caused the injured arm to rise and fall gently. Her long, dark hair spread around her white face, mangled and matted with mud, despite his efforts to clean it.

Cradled in her right arm, she held their sleeping son against her warm, soft body. Jason's stomach did a somersault as emotions pummeled him faster than he could repel them, piercing his every defense—pride, love, tenderness.

The baby moved, and Caroline's eyes flew open immediately. Jason jerked his head away before she could read the undisguised emotion in his eyes, before she could see into his soul. But they drew him like a magnet, this woman and child, this perfection.

Against his will, he turned to gaze at them once again, and Caroline smiled weakly.

"How do you feel?" he asked, his voice strange in his own ears.

"Tired," she murmured.

Caroline drew the child to her breast, gasping as the tiny mouth closed over her tender nipple. Awkwardly, she supported the babe against her shoulder so she could caress his head with her good hand. Her eyes glazed with an emotion that touched him like a shadow.

His own feelings must pale when compared to hers. She'd known this child for nearly nine months, carried him beneath her heart, felt him move inside her body. They were still connected in a way that made him feel like an outsider, an observer with no part in the miracle.

He turned away from the warmth reflected in her eyes. Within minutes, his own pier would come into view and they would be faced with the same world they had left behind two days ago. The same problems would be waiting for them. But for a few more minutes, he reveled in the closeness that had grown between them last night.

When he glanced at Caroline again, both mother and child were asleep.

"Caroline," he murmured. He hated to wake her, but they would be docking soon and she needed to cover her exposed breast and prepare herself before they met the rest of the world.

"Caroline," he said more insistently.

Smiling languidly, she opened her eyes, and the love and contentment reflected there took his breath away.

"We'll be docking soon," he told her. "I think you should, ah—"

Suddenly, inexplicably embarrassed, he could only gesture toward her exposed flesh. She understood and drew her blouse together awkwardly, a touch of pink staining her cheeks.

"We should name him, you know," she said weakly.

"There's plenty of time for that," he assured her, concentrating on the river now that there was, blessedly, something to take his attention away from the yearning in his chest. "We can talk about it when you've regained your strength."

They accomplished the rest of the journey in silence. As they drew near, the pier exploded in activity. Men had already gathered and had begun preparations to send a search party after them. Now they stood at the end of the dock, craning their necks to see whether he was returning alone.

"I see *a senhora*!" someone shouted, and a cheer went up from the small group.

Jason scowled, even though his heart swelled with pride at their admiration. Cutting the engine, he moved to the side of the boat and tossed a thick rope to one of the men on the shore. Quickly the boat was secured and boarded.

"Easy," Jason said as the men tried to crowd around Caroline. "She's still weak."

Ines shouldered her way through the silent, gaping men. "My poor *senhora*!"

"Take the baby, Ines," Jason ordered. "Be careful of Caroline's left arm."

Caroline smiled weakly at Ines as she took the child from her arm. "Isn't he the most beautiful baby you've ever seen?"

"*Sim, senhora*," Ines agreed, her eyes filling with tears. "Out of the way!" she commanded as she made her way back through the sea of men.

Jason moved beside Caroline, carefully arranging the sheet he'd wrapped around her to replace the ruined skirt he'd had to cut away last night. The pressure of her eyes drew his gaze to hers as he carefully slipped his arms underneath her and lifted her off the bed. Immediately she twined her arm around his neck and rested her weary head against his shoulder.

Fear clutched his heart as he held her to him,

trembling through his being, a fear greater than any he'd ever known before. All his life, the things he'd cared about had been stripped from him. He didn't think he could endure it if he lost her, lost them.

He should put them on a boat and take them to New Orleans himself, as soon as they were strong enough to travel. He should take them far from him and see to it that they had a comfortable home and everything money could buy before taking himself out of their lives forever. But if they were so far away, how could he keep them safe?

Never had he been so confused, so trapped by a situation that brought him the fiercest joy and deepest fear he'd ever experienced.

He knew from the rhythm of her breathing that Caroline had fallen asleep again. She'd surrendered herself into his care last night because she'd had no choice. But how could she continue to trust him after what he'd done, what he'd almost done, what he was? He didn't deserve it, any of it. He didn't deserve her or a perfect son or her unreserved trust.

Winding his way through the smiling, gaping men who moved aside to let them pass, he tried to clear his mind, tried to think rationally, but in the blink of an eye, he had lost every ounce of logic he'd ever possessed. In the blink of an eye, he'd been transformed into something he didn't understand or particularly like.

There were no more walls, nothing to protect him from his own emotions. All he had to do was look at his son or at this extraordinary woman who had believed in him when he didn't believe in himself, this woman who had taken his seed and given him a child.

Every time he gazed at them or thought of them, the walls dissolved and the emotions he'd tried so hard to cut off assaulted him with a vengeance.

It was as if his heart had been turned inside out and all his feelings lay bare and unprotected for all to see.

It scared the hell out of him.

Caroline awoke with a start, listening intently for any sound from the crib at the end of her bed. When none came, she relaxed back on the pillow once again.

She'd been dreaming about the storm. Over the last few weeks since Jason brought her back to the *fazenda*, she'd been slowly remembering things about that terrible accident. The memories came to her in the form of hideous nightmares. Tonight she'd dreamed of falling through the air, helplessly buffeted by fierce winds. When her body slammed into the roiling water, the impact had awakened her.

How had she ever survived, she wondered for the hundredth time. Why had she lived when the others had not?

Shivering in the darkness, she remembered waking on the riverbank, covered with mud, racked with pain, unable to move. If Jason hadn't found her, she'd have almost certainly died. He'd saved her life, hers and their child's.

Pushing the covers down, she climbed out of bed, careful not to jostle the injured arm that Ines had set properly following Caroline's instructions. Her heart swelled with joy and love as she gazed down at her little Jase.

Caroline wondered how Jason would react to her decision to name the baby after him. It wasn't official, of course, but she couldn't continue thinking of him as *the baby* or *the child*, as if he were an object instead of a little person. And since Jason had chosen to avoid them both, she'd picked a name herself. Even if Jason objected strenuously, she wasn't sure she'd ever be able to think of him by any other name.

Running her hands lovingly over the raw-wood surface of the small crib, she smiled into the darkness, thinking of how frantically the men had worked to build it upon her return. Jason had bemoaned its roughhewn appearance, but it meant more to her than any expensive store-bought cradle ever could.

And the women had been equally kind, gifting her with potions to make the baby sleep, to make him eat better, to make him grow faster, and though she couldn't bring herself to use any of them, she managed to appear grateful. Their time and their knowledge she did treasure and use, but when Ines had suggested that she find a wet nurse, that it wasn't quite proper for the *patrona* to nurse her own child, Caroline had refused flatly.

Having to nurse the baby herself might seriously curtail her freedom, but she didn't care one whit. There was nowhere else she'd rather be than with her son, unless, of course, she was with his father.

Jason had saved them both from the jungle and the river. If only she could save him from himself.

She closed her eyes with a sigh. Some things never changed, at least Jason never changed. He was infuriatingly predictable. In the weeks since they returned, he hadn't spoken more than three words to her. He'd avoided her, practically living in the orchards, probably sleeping at the *benefício*, even though the fires had long since died out and the danger to what was left of the trees was over.

Well, he might be able to ignore her, but he hadn't been able to achieve that level of indifference where his son was concerned. More than once, she'd caught him standing over the cradle in the main sitting room, gazing down at the infant with such a stark, bottomless yearning that she was forced to turn away. It was as if he was suddenly afraid to touch little Jase, after delivering him and caring for him through that first night.

Assured that Jase was fine and sleeping soundly, she left the bedroom for the sitting room, stopping before the window and gazing down at the courtyard below.

There he was, sitting at the stone table, his head in his hands. She stiffened at the sight of the bottle on the table before him.

Driven by anger and frustration, Caroline tore the door open and marched down the stairs, not stopping until she stood over his hunched form. Reluctantly he lifted his head, his glazed, blood-shot eyes narrowing at the sight of her.

"Is this your answer, Jason?" she asked bitterly. "Will you deal with life by staying drunk?"

She grabbed the bottle, intent on smashing it on the patio as he'd done once before. To her surprise, the bottle was full, the seal unbroken.

Her first thought was that he had dispatched another bottle and this was his second, but when he opened his mouth to speak, she detected not a trace of liquor on his breath. Something else had caused the glazed, lost look in his eyes.

"I can't let you go," he murmured. "I'm sorry,

Caroline. I . . . I just can't. . . . You have no reason to believe me when I tell you I'd never hurt you or our child, not after all I've done. But I won't come near you, either of you. If I can just see you and know that you're here, maybe it will be enough. It'll have to be enough."

Impulsively, Caroline reached out to him, wanting somehow to ease the agony in his soul. She rested a hand on his broad shoulder, feeling the muscles tense beneath her fingers.

"Jason, we can't live in the same house and never see one another. You know that won't work. I can't bear it when you withdraw from me."

"It'll have to work," he said desperately, twisting away from her and coming to his feet. "I'll make it work. You have my word. I'll sleep at the *beneficio* from now on. I'll—"

"Foolish man," she muttered, shaking her head in a gesture of pity and helplessness. "You'll never hold your son again? You'll never want to make love to me again?"

He glared at her, running a hand through his hair. "Wanting and doing are two different things."

"It won't work, Jason." Did he truly believe it would?

"We can make it work. There's no other way because I'm not letting you go. I'll give you a gun and teach you how to use it, and if I ever touch either of you, I want you to shoot me. . . ."

Caroline tried with all her might but couldn't stifle the laughter that welled up from her throat.

"This isn't funny, Caroline." The grimness of his expression pushed her closer to complete loss of control, but she forced herself to appear chagrined.

"I'm sorry, Jason. I can't help it. Are you finished with your nonsense?"

"Nonsense? Is that what you call it?"

"Yes. What do you call it? Listen to me, you've tried to send me away since I first arrived here. And I've tried to leave. We've both failed. Don't you see? We're meant to be together. I have no doubt that if I tried to leave again, another boat would capsize or alligators would pick me up and carry me back. I'm not going anywhere."

"Then we agree. . . ."

"I listened to you, Jason," she said, taking him by the arm and guiding him back to the table. He didn't resist when she pushed him gently into the chair he'd vacated and stood close before him. "It's only fair that you hear me out. I know I talk too much. I know I've pushed you beyond the bounds of human restraint. I'm sorry for trying to force you to change, to become what I thought I wanted you to be. I want you just the way you are. You are everything I want."

"How can you say that? You were right about me. I am a coward. I bully and hurt those who are weaker than me. . . ."

"No, you're a coward because you're afraid of loving and being loved. It has nothing to do with this imagined violence—"

"I nearly hit you," he said. Guilt and torment showed plainly on his expressive face. "Damn! Have you forgotten? I drew back my hand. In another minute. . . ."

"In another minute you stopped, Jason," she said, pressing her fingers against his lips to silence him. "I'll admit you frightened me, enough that I felt I had to leave. But I didn't do it because I was afraid of you for myself. I was afraid for my child. I didn't want him born into a house where there were so many things unresolved. I never, never believed that you would physically harm me or our child."

Jason stared at her dubiously.

"All right, for a flicker of an instant I thought you might. But you didn't. We all get that angry. God knows, I've done nothing but push you and test your patience since I've been here. But you are not your father. You are not anything like him, so you can stop using that as an excuse."

"I see no difference."

He made as if to rise, and Caroline lowered her body gingerly to his lap, careful of her broken arm, intent on keeping him still while she made her point.

"The difference is that you stopped. Your father would not have. That's what separates us from him: not the emotion, the action. I would trust you implicitly with our son, who by the way is in desperate need of a name, unless you want him to grow up being called Boy."

"My God, woman, are you afraid of nothing?" His admiration for her knew no bounds.

"You know I am, Jason. You know what a coward I am."

"You were hurt and confused," he said, realizing that she spoke of the night the baby was born. "You're all right now."

"Thanks to you, Jason," she said, her voice breaking with emotion. "We would have died if not for you. You were so sweet, so gentle that night. You cared for me and for our baby as if you'd been doing it all your life. And now the only thing I'm afraid of is losing you."

"You can't lose me," he murmured against her throat, his voice sending currents of pleasure through her body. "I won't allow it. You are the miracle of my life, Caroline. I don't deserve any of this."

Lifting his face with her good hand in order to look into his eyes, Caroline murmured, "Shut up, foolish man, and kiss me."

Her lips came down on his and his mouth opened to welcome her. Though she initiated the kiss, he soon took control, kissing her fiercely, possessively, caressing her gently, as if she were something precious.

"I love you, Caroline," he said, his voice raw with desire and emotion, "but for the life of me, I can't understand how you could care for me. I can't even understand why you came here, after reading those damned letters I wrote to—" he stopped himself with a laugh, "—I thought I'd written to Derek."

"But that's exactly why I came," she explained. "You let me glimpse your heart in those letters. If not for those letters, I'd have run away screaming a long time ago."

"I don't even know why I wrote those things," he said thoughtfully.

"I think I do," she said with a smile. "When I started writing back, you started opening up. I think you sensed a kindred spirit, even though you weren't even aware of it."

"Maybe you're right," he agreed, his eyes glowing with admiration and love. "But they were filled with dark tales of my past."

"Yes, but they spoke of a man in torment, a man with a beautiful soul who only needed the right woman to convince him of his own goodness and to make him happy, in spite of himself. Are you happy?

Or are you still afraid that if you care for us we'll be taken away?"

Jason buried his face in the crook of her neck, growling deep in his throat. "You terrify me, do you know that?"

"Why?"

"Because you know me so well."

Caroline drew back so that she could look into his eyes. "I'll never betray you, Jason. Never. I'll always love you."

"A miracle, that's what you are," he said, kissing her hungrily again.

Finally Caroline pulled away, gazing into his beloved face. "The miracle is upstairs sound asleep and waiting for his parents to give him a name."

Jason smiled. "I'm not good at this kind of thing. Surely over the months you've thought of names."

Smiling mischievously, Caroline said, "Well, I thought we might name him Jason."

She felt his body tense beneath her and waited expectantly. "After me? But—"

"I like it," she interrupted. "Jason Sinclair Junior. Of course, we'll call him Jase to avoid confusion."

"Do you really want to name him after me?"

"Very much. I can't think of a more appropriate name, Jason. He is your son. And you saved us both. You brought him into the world. You were the first one to hold him, to see him."

"I know," he murmured, his voice thick with unshed tears. "I'll never forget that moment. . . . Neither will you, I suppose."

Caroline shrugged, pushing the memory of pain and fear from her mind. "I remember you talking to me, telling me everything would be all right. I remember you holding him up so I could see him. The pain doesn't even matter now. He's so beautiful, so perfect."

"Oh, God, you'll never know how much I love you."

"Tell me! Tell me!" she teased.

Jason laughed. "I never have told you, have I? I told Ignacio in the wedding ceremony, but I've never told you."

Now it was Caroline's turn to laugh, as she imagined Jason and Ignacio standing before the local magistrate repeating wedding vows. It was funnier than the picture of her and Melanie.

"I've got it!" Jason shouted, coming to his feet and carrying her with him. "We'll have another ceremony. We'll speak our vows to each other."

"That sounds wonderful! We'll wait for the priest—"

"Wait? I don't want to wait. Let's set our new wedding date for three days from now."

"Three days? But how. . . ."

"You just leave the details to me. Three days from tonight, Mrs. Sinclair!"

"But Jason, how . . . ?"

"For once, don't argue, Caroline. For once, just trust me."

"I trust you forever and always, Jason. Never doubt that."

Epilogue

"*I, Jason Sinclair, take thee,* Caroline Marshall Sinclair, to be my lawful wedded wife," Jason said solemnly.

Caroline stood on the empty patio of the *benefício* in a white sarong the women of the *fazenda* had worked frantically to make for her, listening to her husband's strong, beloved voice. Around their necks they wore garlands of flowers, gifts from the *Yanomami* women. Ines stood beside Caroline, tears rolling down her cheeks, little Jase nestled securely in her arms. To Jason's right stood Ignacio, proud and silent.

"To love, honor, and cherish. . . ."

Faust, the *Yanomami* high priest stood before them in full regalia—bird feathers sticking out around his head, leaves tucked into armbands, his body painted in red and black geometric patterns.

". . . in sickness and in health. . . ."

Today was her wedding day. Today they were starting over, starting fresh, she, Jason, and little Jase.

". . . from this day forward. . . ."

From this day forward, they would be together, a family. The scars of old wounds were still there, just below the surface, but they would face them together. Together.

". . . till death do us part."

Turning, Jason and Caroline faced each other expectantly. Joy and love shone clearly in Jason's eyes. No longer were they tormented by a past he could not alter. Now they looked forward to a bright, love-filled future.

Slowly he lowered his head toward her and she lifted hers to receive his kiss, a light brush of his lips against hers that promised more delights to come.

A loud cheer went up from the crowd gathered around the *benefício*. The bride and groom turned to face the onlookers, the *fazenda* workers and their families to the left and the Yanomami to the right.

Behind them, the priest began to chant, his words unintelligible, some kind of incantation to his gods. Caroline didn't think God would mind. They had already been bound together in His eyes, and today was just an affirmation of their commitment to each other.

Drums thundered in the background as Jason bent his head to whisper in her ear. "You'll never know how much I love you."

Caroline smiled, her body suffused with warmth, as she pulled his head down so she could whisper into his ear. "You could show me every day for the rest of our lives."

"I plan to," he replied, his voice thick with desire.

"Starting today?"

Jason gazed into her eyes, uncertainty marring his brow. "Are you sure? It's so soon. . . ."

"It's been weeks, Jason, weeks!"

He swept her up into his arms, walking toward the wagon that had brought them to the *benefício*, and Caroline threw her head back, laughing with the joy that coarsed through her body.

"Starting today, then," he said with an ardent smile.

Caroline settled her head against his broad shoulder, reveling in the feel of his arms around her, in the knowledge that they would be together forever, from this day forward.

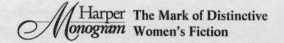

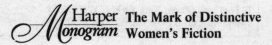